The Walker Diaries 1: Azerica – young, dumb and naive

By Alicia Caldwell Henderson

Let faith & love prevail always...

[signature]

Chapter One

The mirror never lied.

She looked good this morning. She couldn't wait to get to school and prance around in the clothes Trish gave her. She had to be careful though, because there was no way her mom would let her wear half of the stuff her cheerleader friend had given her. But Azerica didn't care. This was all part of the plan to be a new and different person in high school.

It was a new season and this was a new day.

"It's my time to shine," Azerica said smiling to herself.

So far, she was pleased with everything. She managed to use her friend's wave iron the right way, so her shoulder-length black hair crinkled around her face kind of like Ashanti. Her cute tan-colored top flowed perfectly with her faded jeans. The brown boots she could take or leave, but she decided to take them today since it was the first day of school.

If it hadn't been for her friend's fashion expertise over the summer, she would have ended up looking like USG's biggest reject just like the rest of the freshmen class. Fortunately, she met Trish at cheerleader camp and that's not what happened. Trish cared enough to let her know how the public high school system worked. Azerica was clueless.

For as long as she could remember, she'd always attended dry private Christian schools...that is, as long as her dad was doing right and paying child support. When he was laid off from his job two years ago, she transferred to a public school and loved it. She didn't have any dress codes to follow and she could participate in more extracurricular activities. She started cheering that year and fell in love with it. She could hardly believe that she now cheered for USG.

USG was the only high school in Jacksonville to be named after a Union general. Ulysses S. Grant High School, also known as USG, was the newest high school on the Westside of Jacksonville in one of the oldest buildings close to downtown. The Westside started rebuilding so quickly that people from all over the Jacksonville metropolitan area were relocating there because of its new business opportunities. The new growth in the community caused the Westside high schools to overflow. It was necessary for the city to build another high school to accommodate the students. Mayor Kirby decided to break away from Jacksonville's tradition of naming high schools after Confederate generals and introduced USG to the "bold new city of the south."

"Robert E. Lee, Andrew Jackson, Nathan Bedford Forrest," Azerica sighed, naming off the high schools in the area. "Lord, it was about time they did something different."

"Don't you know what time it is?" Candace stormed past Azerica after waking up Melina, Azerica's half sister. "You were supposed to wake her up."

"My bad. I just thought you said you were going to do it, since you haven't found a job yet," said Azerica when her mother walked into the bathroom to brush through the little bit of hair she had. Azerica almost had to exit the bathroom completely. It was too small to hold the both of them comfortably.

"That's what you get for thinking. You and your Dad are just alike, if I let you think stuff on your own, then you always mess up. Melina's hair better be done in ten minutes." Candace said.

She tried not to let them, but her mother's cold words stabbed Azerica with pain. As quickly as it had appeared, her cheerful mood vanished in a matter of seconds. Biting back anger and tears, Azerica turned back to the mirror. Just when joy was starting to find its way back in her heart, her mother came and snatched it away from her. For the past week, this is what life had been like for her. At times, it seemed like her mom had fun tearing her down. And she just couldn't understand why.

"And look here little girl, anytime I tell you to do something, you do it. It don't matter if I'm busy or not, just do it." Candace continued to ramble on while she put on her makeup.

Azerica stopped and turned to face her mother. She couldn't stand suffering through this. Ever since her dad got locked up, her mom couldn't even look at her. When she did, Azerica couldn't recognize the cold, hard eyes staring back at her. Candace was a total stranger to her now. Their relationship had slowly deteriorated over the past two weeks and became completely alien over the past few days. Replacing her mother's smiling, warm face was a bitter, careworn silhouette that couldn't recognize the difference between Jeffrey and Azerica. Anytime Azerica tried to talk to her mother, the conversation ended with Candace enraged and Azerica feeling like an unwanted child.

But there was only so much Azerica could take and she was tired of being treated like a stepchild.

"You know, if you're not working today, why aren't you fixing Melina's hair?" Azerica questioned her mother. "Today's an important day for me, Mom."

"Child, I don't care what today is for you. When I tell you to do something, I want you to do it. Now go fix Melina's hair," her mother said, leaving the bathroom and slamming the door behind her.

Not wanting to continue in this losing battle, Azerica stayed put and finished getting ready. She could still hear her mother griping and complaining and she overheard her ask God why she had such a disobedient and ungrateful child.

Why would she say that? Azerica wondered. After all she's done to help her mother take care of Melina—and even Chauncey, her baby brother. And on top of all that, keep the house clean...never has she complained about the things her mother told her to do.

She just doesn't care anymore, Azerica decided.

For some reason, her mom couldn't get over whatever it was she thought Jeffrey did to her. Azerica never fully understood their situation. He and her mom were never married anyway. They barely even talked. In fact, it wasn't until about six months ago when they actually started getting along and became really good friends.

"Daddy why did you have to go and mess up?" Azerica asked her reflection as if it could talk back. "Mom was so happy about going back to school."

As she finished getting ready for school, Azerica's mind wandered back to six months ago when Jeffrey came over to tell Candace Christian about his new job. She remembered how excited he was.

"God is so awesome!" exclaimed Jeffrey. He glided across the linoleum floor as if he'd just won the lottery.

"What is your problem?" Candace asked half interested. She readjusted her soft blue housecoat so that it would not sit loosely on her shoulders while he was there. The last thing she needed was for him to try and holla at her again. It was bad enough that one night together caused her life to be like this: broke and in despair. If Jeffrey knew the first thing about responsibility, she would be okay. But he can barely keep a job to support himself.

While he talked nonsense, Candace tried her best to keep busy in the kitchen so she wouldn't have to pay attention to him. She really didn't want to let him in, but she knew Azerica hadn't seen him in a few weeks. She tried to maintain a stable relationship with Jeffrey, but it was so hard for her to do. The man just would not grow up. He's a bigger kid than her 8-year-old daughter, Melina. But of course, Azerica loves him. He could do no wrong in her eyes.

"Hey Daddy! I didn't think I'd see you today!" Azerica exclaimed, prancing into the room wearing her USG cheerleader T-shirt and shorts. She made her way to where her father was standing and stood underneath him, becoming his shadow.

"Whatcha got for me?" She asked him.

"Hey baby girl." Jeffrey said and kissed her forehead. "Isn't it about your bed time?"

"Yeah, I'm going in a minute," Azerica said and glanced at her mother who stood at the table across from them.

Candace watched them through slanted eyes and smirked. They were inseparable and it got on her nerves. That child acted like he was the best thing since sliced bread and he barely did anything for her. She sipped her coffee to calm her nerves and silently prayed he'd finish so he could hurry and leave.

"Please get on with it Jeffrey, we don't have time for your antics today." Candace sighed and sat down in the worn oak chair that was part of their kitchen table.

Jeffrey looked at Azerica and winked.

Azerica would never forget that moment. The tension in the air that night was so thick. The usually brightly lit kitchen grew somber and caused the vivid yellow in the wallpaper to seem overcast. The artificial sunflowers on the table drooped as though they hadn't seen the sun in weeks. Jeffrey tried his best to lighten up the room, but to no avail. He knew things would be okay; it was just a matter of breaking through the clouds of her mother's rage.

"Candy, I know I haven't been there for you financially to raise Azerica…"

"Please can you tell me something I don't already know?" Candace interrupted. *"And please don't call me Candy, that name is reserved for only the* special *man in my life."*

Letting him get the best of her, her flesh rose up and she felt herself losing control. She didn't know what it was, but something about him made her go off and lose her head.

"I'm sorry Candace, may I finish please?"

"Go ahead." Candace replied her voice immersed in resent.

"Well, I came here tonight to apologize. Financially, I haven't been there… I've been late on some payments, I couldn't get any of her school supplies and I haven't been able to help support her in cheerleading."

"Please get on with it Jeffrey," begged Candace, drinking the last drop of her coffee.

"All that's 'bout to change. You ain't gotta worry 'bout any of that anymore, and I'm gonna give you extra to make up for what you had to do," said Jeffrey as he returned back to his normal vernacular. It was hard for him to speak proper for too long. After a while, the sloppy speech crept back into his system.

As he continued to talk, the same winning smile that melted Candace's heart when she was only 16 remained plastered to his face. He smiled as though he were about to give her the world.

"…And Candace, this is for you." He said, walking over to the old oak table. He handed her an envelope and sat across from her, just waiting for a pleasant reaction.

young, dumb and naive

Candace stared at him in shock when she opened the envelope and found five hundred dollars cash. She didn't know what to think. The money was exactly what she needed to survive. She'd been in a rut for so long, she never thought she'd be able to get back on her feet.

"Girl, I just want you to know, you can get some money from me every Friday. It might not always be so much, but I'm here to help you," Jeffrey smiled.

All she could do was bubble with joy. He was finally acting responsibly and thinking about Azerica. But then realization hit her. Jeffrey had not had a job in over five months. He wasn't working now and he didn't have any rich family members who would just give him this much cash.

Just as soon as it appeared, her blissful glow vanished and she became angry.

"Are you selling drugs?" She asked. "Because first of all, drug money is dirty money and as a Christian, I don't want to be associated with any part of it. Drug money is not acceptable in my house Jeffrey! Where did you get the money from?"

Jeffrey laughed.

Azerica watched in silence as her mom continued to question the origin of the money. Her voice got louder as Jeffrey continued to make it a point not to answer. His calm demeanor caused her mom's to flare up. Azerica crept over to the doorway in the small room, just in case she needed to leave and tend to her newborn baby brother or get some help. Her mother had a tendency to get violent with her dad when she was upset with him.

"You don't change. Woman, you always get yourself so worked up. Relax, this money is all legit," he said, trying to persuade her.

"Then where'd you get the money Jeffrey!" Candace exclaimed, her voice getting higher.

"Candy... I mean Candace, trust me."

"The last time you said that, I was almost put out of my house because I couldn't pay the rent because you didn't pay the child support you promised. Now tell me where *you got the money 'cause I know Wal-mart don't pay you that much."* Candace said, *walking up to his face.*

"Trust me, it's legit."

Azerica remembered watching silently as they continued to argue that night. She remembered it took everything in her mother's power to keep from cussing Jeffrey out. It wasn't until she threatened to call the cops before Jeffrey finally told Candace he was promoted to customer service manager at Wal-mart. He told her the five hundred dollars was part of the sign on bonus they offered him.

"Yeah, Dad. Wal-mart give a sign on bonus? We should've known better." Azerica said sarcastically, talking to her reflection once again. "I guess Mom just really needed the money."

Azerica knew her mom blamed her dad for the way her life turned out and she knew her dad wasn't the best father, but she was able to accept him for who he was. She just wished her mom could do the same thing.

Ever since she was a little girl, her mother always spoke ill of him. Azerica had never been able to carry on a positive conversation with her mom about her dad. Her mom never passed up the chance to ruin his name. Azerica tried to understand and even asked her mom about their history, but she would never tell Azerica anything. Even her father wouldn't tell her what happened between the two of them. All Azerica knew was that her mom got pregnant, and according to her mother, her life has been in turmoil ever since.

Why are you thinking about this now? Azerica asked herself. *Today is not the day to be upset. You are here for a reason. Don't let anything tear down your spirit. Get yourself together and finish getting ready for school. You're a beautiful person and you are loved.*

Azerica sighed. It was sad, but she knew she had to make herself happy and think happy thoughts. She had to make herself laugh to overcome feeling worthless.

She closed her eyes and allowed herself to think about the day she tried out for cheerleader for high school. She felt so good that day. The judges loved her cheers, the girls on the squad couldn't wait to start cheering with her and her dad was there to support her. That was a beautiful day for her. She let those same emotions come rushing back to her. Then she opened her eyes. But this time when she saw herself, she didn't frown. Something in the way she looked made her smile.

For once, she stopped thinking about the turmoil in her family, and she focused on herself and the day ahead of her. It took her a moment, but finally, she was starting to feel good about the person staring back at her.

While her daddy's million-dollar smile and his bright eyes are the features that tear at her mother's heart, they make her personality glow. If they remember nothing else, people always remember her smile and her shining eyes. And then there are those who only remember her because of her hair. She had the good stuff, the kind that only needed to be washed. She had to give credit to her mother for that. But unlike her mother, whose hair was styled kind of like Halle Berry, Azerica's black hair was shoulder-length and quickly growing.

She took one last look at herself and smiled. Every hair was strategically in place. Her clothes fit perfectly and she was wearing Curve, her favorite perfume. But in the back of her mind, her mother's cold words haunted her and caused her to feel insecure once again.

God, I really don't need this today, Azerica prayed silently on the way back to her room. *Please help me to deal with her. Lord I know she's having a hard time, but why is she taking it out on me? I can't help it if I'm Jeffrey's child. I'm her child too. I need her just as much as Melina and Chauncey do.*

When she walked into the room, Melina was sitting on the floor on Azerica's side waiting for her.

"Melina, how do you want your hair today?" Azerica asked her 8-year-old sister and sat on the bed above her.

"I think I want braids."

"Girl, you know we don't have time for braids. Try again," said Azerica.

"Okay Azerica. I want one braid and some hair left down," said Melina, demonstrating exactly how she wanted Azerica to do it.

As Azerica fixed Melina's hair, she looked up and saw the Power Puff Girls staring at her. Everywhere she looked on Melina's side of the room the cartoons were smiling at her. Melina's bed and rugs had the animated figures all over them. And then the girl was even wearing a Power Puff Girl T-shirt!

"Mel, we gotta talk about your side of the room. The Power Puff Girls are cool and all, but I think you're getting too old for them."

"Mom said you would say that, but I like them," Melina said. "And Mom won't let me put up my posters of Bow Wow anyway."

"Good, he's way too old for you. L'il Romeo is closer to your age, stick to him."

"But I don't like him. He acts like a little kid."

"Mel, you are two years younger than that boy. What do you think you act like?" Azerica asked.

"He's..." Melina started to reply.

"It don't matter, your hair's finished. Go to the front, Mom's waiting for you."

Melina grabbed her purple Power Puff Girls backpack and walked towards the door. Then she stopped and stared at Azerica.

"What?" Azerica asked, a little irritated.

"I just have one thing to say." Melina said. "Bow Wow gives me butterflies, not L'il Romeo."

With that, Melina bounced out of the room, singing *Butterflies* by Michael Jackson. All Azerica could do was stare and laugh at her little sister.

Melina had so much energy and she was so animated, but she was also very irritating. Azerica loved her sister to death, but Melina had a tendency to talk too much and complain about almost everything. At times, she could liven up any room with her bright smile and sarcastic jokes. But the majority of her time was spent talking nonsense to anyone who would listen.

Azerica had to admit, that even in her silliness, she still enjoyed being around Melina because she made her smile.

-ydn-

"Well, you know. I called Jacob back, right. And he said Lenni's mom is over there every night trying to get high for free. I was like goodness I didn't know her mom is that bad! That must be some for real stress or she's doing something serious."

Walking towards the complex exit, Azerica was barely listening to her best friend's dramatic tale of Lenni's mother's smoking habit. She just didn't care. Instead, she focused her attention on their surroundings. Even if she didn't already know it, she could tell school was back in session. Just like any other first day of high school, commotion filled the air. Cars beeped in frustration at students jaywalking, and traffic on Lexington Avenue was backed up because of school buses trying to turn into USG. Unlike years prior, Azerica didn't wish to be part of the high school atmosphere, she already was.

They hadn't walked out of the complex yet and Azerica could already hear the hums of the school buses off-loading students. Raintree Apartments and USG sat at opposite corners of the intersection of Lexington Avenue and Lincoln Boulevard. The school and the complex both faced Lincoln Boulevard, but Lexington Avenue made the intersection the most popular intersection in the area because you could get anything on Lex Av.

Still taking in the scene before her, Azerica barely noticed her friend still carrying on with the conversation.

"And then, he said Lenni and her mom smoke together on the weekends. I told him, my mom would shoot me if I even thought about talking about weed. But you know I've never had a desire to do that anyway."

young, dumb and naive

Devin Roberts stopped in the middle of the road to get Azerica's attention.

"Azerica, are you listening to me?" Devin asked.

"Yeah, I'm listening. I just don't know why you listen to Jacob's stories 'cause you know his information comes from DeShae. And all DeShae does is stay inside and watch people from out the window. And half the time he can't see what's going on."

"Yeah, but Azerica, has he ever been wrong?" Devin challenged.

Azerica stared at her friend, her blood beginning to boil. "You know you're right," she said. "He wasn't wrong when he said Mom was smoking. He wasn't wrong when he said Dad was selling the stuff. And he wasn't wrong when he said how Dad got caught. The man is never wrong, what do you want me to say? That I'm happy Lenni's business is out in the street?"

"Azerica I'm sorry. I didn't mean to hurt you with that. I didn't mean anything by it. I promise," Devin said. "Can we pray?"

Azerica just shrugged her shoulders as if to say whatever. Every time her friend did or said something crazy, she always wanted to immediately stop what she was doing and pray. *God why don't she ever think before she speaks*, Azerica asked silently.

When they stopped a few feet away from Raintree Apartment's exit, Azerica reluctantly allowed Devin to grab her hands.

"Father, you said we shall not be false witnesses and God that's just what I've done. Please forgive me. We don't know what's going on with Lenni and her mother, but we pray for them. We ask that you encourage and protect them. Father, you know what they need. We ask that you provide for them and meet their needs. We ask this of you in the name of Jesus Christ. Amen."

"Azerica, I really am sorry. Please don't be mad at me," Devin pleaded, staring at Azerica with puppy dog eyes as they continued their walk to school.

But this morning, Azerica didn't have time for her friend's antics. Without looking up, she said, "That's okay."

Every time Devin says something insensitive or just speaks out of her head, Azerica is always so quick to forgive her. But not this time, Devin just has to learn a lesson, Azerica thought to herself. This time, she went way too far. How could she not remember that Jeffrey was arrested a few weeks ago? She knows everything that goes on with me, Azerica thought. I've told her about everything. The only thing I haven't mentioned to her is Mom's recent attitude towards me. But I can't help it if my life isn't as perfect as hers.

Compared to Azerica's, Devin's family life resembled the Cosby Show. Both her parents are married and happy. Her brother, Jason, is a high school athletic star. And he's so *so* fine, Azerica thought, and smiled as her mind drifted to his sexy green eyes, tall stature and beautiful brown skin…he's what every 14-year-old girl dreams about. He's actually part of the reason why Azerica was so thrilled about attending USG.

Then there's Devin. She's just as attractive; with her peanut butter complexion and green eyes, you'd think they were twins, but she's 14 and he's 16.

All summer Jay joked around with she and Devin, telling them he owned the school and when he graduated he would leave it to them in his Senior Will. Azerica always told him she didn't want that inheritance because she heard it was haunted. She didn't know whether or not it really was, but it scared her sometimes. Although it was renovated and remodeled, the three-story brick building still scared her. It stood menacingly over Lincoln Boulevard. Even though the school had a huge courtyard preceding the entrance and flowers and palm trees to make it more inviting, something about it made her feel uneasy. Then again, that could be because this was her first day of high school.

"Do you have practice today?" Devin asked shyly, interrupting Azerica's thoughts.

"Yeah, 'til 4," she replied, not realizing they had walked in silence for so long. They were already walking up the steps to the entrance of old Public School No. 2, or the freshly created Ulysses S. Grant, also known as USG, as nicknamed by Jason and his friends.

"Well, if I don't see you the rest of the day, I'll call you sometime after school," Devin said.

"Sure."

Azerica watched as her friend hurried through the crowd to make it to her first class. Devin could be so melodramatic sometimes, especially when she didn't get her way. And today was one of those days. Azerica refused to accept her apology just yet. She wanted to make Devin suffer a little while longer. It didn't matter how long Devin sulked; she wasn't going to ruin Azerica's day. And neither was Azerica's mom. They could both go to hell for all she cared.

"Sorry God, I didn't mean it like that," Azerica said and looked up towards the sky. "They just get on my nerves sometimes, but I still love them."

"Who are you talking to?"

"Oh, hey Trish," Azerica turned to face the voice behind her.

"I know crazy people talk to themselves sometimes, but just don't go answering yourself or we'll have to check you in to Charter Ridge."

"Oh Please. And Hoochie! What are you wearing?" Azerica gawked at Trish's attire. "Who are you trying to look good for? You ain't got no man."

"That nigga Jay," Trish said glowing as she smiled.

"You talking 'bout Jason Roberts?"

"Yeah, girl. That's my future man."

"Trish, I don't mean to hate, but he don't know you're alive," said Azerica.

"Ok. Just wait 'til school's over and I bet I'll have his number or he'll have mine."

"Trish, he don't talk to freshmen."

"So I may be a freshman, but he don't know that. I mean look at me, do I look like a greenhorn?"

Azerica laughed as her friend modeled her form fitting T-shirt dress. She couldn't ignore the way the dress enhanced her friend's figure and revealed virgin curves. She definitely didn't look like a 14-year-old. And her make-up was perfect.

"Well, you do look a little older." Azerica said. "Your mom let you outta the house with all that make-up on your face?"

"She was passed out when I left. She was at the club last night and didn't come home 'til like four this morning, so I didn't have to worry about hearing her mouth," Trish said and rolled her eyes.

"Next time she goes, you should get her to take my mom with her. Maybe she'll lighten up a bit," suggested Azerica.

"Why you say that Azerica?"

"Nothing. Are you going to practice today?" Azerica changed the subject quickly. She didn't feel like sharing her dramatic life with Trish. Not today. She wasn't ready emotionally.

"I hate cheering, but I love seeing Jay sweat! I'll be there as soon as the bell rings." Trish said laughing when the bell rang to start their day. "And I'm for real."

"Ok, I'll see you at practice," Azerica laughed and walked to class.

Chapter 2

"Mom, what am I going to do?" Candace whined into the phone. "I have no job, Chauncey is just six months old, Mel's in school and Azerica isn't old enough to work—I can't believe that negro got busted. How could I be so stupid?"

Every time she mentioned her reality, Candace cringed. There was no way she was going to make it without that extra money. She hated to admit it, but she considered all that extra cash a blessing. It helped to keep her bills paid and food on the table while she was able to stay home and take care of her baby.

"Sweetie, you shouldn't have trusted in him in the first place. You knew where the money was coming from," her mother reminded her.

"But Mom, I needed it. I wasn't ready to go back to work when Chauncey was born and Jeffrey was giving me so much money 'cause he was trying to make up for Azerica and it was taking care of the bills that child support didn't pay."

"Well, where are my babies now?" Sheryl cut her off, not wanting to hear any more of her daughter's excuses.

"Azerica and Mel are at school and Chauncey is here with me," Candace replied. "Mom?"

"Yes."

"Are you sure you can't come down and stay with me for a while. I really need you." Clearly, her mother could see she couldn't go through this on her own. Candace needed family support. Who else did she have to turn to?

"Candace, dear. I can't always come and rescue you. You need to stop depending on everyone else and do things for yourself. That's part of the reason why I moved to Orlando," said Sheryl. She wanted so badly to help out, but deep in her heart Sheryl knew that would defeat the purpose. She left Jacksonville so her daughter could mature as a mother. "Just pray about it. God will help you."

"Mom, I don't think God hears me anymore," Candace sulked. She hoped her voice oozed with pity so her mom would feel sorry for her and change her mind.

"That's ridiculous! God hears all of his children, just call on him." Sheryl replied sounding as unconcerned as possible.

"But Mom," said Candace, thinking about the mess her life had become. "I've messed up. I wouldn't even know how to call on him."

"Baby, it's easy, just say Jesus, I need you." She paused to let the words sink into Candace's heart.

"Mom you know I was with Greg for eight years. And all that time, I waited for a ring. I thought we would be married by now." Candace drowned in sorrow. "He was so awesome. He treated Azerica like his own child and he was always there when Mel called on him. When he came to see me and Chauncey at the hospital, I thought he was going to propose when he said he had to talk to me. Just the week before we were talking about how much we meant to each other. I never thought he would risk our relationship. He was so smooth, I never imagined he would be with another woman…"

"Candace, I don't mean to interrupt you. But child, you have got to move on with your life. You can't sulk forever and there's no way you could ever understand what was going on in that man's head. Just pray that he will continue to take care of Melina and that he'll have the same love for Chauncey. And go back to work, you need to be able to support your family," Sheryl said with more force.

"But Mom, that's the thing. I can't afford to pay for daycare for Chauncey and I don't trust Azerica enough to keep him at night while I work."

"Candace, If I could beat this into your head I would," Sheryl said. "But I'm just going to tell you one more time. Pray about it. Trust in your God. He will never leave you nor forsake you. Make your peace with him, repent from your sins and return back to him."

"But Mom…" That's not how Candace planned to fix her problems. She knew it was possible, but she just didn't have it in her to do. Saying 'Jesus I need you' wasn't going to pay her bills.

"Candace, where is your faith? You sound like Jesus' followers in Matthew…hold on, I'll find it for you," Sheryl responded.

"Mom, that's okay." Candace tried to interrupt her. "I know the story already. You don't have to get it for me."

"No, you need to hear this," Sheryl said as she flipped through the pages in her Bible. "I'm getting there, but basically they had no faith. They tried to cure a boy from epilepsy and couldn't do it because they had little faith. And they went to Jesus to do it and he did. The boy was cured! Jesus told them they couldn't do it because their faith was too small. And that's your problem. Increase your faith. All things are possible when you believe."

"Mom," Candace droned. That didn't have anything to do with her needing her mom's help to make it through this. "Please just come and help me. I'm sorry for whatever I've done."

"I found it," Sheryl said ignoring her daughter. "I want you to read Matthew 17:14-21. It's there. Now I have to go, tell my babies I love them."

"'Bye Mom."

Reluctantly, Candace grabbed the worn black Bible sitting on her table. Wanting to read the story, but determined not to, she quickly sat it back down. She picked up the phone ready to dial another number, but she couldn't think of one. She thought of her best friend Leesa, but Leesa wasn't much better off. She had just enough to survive. She only had one child, but she still didn't have anything extra to give except for her time. And Candace wasn't going to do her that way.

Still holding the phone, Candace sat as if she were waiting for someone to tell her what to do. But there was no word, no advice and once again, she was alone with her problems. She couldn't even remember when things started getting bad. She could say it was when Chauncey was born or even before that, like the day she met Greg, or the day she found out she was pregnant with Azerica. Her involvement with Jeffrey seems to keep her life in shambles and it all began with one night of lust and passion 14 years ago. If she could go back and do it all over again, she would have stayed home that night. The passion wasn't worth the turmoil her life is in now.

If I'd just kept my legs closed I wouldn't be in the mess that I'm in now. I've got two baby daddies who aren't worth the shoes they walk in. They make promises they never keep and can't stay out of trouble long enough to do right by their children. Candace thought of Jeffrey. *I was just so stupid in high school, young and stupid. We only had sex one time and I got pregnant. All it took was one time. No one ever told me that. If I'd known this was what my life would turn into, I would've never had sex with the man.*

"But I will never be rid of him," she sighed.

She reached to turn on the TV but forgot what she was doing when she saw her sleeping baby. Chauncey was going to grow up to look just like Greg. He already had his features. How she was going to survive, she didn't know.

And Greg just broke my heart. I loved him. I thought we were going to get married and be a real family. I still can't believe he would cheat on me after all these years we'd been together. I won't be able to look at Chauncey without seeing Greg. Why do these things always happen to me? Candace wondered. She didn't know how her life came to be this way, but she knew it was time to explore other options. She had to do something to make it better and she knew exactly who to call.

"Hello Memorial Hospital. How can I help you?"

"Hi. I'm trying to reach Dr. Craig Pearson. Can you tell me if he's available?" Candace asked, surprised her call was answered so quickly. The hospital was usually so busy that the phone rang off the hook.

"Are you a patient of Dr. Pearson's?" The receptionist asked.

"No."

"Do you have an emergency?" She continued to inquire.

"No, I'm an old friend. Candace Christian," she responded.

"One moment please. Let me see if he's available."

Candace hummed along to the jazz hold music while she waited, hoping he'd be available. She needed his help out of another mess. The last time she needed his help was ten years ago and she hadn't spoken to him since then; she hoped he hadn't forgotten who she was.

He could never forget me, Candace smiled to herself, remembering their high school history. How could he? She always trailed behind him when her friends weren't around. She never cared if she got on his nerves. He was like the big brother she never had, but always wanted.

"Dr. Pearson." A deep voice finally came through the line.

"Craig." Candace said, her voice slightly rising.

"Yes, who is this?" He asked recognizing the voice, but not able to place the voice with a face.

"Candace. Candace Christian. I know you've got to remember me," she joked.

Craig chuckled lightly on the other end. "Of course I remember you Candy. How's my little girl Azerica?"

"She's fine, but not a little girl anymore. She started her first day of high school today," she told him. "I can't believe it's been that long since we've talked."

"Wow, she's really grown," he momentarily continued with the conversation, ready for the punch line so he could get back to work. "But I know you Candace and I know you didn't call to talk about Azerica. How is everything, really?"

"You're right. I'm stuck and out of options. I need work and no one is hiring me right now," she said, trying not to whine. "I don't like to always call you for help, but I'm desperate. I need something."

"Well, I can help you. I just don't have time to talk right now." Craig replied quickly. "I need you to meet me at Milano's Thursday night for dinner. Don't worry about money, just dress nice. I've got you covered."

"Thanks Craig. I knew you could help me." Candace felt the world lifted from her shoulders.

"You're welcome," he said. "I have to get to my patient, but it was good to hear from you again Candace."

"I feel the same," she smiled. "I'll see you Thursday."

Azerica glared at the clock, willing it to turn to 2:24. It had been a long day and Azerica was ready to start practice so she could go home. All her classes that day had been fairly decent. It was just like junior high except the teachers were meaner and stricter, and there were lots of older people here. She couldn't believe how old the majority of them looked. Compared to them, she looked like a little girl. She needed Trish to help her perfect this new look she created. It just wasn't quite working.

"Yeah, Trish will know what I can do," she said softly.

"Azerica, is there something you would like to share?" her history teacher asked.

"No Mrs. Armstrong, I'm sorry," Azerica replied. Azerica couldn't believe she was just thinking out loud. The people sitting around her probably think she's crazy. Well, she went to junior high with most of them anyway, so they probably weren't paying attention to her. She hoped. It's not like Jason and his click are in this class. Only freshmen take European history.

"Well can you tell us what you enjoy the most about European history?" Mrs. Armstrong asked, still irritated that she interrupted class.

Oh Lord, why is she putting me out there like that? Azerica questioned herself. *I don't know anything about European history. I don't even like Europe!*

"Well," she finally replied. "I don't really know about European history, but I would like to know about Spain, France and I guess Italy."

"Well Ms. Christian, in order to learn more about them, you will need to pay closer attention. If you hadn't been talking, you would've heard the last part of the overview for this class. In that overview, I discussed a little bit about the cultures of Italy, Spain and France."

Turning to face the board, Mrs. Armstrong began writing their assignment for the next day.

"I want all of you to read chapter one in the World Civilization book I handed you in the beginning of class," she said as she gave out a worksheet. "And have this outline of the chapter completed by class tomorrow."

"And remember, no talking during class," she said and looked sternly at Azerica.

Azerica stared back at her for what seemed like hours until the bell rang. She could already tell that she and Mrs. Armstrong would be at each other's throats for the rest of the semester. It's a good thing they have block scheduling at USG, 'cause after December, she'll have a whole new set of classes and no more Mrs. Armstrong.

When the bell finally did ring, Azerica grabbed her books and headed straight for her locker. She had to get her clothes so she could change for practice. She didn't want practice to be too long or hard today since she'd promised her dad she would be home at exactly five so he could call her. Lately, it seemed like every time she made an attempt to keep contact with him, something always came up. Most of the time it was her mother staying on the phone and not answering the beeps. But today, Azerica planned to stay on the phone so she could answer his call. The last time they spoke, he said he would call to see how her first day of school went. She really needed to hear from him, he always knew how to make her laugh especially when her mom was driving her crazy.

She walked with the flow of traffic down the stairs and through the halls to get to her locker. She knew she was small, but she never realized how little she was until that moment. She kept getting bumped into. It was like no one in the halls noticed her. All around her, she heard their laughs, jokes and chatter, but they didn't acknowledge that she was walking in the midst of it. *Am I that little?* She wondered.

It was definitely time to find Trish; it was time to do something about this. She was tired of feeling like a little girl amongst a school full of adults.

When she finally turned the corner and approached the freshman hallway, she saw Trish standing by the water fountain talking to Jason. And Jason was all over her. It looked like her cute little dress and make-up worked.

"Hey Z," Trish exclaimed when Azerica walked closer. "Jason, you know Azerica, don't you?"

"Yeah, she's like my little sister. We live in Raintree." He said. "How's your first day at USG?"

"It's been alright," Azerica told him. "I'm trying to get used to this block scheduling thing."

"The classes seem really long for a minute, but you'll get used to it," Jason said smiling and trying to encourage her.

"Jason was just telling me about this party Darren Lewis is having after the game Friday. Do you want to go with me?" Trish winked at her. There was nothing like a party to set off the first week of school. She couldn't wait to socialize with all the upper classmen.

"Well, normally freshmen can't come, but you're a cheerleader, plus you're my little sister's best friend, so we'll make an exception for you." Jason smiled. "After all, freshmen need love too."

Please don't let Trish hear what Jason just said about me and Devin.

"Right after the game, right?" Azerica rushed the conversation along.

"Yeah, just don't tell too many freshmen you're going," said Jason. "The last thing we need is to baby-sit a crowd of ninth-graders."

"Don't worry, I don't even talk to them," Azerica laughed.

"Well, Trish, I guess I'll see you on the field. Make sure you call me tonight." Jason winked then he walked off.

"How did you get Jay's number?" Azerica asked when he was out of hearing range.

"I can't believe you were questioning this," said Trish pointing at her curves. "He took one look at me and couldn't help himself."

"And now you're going to Darren's party?"

"Yeah and so are you, we just have to work on more new clothes for you." Trish said, shaking her head. Azerica had to be right to hang out with her. "You're outfit's alright, but you still have that little girl look."

"I was just going to ask you to help me. I'm tired of looking young and small. Help me!" Azerica pleaded. "I need you desperately."

"Girl, I got you. What are you doing tonight?" Trish asked.

"Nothing," Azerica said. "My dad is calling me at five."

"Can you come over afterwards?" Trish asked. "Well, like around 9. Mom goes to Martini Mondays. She usually leaves around 8:30 to go to her friend's house so they can eat and get ready together. So I'll have everything ready for you by the time you get there."

"I should be able to get back out the house."

"Azerica, don't tell me your mom still be tripping about a curfew!" Trish exclaimed. "Don't she know that no one has curfews anymore?"

"Yeah, well tell my mom that," said Azerica. "She still believes in no dating 'til your 16."

Trish shook her head again. She didn't know very many people who still lived in the dark ages. She thought curfews went out with cassette tapes! Azerica's mom was going to bring them both down fast if Trish didn't do something. *Hell, Azerica's old enough to live without a curfew. It's not like she's ten.*

"Well look, we don't want to have a problem with the game Friday, so just spend the night with me. My mom will be out all night, so we could have a little after party for the party if we wanted. It just depends on how long Darren's party lasts." Trish suggested. "But anyways, we can talk about that later. Are you ready to go to practice?"

"No, hold on. I have to go to my locker." Azerica turned and walked a few feet to her locker.

"Girl, hurry up. I don't want people to think I'm a freshman." Trish looked nervously down the hall.

"But Trish, that's what you are."

"Yeah, but they don't need to know that." Trish hid her face. "That's on a need-to-know basis and you'd better not tell anybody!"

Azerica rolled her eyes and laughed. Sometimes she wondered how she ever became friends with Trish. The girl is so crazy! But cheerleading kind of does that to you. It's funny, but they didn't even know each other last year. Actually, they had just met at cheerleading camp over the summer. Since then, Azerica's been laughing at her friend's deranged personality ever since.

"Hey Azerica."

"What Trish?"

"Isn't that Jason's sister walking this way?" Trish asked.

"Yeah, her name is Devin." Azerica replied.

What could Devin want now? I hope she doesn't try to pray with me again. I don't want Trish to think I'm weird. Ok, so if the subject starts turning in that direction, I'll just change it, and God please send her away. I just know that if Trish saw or even heard about the praying thing, she wouldn't want me to go to the party with her.

"Hey Azerica. How were your classes today?" Devin asked when she walked up to join them. She didn't want to intrude, but she hadn't seen her friend since they got to school.

Maybe she forgot about this morning, Azerica hoped.

"They were alright," Azerica responded half-heartedly. "Do you know Trish?"

"No." Devin had seen her around before, but never knew her name. *So this is who Azerica's new best friend is.*

"Well, Devin, this is Trish Jackson, she cheers with me and Trish, this is Devin."

"Hello Trish," Devin politely held out her hand.

"Hi," Trish smirked and shook her hand. Trish didn't know her, but she could tell Devin was the biggest goody-two-shoes she'd ever met. Not only did she shake her hand, but the chick also spoke very properly. That made Trish want to gag. No one is that perfect. No one acts like that anymore. No real black person anyway.

"Azerica, will you be busy after practice tonight?" Devin asked. "I was wondering if you'd like to study with me."

"Sorry, Devin. I can't tonight. I've already made plans."

"Ok. Well maybe tomorrow." Devin said. She let Azerica off the hook this time, but she promised God she would keep asking Azerica to study with her until she got convicted. "Are you two on your way to practice?"

"Unfortunately," said Trish. "But the highlight of practice is being able to see your brother sweat."

"You know my brother?" Devin laughed. "You probably wouldn't like the sweat if you knew what his clothes smelled like when he got home. They're so nasty and Mom always tells him his love for sports would drive any woman away."

"Not me. I'd do anything to keep him, if I had him." Trish said, thinking of Jason's sweaty body close to hers.

Out of the corner of her eye, Azerica watched Devin's natural glow disappear. She knew Devin was saved and sanctified and was extremely sensitive to talk about sex. She could see in her best friend's eyes that she didn't approve of Trish's actions. She probably didn't approve of Azerica being friends with Trish. But who cared? Who was she?

Azerica remembered last year when she and Devin were both living for God and setting out to do his will. But then high school and cheerleading, her mom, her dad…Azerica just stopped and slowly started living life for herself and having fun the way she wanted to. She finally realized she couldn't wait for everyone else to make her happy. They always ended up disappointing her. And in the midst of it, God just seemed to take way too long. Who knew things could change so much in one year?

"Devin, do you think you and Jay can give me a ride home today?" Azerica asked.

"Yeah girl, of course. You live right next door. Just make sure the two of you come to get me from the library after practice. I'll be in there studying. I'll just do that today since you can't study with me tonight." Devin tried again to get Azerica to see how important studying the Bible was.

"Oh, alright Devin. Well, I'll see you after practice." Azerica said, cutting Devin off.

"Ok. It was nice meeting you Trish." Devin said sweetly.

"Same to you," Trish replied, mocking Devin's tone.

Azerica and Trish watched Devin walk down the hall to the library.

"What's with her? Do you have class together?" Trish asked trying to figure out Devin's motives.

"No."

"Well, why does she want you to study with her so bad?"

"She needs help in English," Azerica quickly lied.

Sorry God, she said silently. *I didn't want to lie, but I can't tell Trish the truth. She would disown me as a friend and tell all the other cheerleaders if she knew me and Devin studied the Bible every week. I can't let them think I'm weird. My high school life would be over before it even started.*

"Devin seems real proper, I would've thought that she needed help in math or something, oh well. I just can't believe you're going to ride home with Jay! Why didn't you tell me he was your neighbor? I would've been coming to your house everyday."

Azerica smiled and laughed. "Come on Hoochie. We're about to be late and it's the first day of practice on our first day of school. We don't want to have to do extra work."

"I know, right! Plus Jason should be real sweaty by now."

"How can you even tell who he is? They are always wearing their football stuff?" Azerica asked.

"He's got the tightest ass. And besides, his number is 16." Trish smiled.

"Girl you are a trip!"

-ydn-

"How's that daughter of yours?"

"Oh, Mr. Henry, she's as stubborn as ever." Sheryl said, happy to talk to someone about it. "I moved away so she could grow up and learn to be responsible, but I'm going to have to make a special trip back to Jacksonville to help her out."

"Well what's the problem?" the old man reached and grabbed her hand.

"Are you getting fresh with me Mr. Henry?" Sheryl teased. "Because if you are, I'm going to have to start volunteering at another nursing home."

"No, young woman. I don't want to run you off. I just want you to know my ear still works even if the rest of me don't work properly," Mr. Henry said squeezing her hand.

"Well thank you Mr. Henry."

Sheryl returned his squeeze and grabbed his newest edition of JET Magazine so they could look at it together. That was one of his favorite things to do when she came to visit him. He enjoyed seeing popular black faces in the news because they didn't have many chances to be in magazines and newspapers back when he was young.

"Mr. Henry, look who made it on the front cover!" Sheryl exclaimed. "I know you'd know this face anywhere."

"I done already looked at that magazine Sheryl. I seen Bill Cosby on there many a times. Put that magazine down and tell me what's troubling you." Mr. Henry commanded.

Sheryl couldn't help but to laugh. At his ripe old age of 96, Mr. Henry still had his sharp tongue. He wouldn't let anything get passed him. If he told you to do something, you'd better do it. *I don't know why I thought I could avoid telling him my problems.*

"Mr. Henry I don't want to burden you with my burdens. Let's just look at this JET." Sheryl suggested.

"Now girlie, you and me's both Christians and it's my duty as your brother in Christ to help you through your problems. I might be old and 96, but that don't mean I'm senile. I been around and could tell you a thing or two," Mr. Henry said getting onto her. "Don't let this gray hair fool you. Believe me, I earned it."

"Now that my grandbaby is 14, I think I know everything," Sheryl smiled. "I'm sorry Mr. Henry, I keep forgetting that wisdom comes with age."

"That's right. Now, tell Mr. Henry what the problem is," he encouraged her.

"After all these years, my daughter still has no faith. We've talked and prayed together and I keep praying that God will give her faith, but she still hasn't received it." Sheryl began to open up. "And now she really needs God to move in her life. She's not working and she stopped getting child support and she has three children to care for."

"Girlie what is it that you were going to do?" Mr. Henry asked.

"Mr. Henry, I don't have much. I was going to give her some of my retirement money. I don't want to see my grandbabies without a home because she's irresponsible," Sheryl sighed. "It's just so hard to sit and do nothing for her."

Mr. Henry sat silently so she could get all her thoughts out.

"I know Mr. Henry. You don't have to say it. I bail her out all the time. She'll never learn how to be responsible if I keep giving her money. I just worry about the babies." Sheryl continued.

"Sheryl didn't you tell me you moved from Jacksonvillage so she could learn to depend on just herself?" Mr. Henry asked.

"Jacksonville, Mr. Henry." Sheryl corrected. She hated correcting him because he never listened to her when she did it. But she didn't want him going around saying the wrong things.

"Girlie, I know what it's called. Just answer my question."

"You're right," she answered. "I moved so she could stop depending on me."

"If you go giving her money, it'll be the same thing all over again. Let the girl grow up. She needs to find a job and start working. Does she know how to clean? She can start cleaning houses. My wife did that for years when we needed extra money. And they even have that thing the govment does now…what's it called?"

"Welfare?" Sheryl offered.

"Yeah, that's it. We never had such a thing. If you had told black folks back then that the govment was going to buy our food 'cause we were po we would'a always had sumthing to eat. Young black folks now don't wanna work and if they git welfare, they wanna keep it 'til they die," Mr. Henry shook his head. "I tell my grandkids now don't ever come see me if you on welfare 'cause you don't wanna work."

Sheryl laughed. She loved her weekly visits with Mr. Henry. He reminded her so much of her grandfather who was 94 when he passed away. The man could go on for days about the same stuff Mr. Henry complained about. It amazed her they were so alike and had never met. After a few visits with Mr. Henry, she felt like she'd known him all her life. And she's only known him for about five months. But he was already like family to her.

What would I do without Mr. Henry, she asked herself. *If daddy or even granddad could see me now, they would be happy to know that I'm still getting advice from my elders.*

"Girlie, I'm about finished talking to you. I gotta take my nap so I can go to Bingo tonight. Old William thinks he can break my winning spree."

Sheryl stood up to leave.

"Now, Sheryl I said about. I still got some more to say to you." Mr. Henry pointed his finger at her.

Sheryl sat back down in her seat; she didn't want to get in trouble with Mr. Henry.

"Sounds to me like God is dealing with your daughter. You can't go fighting her battles for her and you can't hold her hand while she's fighting 'em. She's a competent woman and she knows the Bible. All you can do is what you done did. Tell her to pray and have faith. Now, don't you stop praying for her. You know God will answer your prayers. It's time for you to have some faith too. You hear me?" he asked her.

"Yes, Mr. Henry," Sheryl felt like a schoolgirl again. Mr. Henry made it sound so simple.

"Now I'm not sayin' don't give her any money. I'm just sayin' don't go givin' her any money 'til after she finds a job that she's goin' to keep. We all need a little help, we just gotta help ourselves a little first."

Thank you Lord, Sheryl said to herself. *Sometimes I just need a little confirmation to know I'm doing what you want me to do.*

"Mr. Henry I always enjoy coming to see you. Please be nice to Mr. William tonight. You know how easily his feelings get hurt," Sheryl said, adjusting the lights for him.

"Don't you worry 'bout me and William. He ain't as soft as you think he is," Mr. Henry said. "Now go on home and pray."

"Yes, Mr. Henry." Sheryl said. "When can I come see you again?"

Mr. Henry winked at her. "Girlie, you know I gotta open door for you."

Sheryl laughed. She placed the JET back where she found it beside Mr. Henry's bed. He had to be one of the only seniors she knew in this nursing home with a single room. He was blessed not to have to share his space. Even if he had to, he'd probably confine his poor roommate to the smallest section of the room.

"Mr. Henry," Sheryl kissed his forehead. "I will see you this weekend."

"'Bye Sheryl," Mr. Henry said as he settled down in his bed for a nap.

"'Bye Mr. Henry," Sheryl whispered and quietly closed the door behind her.

Everything Mr. Henry said made so much sense. How in the world could she continue to preach faith to her daughter, if she herself couldn't show that she had faith in Candace?

And in my heart, I don't really know if I have a lot of faith in her, Sheryl's mind wandered as she found her car and made her way home. *Candace means well. She's always tried to do what's right, but it never happens for her. Every time it seems she's found her way, something happens and she falls off the wagon again. And my poor grandbabies suffer from her mistakes. Luckily I've been there to help her with providing for them, but what's Candace going to do when I'm not here anymore? I can't keep doing everything for her if I want her to learn on her own.*

Candace is thirty-something and still struggling with everyday life. Sheryl's never understood what she doesn't get and why she can't understand. She never taught Candace life was easy, but even the simple things she can barely do.

God, I'm running out of options here. Tell me what you want me to do. Lord,

Candace needs you. Please show her faith and make it strong. Please bless her with a job so that she can take care of her family. Lord, please ensure they will always have food to eat, clothes on their backs and a roof over their heads. And Lord, please increase my faith in her. Help me to believe that she can and will be a responsible adult who is able to nurture all her children's needs. Because right now God, I just don't see it.

Chapter 3

Staring at the bland gray walls drove him crazy. He couldn't wait until he was able to see the bright smile of his baby girl again. Her face alone always lit up the walls of his heart. Her laughter was his favorite song. Since the day she was born, it played to the beat of his heart and hasn't stopped since.

He hated himself for always being the reason why she was never able to see him. If he didn't always get himself into these types of situations, he would be able to support her the way a father should. Instead of working towards building an empire, he always looks for the easiest ways out. That's what he was doing when he was arrested for drug trafficking. He thought he could sell a little something on the side while he worked legitimately at Wal-mart in his management position, but the plan backfired in his face. He never thought about the consequences until it was too late. Now he's facing three to five years in prison and he's going to miss some of the best years of Azerica's life.

All he wanted to do was provide for her and give her what he never had. Now he has nothing and nothing to give but his love. His angel could accept that and appreciate it. She never asks for anything other than his attention. But Candace, on the other hand, demands the world from him and when he can't provide it, she raises hell. He was so happy to pacify her when he was selling drugs. She felt taken care of and for the first time, she felt like he was doing his job and taking care of Azerica consistently.

But now that he's locked up, he knows Candace is tripping and is on one of her rampages. She gets nervous when things don't go the way she wants them to. She don't know how to handle tough situations.

"That chick is like me," Jeffrey said to himself. "When things get tough, she looks for the easy way out just like me. Except when I do it, I'm immature and irresponsible. But when she does it, she's handling business."

Jeffrey sighed a long sigh. The history the two of them shared was a long, bumpy road of ups and downs. He loved Candace with all his heart but could never really express himself and show her. Every time he tried, it ended with him causing her grief and pain.

He will never forget the first time he saw her almond-shaped brown eyes and beautiful smile. Until he saw her, he had no clue what love at first sight meant. She was absolutely beautiful. The day her beauty first beckoned him, he was on his way home from school. He had just gone to his locker to put up his books and he happened to walk down the wrong hall thinking that he was going to see Coach Johnson. That's when he saw her. She stood in front of her locker talking to a few of her girlfriends. He don't know how many of them were with her or what they were talking about, all he saw was her. And her face glowed with every word that flowed from her mouth.

That was 1987 at Robert E. Lee High School in Jacksonville. He was 17 and she was 16. He didn't know her name then, but her face stayed embedded in his memory.

Why am I putting myself through this, he thought. *That was 14 years ago and since then, she's had two more children by another man.*

Jeffrey sighed another long sigh. It had been a long morning and he could tell it would be a long evening.

-ydn-

She'd finished all her homework for the evening. She used to hate waiting at school for her brother while he was at practice, but Devin learned to use the time wisely so she was able to go home, eat and study her word. She really wished Azerica could study with her tonight, but she knew how busy Azerica had been with cheerleading.

The first week of school was always hectic especially as an athlete. Devin knew from watching her brother and the hours he spent practicing after classes. Cheerleading was obviously no different. Azerica hadn't had the time to do many of the things they used to do on a daily basis. They'd barely even spoken on the phone.

"Lord, I hope that's all it is," Devin thought out loud. "God, I pray things are okay for her at home. I ask that you strengthen her and give her a mind to continue to seek and know your ways. God don't let her part from you during this time in our lives. High school can cause grief and confusion for so many but I know Lord that you've set a different path out for her. I thank you for her friendship and for knitting our hearts together. In Jesus name I pray, Amen."

After finishing her prayer, Devin felt better. She enjoyed praying and speaking life into those who she knew really needed it.

She gathered her things and walked over to the computers so she could check her e-mail. When she finished she walked upstairs to the newsroom. She wanted to become part of the newspaper staff, but the desktop publishing classes filled up so quickly this year that she wasn't able to get in. Even though she couldn't take any of the classes, she still wanted to meet the staff and maybe be able to contribute articles to the paper this school year.

When she got there, she saw several students busy and typing away to meet deadlines.

She walked inside to find a teacher sitting at a desk towards the back of the room. Devin walked over and introduced herself. She told him her position and how much she would love to write and contribute something.

"Well, Devin it's seems like you came at a good time. A few people decided to drop the class and now there are some open spots. Why don't you go see your guidance counselor and I'm sure you're schedule can be re-arranged," Mr. Hensley told her.

"Are you serious?" Devin asked. She was ecstatic. She couldn't believe this was happening!

"Yes. One of them is a senior this year and she's decided to do the morning announcements instead. The other student moved to another city."

Thank you Jesus!

"In this class you'll find everyone from freshmen to seniors. Sometimes the counselors have to register them under a different class name, but they're all newspaper. Let me write a referral for you so you don't have any problems," said Mr. Hensley reaching for his pen and paper.

God it's amazing the way you work. I bless Azerica through prayer and you bless me by allowing me to write for the school paper.

"I'm so glad you came when you did, I was just going to close the class and keep the students who are already enrolled." Mr. Hensley said. "I really didn't want to do that because the paper needs some good writers. We have some, but we could always use more."

"I'm glad I came when I did too. I love to write and I wanted to be able to write for the school paper. We didn't have one at my junior high," Devin said. She felt her spirit shining through her.

"Well, as soon as you're in, I'm going to have them close the class. If you don't see you're guidance counselor today, make sure you go first thing in the morning so you can be in class tomorrow. We have some work to get you caught up on," Mr. Hensley said as he handed her the referral.

"Thank you Mr. Hensley," Devin glowed. "I really appreciate it."

"No problem. We need you."

They need me, Mr. Hensley's words repeated in her mind.

Devin felt like she was floating on air. She had no idea that would happen, but God had set it up for her. All she had to do was walk in faith.

I only expected to be able to contribute an article or two this year. I didn't imagine I could get in the class and learn about it. Lord I'm so thankful. You keep me on my toes. There's no way I could ever renounce you as my Savior. You do so much for me without me even asking. Help me to spread this cheer to all those I come in contact with. I don't want this day to go by without me sharing this testimony with someone.

Basking in His glory, Devin walked back downstairs to the library to wait for her brother and Azerica. She couldn't wait to tell them about what God just did for her. But until practice was over she would just study her Bible.

Inside there were only a few students, mostly science students who were working on their research for their science fair projects. She quietly walked by them towards the study room and sat down on the big, cushioned chair in front of the door. She sat her bag at her feet and unzipped the front pocket where she kept her small study Bible. Her mother gave her the Bible for her birthday last year. She remembered she didn't want anything else but it because she wanted to be able to have something small and compact that she could always refer back to when she felt in need of a word.

She opened the small Bible to read some more in Hebrews. She started reading the book last week, but when she came to chapters ten and eleven, she continued to read them over and over. It was hard for her to admit, but she needed the faith reminder. Azerica had changed so much over the summer it was like they were never friends. It hurt Devin, but she knew in heart that God was telling her to continue to be a friend to Azerica even when she knew Azerica would continue to let her down. She could feel God tugging on her heart, and Hebrews 11:1 played over and over in her mind: *Now faith is the substance of things hoped for, the evidence of things not seen.*

Devin lost herself in her Bible, reading and rereading. She wanted to make sure she heard what God was saying even if she didn't understand. She didn't realize how much time had passed until she heard her brother's voice. When she looked up she saw he and Azerica walking towards her. They both looked exhausted and ready to go home.

"Dev, you ready?" Jason asked when they got closer.

"Yeah, let me put my Bible up," she answered. She'd been so enveloped in her studies that she hadn't noticed them and they caught her off guard. The glow and sparkle she had before she started studying slowly disappeared.

Oh great. Jason and Azerica are in one of their moods. It would be an answered prayer if they ever decided to acknowledge God's presence in their lives. I know Jason never really fully dedicated his life to God, but he's experienced the Lord. And Azerica is just tripping. Lord, please help me to stay positive and to testify what you've done. I'm going to really need you.

Devin struggled trying to start a conversation with them. She had no idea what personalities she would get this afternoon. They both acted funny anytime she was around. She was used to it from her brother, but it really hurt that her best friend treated her that way now too. As far as she was concerned, they both were spiritually disconnected. She knew she just needed to pray for them right now, but their attitudes could really be discouraging.

"How was practice?" Devin finally asked as they walked out of the school.

"You know Coach is trying to get us ready for the game Friday." Jason said nonchalantly.

"Who do you play?" Devin asked. She wasn't that interested in football, but she pretended to be for her brother's sake.

"Lee."

"Are you serious!" Azerica exclaimed. "I thought we were playing Forrest. That's why Coach is running y'all to death on the field."

"Yeah, you noticed?" Jason asked.

"Yeah, man. I'm sorry." Azerica apologized. "I felt sorry for you guys when I saw you over the summer, but I really feel sorry for you now. Y'all looked about dead today."

"No problem Z. We're used to it." This was Jason's second year on varsity. They always had severe practices during the start of the season. USG football practices get less intense after the team has proven themselves.

"So this game will be good," said Devin. "Have you told Mom and Dad about it?"

"Yeah, they got one of the schedules on the fridge. I put it up for 'em last night."

"You know what? I'll be taking pictures at the game." Devin smiled.

"For what?" Jason asked shocked. "Are you starting a new hobby or something?"

"I'm going to be on the newspaper staff. I have to go to the guidance counselor tomorrow so my schedule can be changed," Devin smiled even bigger.

"That's great," said Azerica, forcing a smile to form on her lips.

"Yeah, Dad will be real happy that you're finally doing something," Jason joked.

"Oh, whatever," Devin smiled.

They had a running joke in the Roberts family that if it didn't involve prayer, Devin wouldn't do it. She remembered back to a few years ago when their dad thought she'd become an introvert because she didn't get involved in any school activities. But it wasn't her fault. Nothing ever interested her. Everything was always about the school and not about God. And she was about God. She wanted so badly to go to a Christian school then, but her parents couldn't afford it.

And they still couldn't.

"How's your dad doing?" Devin changed the subject and asked Azerica.

"He's doing alright, I guess. I talked to him the other day... I think it was. He's just ready to get out and come home." Azerica said. Her heart ached when talked about him. It killed her to hear him like that. She hadn't visited him yet. She refused to see him that way. "I wish I could talk to him more. I don't really get to talk to him as much as I want."

"Why is that?" Devin asked.

"I guess our schedules don't really match up now that school has started," Azerica said, not wanting to mention her mother's phone games. "Hopefully, he can call me today."

"I'm sure he'll do his best to call you." Devin tried to reassure her. "You two are so close, I really admire that."

Azerica smiled. "Yeah, that's my dad. I love him to death."

"I know." Devin looked at her and smiled.

Azerica felt a warmth that she hadn't felt in a long time. Even though she and Devin were living their lives a little differently right now, they still had a connection. No one else knew her like Devin did and deep in her heart she knew she would have no other friend as wonderful as Devin. As soon as she redeveloped her image, she would work on bringing Devin in to the circle. It wouldn't be hard with her brother being the school's best athlete and her friend a cheerleader. She would just need to chill a little with her holier-than-thou attitude.

"Let me tell you what happened to me today," Devin said smiling. They both seemed to be in a better mood now.

"What's that Dev?" Jason asked, happy the topic changed. He never really knew what to say to Azerica about her dad. All that made him a little uncomfortable.

"Well when I finished my homework, I decided to go upstairs to the news room to introduce myself to the staff. You know I really wanted to write for the school paper but the classes were all full. When I got up there I found out two spots were opened. One person changed classes and the other moved to another city. I spoke to the teacher and he gave me a referral to take to my guidance counselor so I can get in the class. Ain't that so awesome!" Devin exclaimed.

"Yeah, it's great," Jason, said nonchalantly. He was going to have to make a new conversation rule for his passengers. No talking about God and no talking about Azerica's dad in jail. *Those two subjects I can't handle.*

"Wow, that is good," Azerica tried to sound as enthused as Devin.

"God really just worked that one out for me. He gives you the desires of your heart as long as they're in His perfect will." Devin tried to explain to them. She knew they weren't listening to her, but she needed to say it anyway. *Maybe the seeds will find some good soil in their hearts somewhere.*

Azerica sat in silence while Devin continued to talk. She stared out the window at the scenery before her. She really didn't feel like being preached to. Whenever Devin got started that's where all her conversations ended. With everything going so well in her life right now, Azerica didn't want to hear it.

"Dev, when will you start the class?" Jason asked, interrupting Devin's flow.

"Hopefully tomorrow. That's when I'm going to see my counselor. I already have so many ideas for articles that I want to write," she answered with excitement still fresh in her voice.

"That's good," he said trying to keep a conversation with her that he wanted to have.

For the rest of the drive Azerica listened to Jason and Devin talk. Her mind wandered from their conversation to thoughts of her dad. She hadn't seen him since the day after he was arrested. That day he was miserable and he waited almost a week before he called her for the first time. Now that they had established a somewhat consistent form

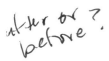

young, dumb and naive

of communication, she wasn't sure if she could handle it. She didn't know what she would say or how to keep a positive conversation going.

What do you tell a man in prison?

Chapter 4

Maybe he'll call today, Azerica thought to herself. She couldn't imagine why he wouldn't call, but she couldn't imagine why he wouldn't call yesterday, either. She waited all day after school yesterday for her dad's phone call, but the phone never rang. *I hope he didn't forget about me. I really want to hear from him. I hope he's okay and he didn't get hurt. They always talk about men getting raped in prison. Oh God, please don't let my daddy get raped.*

Azerica flipped through the channels to occupy her time, but she couldn't help worrying. Her dad always did what he told her he would do. Well, other than the money thing, but he always made those promises to her mother.

Azerica gripped the raggedy cordless phone and brought it close to her chest, so she could answer it on the first ring when it did ring.

The last thing she needed was for it to ring more than once. If her mom knew she was accepting collect calls from her dad, she would be in so much trouble. Azerica knew her mom would eventually find out. The phone bill doesn't lie. But Azerica was just going to have to cross that bridge when she got there. It was worth getting into trouble so she could talk to her dad.

Azerica pressed mute on the TV to listen for her mother. Twenty minutes ago she and Chauncey went to the back because he needed to be changed, but they hadn't come back to the front yet. Azerica strained her ears and heard nothing but silence. She loved the sweet sounds of silence, but too much quiet made her nervous sometimes.

The apartment was already unusually quiet with Melina playing outside with some of the other Raintree children. And they all were enjoying their quiet time. But it was just too quiet for Azerica.

Let me see what Mom and Chauncey are doing, she thought. *Chauncey really doesn't make a lot of noise, but Mom does. Even when she's just changing his diaper.*

She walked to the back and peeked inside her mom's room and found the two of them sleeping.

Great! They're asleep. I don't have to sneak around when he calls...If he calls. Daddy just please call me! Azerica silently whined.

As if her wish had been granted, the phone rang.

"Hello?" Azerica asked softly.

"Hey baby girl!" It felt like years since Jeffrey heard his daughter's voice. "I miss you so much."

"Daddy! Hey! Why didn't you call me yesterday?" Azerica asked excitedly. "I waited by the phone all day. And you know how nosy Mom is. She was tripping and she kept watching me. She knew what I was doing."

"I'm sorry baby. Where is she now?" Jeffrey asked.

"She's sleep. She and Chauncey are back there knocked out." Azerica said as she walked back to the living room.

"What'd you do? Give 'em some Nyquil so she wouldn't bother you?" Jeffrey teased.

Azerica laughed. "No Daddy!"

"Yeah, it'd probably take more than Nyquil to knock that woman out," He laughed hard at his own joke. "You'd have to go ol' school and give her some Moonshine."

"You're crazy Daddy." Azerica laughed with him. She couldn't remember the last time she ever laughed this hard. And what he was saying was true. Her mom was a real stubborn lady. "Laughter really does good like medicine."

"Baby it's so good to hear your voice. Did I tell you miss you?" Jeffrey finished his fit of laughter. "You are very important to me."

"Yes Daddy. You did. I miss you too. So what happened to you yesterday?" Azerica asked him again. She felt like he was getting all mushy and avoiding her question. "There couldn't have been anything more important than calling me?"

"No, there's nothing more important than you," he replied, playing her attention game. "Sweetheart. I just couldn't get to the phone. But don't worry about that. How was your first day of school?"

"It was alright. I feel like a baby. I am so small! Everyone else is so big and they bump into me all the time. Trish gave me some clothes and she's going to bring me some more this week. Daddy you should see her clothes. They are so cute! And they don't make me look so little," Azerica ran through this week's emotions all in one breath.

Jeffrey laughed. He envisioned sitting right beside her while she told her story. He could see her animated facial expressions and hand movements.

I can't wait to be outta here so I can see her again.

"Daddy are you listening to me?" Azerica asked him.

"Yeah, I'm listening." Jeffrey smiled through the phone.

"Well aren't you proud of me? I'm one of two freshmen who got picked to cheer with the varsity cheerleaders. We have practice everyday after school. I met all the varsity cheerleaders yesterday. When we were in camp, we had an idea of who would make it, but I had no idea they would choose me..."

"I am very proud of you girl. Just make sure you keep good grades," Jeffrey reminded her. "That's what's really important. You don't wanna be a dumb jock when you get older."

Azerica laughed. "Daddy, I'll never be a dumb jock."

"You will if you don't have good grades. I know you don't plan on cheering for the rest of your life. Cheerleaders don't have much of a career after college, unless you think you're gonna cheer for the Jaguars or something. But their salaries aren't much to brag about." Jeffrey tried to school her. "I need you to be a lawyer or doctor or something so you can take care of me when I get old."

"Now you sound like Mom." Azerica sighed. She never gave much thought to what she really wanted to be when she grew up. *I still have plenty of time though.*

"Whatever you do, don't put us in the same nursing home. We might end up killing each other." Jeffrey could see them arguing about child support during Bingo or something. He'd be waving his cane at her and Candace would be trying to run him over in her wheelchair.

She'd definitely be the one with a wheelchair. I work out. My legs will make it through old age.

"Alright Daddy. I know. But let me tell you what happened to me yesterday in my history class. I don't think my teacher likes me much, but I'm going to try to keep at least a B in that class. But I accidentally said something out loud. I forget what I was thinking about, but Mrs. Armstrong heard me. She asked me a question. She knew I hadn't been paying attention to her, and she asked me anyway. Daddy I was really embarrassed." Azerica rambled.

Jeffrey laughed again. He loved hearing her ramble and he loved the innocence in her problems. "Oh Pumpkin, she didn't mean anything by it. She just wants you to listen to what she's saying. That's what's supposed to happen in class."

"But I was. Daddy, I should've known you wouldn't get it. You're one of them," she sighed dramatically. All parents were just alike.

"Yeah, because I'm acting like your dad right now, I'm one of them. You'd better be glad someone cares enough to tell you." Jeffrey said.

Azerica sighed dramatically again.

"Well Baby, I have to get off the phone now before they kick me off." He said reluctantly.

"Ok Daddy," Azerica's voice dropped a little from disappointment.

"I promise to call you as soon as I can. If I can't call tomorrow, I'll wait until Saturday so I can hear about your first game." Jeffrey said. He tried to sound cheerful, but it wasn't working for him.

"Ok Daddy." Azerica's voice drooped a little more.

"I love you baby." He said sweetly.

"I love you too Daddy," Azerica said softly. She sat the phone down, walked back to her room and closed the door.

"I miss my daddy," she said softly to herself. *I never thought I would miss him so much. But I never thought he'd be in jail either.*

Her dad meant everything to her and now he was so out of reach, she couldn't cope. She'd been fine the past two days, but hearing his voice just now made it hurt so much more.

Azerica clung to her teddy bear, lay down on her bed and allowed two weeks of pain to flow through her eyes. It was always easy for her to keep her gameface at school around her friends, and even around her mother. But every time she was alone, all she could do was cry.

-ydn-

"Trish, don't you have somewhere to go?" Denise Jackson walked into the room and asked her daughter.

Trish glared at her. It was 9:30 and dark outside. She wasn't about to go anywhere or visit any friends at this hour. All her friends' parents had normal rules for their daughters: in by ten on weeknights and by midnight on weekends. Trish hated their curfews on the weekends because she could always come and go as she pleased. And usually, she left because she was forced out. But sometimes, she secretly wished her mom would give her a curfew. Then at least she would know her mom worried about her.

"Oh, Neesie. She don't have to go anywhere," breathed a strange man walking up behind her mom. He grabbed her and pulled him close to her. "We can just close the door and turn some music on."

Trish kept her eyes glued to the television while her mom giggled and let the man grab her. After ten years of seeing her mom sleep with man after man, Trish thought she would become immune to hating it. But she hadn't. And she finally realized she never would.

"Eric, we can't do this while she's here," Denise rubbed his baldhead. "Why don't you come by tomorrow morning before work? Breakfast in bed. I guarantee you've never had breakfast like this."

Trish's skin got hot. Didn't they know she could hear them?

"Neesie, I'm not playing anymore games with you," Eric pulled her more tightly towards him so she could feel him. "You called me, like you always call me. I didn't call you."

"Eric I know," Denise pleaded, her eyes begging him to work with her. "I didn't know. I swear I didn't know or I wouldn't have called you."

"What's it going to be?" he asked her sternly. "If I walk out that door, don't ever call me again."

Denise knew he was serious this time. He didn't need her anymore since everything was better at home. He always made it a point to throw that in her face, but Denise still calls him anyway because she still needs him, even though she's his client now and now they have to play by his rules.

"Neesie, I don't have much time before my wife starts calling to see where I am." Eric rubbed her thighs.

Denise turned back towards Trish. "Trish can you pick up some milk for tomorrow?"

"I did that on the way home from practice," Trish avoided looking at them.

Refusing to wait any longer, Eric began pulling Denise back towards the room.

"Eric, wait. She has no where to go." Denise stopped him from pulling her.

"Hell! I hope you find another million-dollar nigga out there willing to put up with you 'cause I ain't doing it no more!" Eric burst out in frustration.

"Fine." Denise gave in. She needed his support until she could find someone else. She glanced one last time at Trish and then walked towards her room.

When Trish realized they were going to have sex whether or not she was present, she turned the TV off and threw the remote down. "Don't worry Mom. I do have somewhere to go," she said and slammed the door behind her.

She didn't know where she was going. She just had to get out. She didn't want to hear or see what was about to take place with her mom and the married man. Her mom had been doing this for years, but this was the first time her mom was going to go ahead and have sex while she was still there. *Mom must be desperate for money.*

Trish walked out of their apartment complex and to Lex Av, gazing at the stars. With all the city lights, they were normally hard to see. But she could see them tonight. She picked one and made a wish.

"I wish I may I wish I might have this wish I wish tonight," she said softly. "I wish that when I find the right guy that he knows it too because he's never had anything better than me. I don't want him going off and having sex with millions of women all the time."

Trish knew her mom was pretty bad about sleeping with a lot of men, but she knew the men were just as bad. Many of them were married and they've been sleeping around for years. Trish didn't understand and she didn't want to understand.

"I just want to marry a fine man who doesn't sleep around," she said out loud. *But until I get there, it's free reign. I'll just be better than my mom and not date anybody that's married. Why would any woman do that to herself? No matter how much money he has, Eric's never going to be hers.*

"Which reminds me. I've gotta take Azerica through my class. She's got to learn to flirt and act a little older," Trish said. "I can give her all the clothes in the world, but until she starts acting a little more grown, she's gonna keep looking like a little girl."

Trish tried, but she couldn't be Azerica's savior. Azerica needed a boyfriend who could take her through a few things. She needed to live a little and have fun.

Trish decided to find some random guy for her at Darren's party and encourage Azerica to open up to him. She would plan some unexpected alone time for them and leave a few condoms in the room or something. That should work. That was always a foolproof plan when she was dealing with rookies. It didn't really matter if Azerica had ever had a boyfriend because she and whoever the guy will be will work things out.

Trish smiled, happy that she finally had a plan. Now she had to call Azerica and let her know what was up.

She walked over to Krystal's to use the payphone outside the restaurant. She wanted to prep Azerica for the weekend so she had an idea of what might be occurring. Girls like Azerica always chicken out because they don't realize how immature it is to not participate.

"Hello." Answered a female voice.

"Hi. This is Trish. Can I speak to Azerica?"

"Hold on a sec." Trish listened while Ms. Christian yelled for Azerica to get the phone.

"Hello." Azerica said after about a minute.

"Hey, it's Trish. What are you doing?"

"Watching TV," Azerica said. She didn't really feel like talking on the phone. She still missed her dad.

"I can't wait for Darren's party and I know you can't either. We've got some work to do with you before you're ready to go," Trish jumped right to it.

"So what are you thinking about?" Azerica got a little excited. She liked talking about redefining herself. She could talk all day long about that.

"I need you to call me back at this number before I tell you," Trish said.

"Where are you?" Azerica asked, hearing the traffic in the background.

"A pay phone." Trish said nonchalantly. "Just call me right back at this number. You have caller ID, right?"

"Yeah. I'll call you right back." Azerica said and hung up the phone.

Trish placed the phone on the receiver and looked around. Traffic was pretty heavy for ten 'o' clock at night. That was unusual for Jacksonville especially during the week, but Trish didn't care enough to wonder.

"Hello," she answered when the pay phone started ringing.

"Trish, what are you doing at a payphone?" Azerica asked. "I know your house phone works."

"I don't wanna talk about it," Trish answered, thinking about her mom and Eric. "It's a long story that we don't have time for."

"Alright." Azerica said, still wondering what was going on.

"Anyways, I've got some more clothes I wanna give you. Can you come over Thursday night? We can go through them and pick out some clothes for you to wear to school and to the party. 'Cause you gotta be stacked at the party. I heard Darren's brother's friends are going to be there too. And his brother has some fine friends." Trish said. "They make me hot."

Azerica blushed at Trish's comment. "Do they look that good?"

"Yes! I saw them at the mall a few weeks ago. They were like thugged out Chippendale's." Trish could still see them in her head. "I wanted some thug passion!"

"But you got Jay, remember Hoochie?" Azerica teased.

"Yeah, but you're free. Thugs need love too."

"I never thought about dating a thug," Azerica admitted. She thought they sold drugs and carried guns.

Trish laughed at her. "Azerica, they're not thugs for real. I just say that because they wear real baggy clothes. Girl, they all go to school. I think they go to the community college."

"Oh," Azerica felt silly.

"Anyways, Z. They're real cool. It would be good for you to start talking to one of them. You can't act like a baby though. If they give you a drink take it. If they kiss you, kiss 'em back. 'Cause if you don't, they will talk about you." Trish tried her best to advise. "Be ready. Anything goes."

"Ok." Azerica replied. She wasn't sure if she could be ready for this.

"Z, let me get off this payphone. I'm gonna go back home and go to bed. They should be finished by now," Trish said.

"Who?" Azerica asked curiously.

"Oh, don't worry about it. I'll see you at school."

"Bye. Trish." Azerica said.

"Bye Z." Trish put the phone on the receiver and walked back down Lex Av. Now Azerica had something to think about. *I hope she's ready to prove herself. My reputation's at stake too since we're friends. I guess I should've just come out and said it, but oh, well, too late now. The party ain't until Friday anyway.*

The walk back home seemed to take twenty minutes longer than it took for her to leave. Normally, Trish didn't mind, but tonight it got on her nerves because she was trying her best not to think about what she might find when she made it home. She hoped the man was gone so she could just climb into bed and go to sleep. She didn't like the way he spoke to her mom or the way he groped her. But she couldn't control it. Her mom would let it continue no matter what Trish had to say.

I guess I can't complain. That's how we get everything we have. Trish said to herself. *Mom's with me all day after school except for when she's with her men. And she's not strict. I guess most teenagers would love what I have.*

That didn't convince her. Trish could tell herself that all day, but she would never shake the churning she felt in her stomach until her mom changed her lifestyle.

"That's not happening anytime soon," Trish rolled her eyes and unlocked the door.

She felt her way back to her mom's room, careful not to run into anything. It took a few moments for her eyes to adjust to the blackness. Outside of her mother's bedroom door, Trish bent down to listen for any sounds of movement. There was nothing. She went inside and found her mom and no Eric. Her mom was sprawled across the bed in a deep sleep wearing one of her large t-shirts.

Trish pulled the covers over her and kissed her forehead. "I love you Mom."

She closed the door back and went to her own room. In spite of everything, she really did love her mom.

Chapter 5

So far, this week hasn't been so bad, Azerica said to herself recounting the events so far. Monday started out horribly, but ended alright. The first day back was always fun, but even more fun at USG. She finally got to talk to her dad Tuesday. That made her day. And she found out Trish had more clothes for her. And then Wednesday was just another day.

I am so glad tomorrow is Friday!

Azerica flopped on her bed and gazed at the ceiling. She couldn't help but see all the glow-in-the-dark star stickers she and Devin put up last summer. Azerica wanted to create a space-like atmosphere in her room, but found it hard to do with Melina's Power Puff Girl accessories. Nonetheless, she was able to paint the walls navy blue and even paint silver stars around the room.

The thought of being in space relaxed her and helped her think. Every time she was alone in her room, she reflected on situations in her life.

One of her biggest challenges right now was adapting to high school.

I guess for my first week in high school, everything is going ok. It's just so hard being at the bottom of the food chain. At least when I was in eighth grade last year, everyone knew who I was. Now, no one knows me other than the other freshmen and a few cheerleaders and football players. My junior high friends are still cool, but they're nobodies like me. If it weren't for Trish, no one would ever know me. But unfortunately that means I am popular by association. That definitely needs to change, but I don't think I'm ready to make the changes Trish is suggesting. What if I don't want to have sex right now?

"Oh well. I can cross that bridge when I get there. But at least, I'm going to Darren Lewis' party tomorrow," Azerica said to herself and smiled. She jumped up to look at the clothes in her closet. She really needed to wear something that would say young, beautiful and sexy.

I hope Trish remembers I'm coming over tonight. I wonder where that chick is. She was supposed to call me by now.

Azerica reached for her phone and dialed Trish's number.

"Hello," answered a raspy voice.

"Umm. Is Trish home?" Azerica asked uncertainly.

"No, sweetie, she isn't home," the voice breathed into the phone. "Who is this?"

"Azerica."

"She'll be home in about half an hour. Can you call back then?" the voice asked, slowly fading.

"Sure." Azerica said and hung up the phone. "Ok, that was weird."

"Are you talking to yourself again Azerica?"

Groaning, Azerica rolled her head from the wall to the bedroom door to see Melina glide into the room.

"It's called thinking out loud. What do you want?"

"Mom said she needs you to make dinner 'cause she's got a job interview." Melina said matter-of-factly.

"A job interview? Tonight?" Azerica asked.

"That's what she said and you can't go anywhere. You have to watch us."

Her mom was really starting to ruin her night. How could she work on her new look with Trish if she had to be home playing mom? And where did her mom think she was going for a job interview anyway? The strip club! It's bad enough that her dad was in jail, but if her mom started stripping, that would be it.

"Let me go ask Mom, I don't think you know what you're talking about Mel." Azerica tried to believe differently.

"That's what Mom said!" Melina exclaimed. "I know what I'm talking about."

Azerica rolled out of bed and walked to her mother's room. The door was cracked open just a little. Azerica quietly stepped closer and peered in to see what her mother was doing. She certainly wasn't dressed like she was going to an interview. She didn't exactly look business-like in a form-fitting, short black dress. The dress accentuated her curves and fell just a little above her knees. It was spaghetti strapped with a cute little belt that tied around her waist.

Azerica knocked quietly at the door. "Mom."

"What Azerica?" Candace replied while she tried to apply mascara to her eyes.

"Mel said you need me to cook and stay home and baby-sit tonight."

"That's right."

"Where are you going Mom?" Azerica questioned as if she were the mother and Candace was the daughter.

I don't know why she thinks she can use that tone with me. She is far from the parent. Candace sighed and rolled her eyes at her daughter. *I'll let the tone go for now. I'm just not in the mood to address it tonight. I'm sure it will come up again.*

"I was supposed to go and study with Devin tonight." Azerica lied, knowing she was going to go to Trish's house to work on upgrading her new high school look.

"She'll just have to come over here. I have to be somewhere." Candace used her authoritative tone.

"Where are you going?" Azerica couldn't help to challenge once more.

"It really isn't any of your business, but since your dad is the reason I'm in this mess in the first place...I'm going to a job interview, if that's okay with you," said Candace heatedly. She slammed her brush down on the vanity.

"You look like you're going on a date and I don't know of any company that does job interviews after business hours anyway?" Azerica stood with her arms crossed.

"Azerica I don't know how many times in a day I have to tell you, you are *my* child. You answer to me, not the other way around. You think you're too grown to get beat, but just keep up this little attitude and it'll come your way." Candace said, her voice rising with aggravation.

Azerica didn't budge.

Calming down just a little, Candace said, "I'm meeting with the night supervisor at Memorial Hospital. He's considering me for a position and he asked me to dinner. While I'm out, you have to stay home and watch Mel and Chauncey."

"Mom, you always do this to me!" exclaimed Azerica. "I can't stay home. I already made plans!"

"I can't help that, you gotta stay home."

Azerica shook her head. She couldn't believe it.

I am in high school now. I finally have a life. I shouldn't have to keep raising my sister and brother. Azerica's anger boiled inside her. But before she could say anything else, her mom closed the bedroom door in her face.

I can't believe she just did that, Azerica thought. *She's just not ready to hear the truth. All she has to do is call their daddy to come and get them. He'd do it. He does everything that Dad can't. And she's pushing the man away.*

On her way back to her room, Azerica grabbed the raggedy cordless phone they'd had since Mel was real little. Even though the antenna always fell out and the numbers were faded to nothing, it was still her favorite phone to use. Every time her mom gets the itch to throw it away, Azerica hides it and tells her that she doesn't know where it is. But the only reason her mom wants to throw it away is because Mel's daddy bought it for her and she says she has to get rid of everything that reminds her of him, which she could never do because Mel and Chauncey are with her for life.

"That's Mom's life, not mine," Azerica muttered to herself. Sometimes, she just wished her mom wouldn't make her such a big part in their lives. She didn't want to be. She didn't ask to be. Sometimes she wished she could move to Orlando with her grandmother or go live on the Southside with her dad's parents.

Mom would never have that, Azerica thought to herself. *No, 'cause that would mean she would have to take care of Melina and Chauncey fulltime.*

"Let me call Trish and tell her I can't come," Azerica said out loud.

Before she could even start dialing numbers, the phone rang. The unexpected noise made her jump and she fumbled to answer it.

"Hello," said Azerica.

"Azerica, what's up? How's my l'il man and l'il momma?" asked the husky voice on the other hand.

It didn't take long for Azerica to recognize the deep, husky voice.

"Hi Greg. They're doing fine." Azerica replied quietly and quickly. "But what are you doing calling now? You know Mom is home. She'd have a heart attack if she knew you were on the phone and she'd kill us both"

"I know it's not Friday, but I just wanted to check on my babies." Greg missed them so much, especially his loud-mouthed Melina. He didn't want to lose his presence in their lives. And he never wanted Chauncey to grow up thinking he was never around to be his dad. "Azerica, life gets kind of hard without them."

"Greg, I know." Azerica sympathized with him. "Look, Mom's going out tonight. If you call back in an hour you can talk to them or come over if you want to get them, but I gotta get off the phone now before she walks by or picks it up."

"Thanks Azerica," Greg said graciously and hung up.

Poor guy, Azerica thought.

Candace had been giving him hell since they broke up and she only lets him see Mel and Chauncey on weekends all because she says she doesn't trust him. He cheated on her with an ex-fiancé. He says they didn't have sex but Candace just knows they did. Since she can't trust him with her heart, she can't trust him completely with her children, so she says. But Azerica knows she's just being ridiculous because she's hurt and when she isn't around, Azerica lets Greg see Mel and Chauncey.

"Who was that?" Candace asked, as she walked passed Azerica's room.

"My friend Trish."

"You got off the phone fast, what's wrong?" She could tell Azerica was lying.

"Nothing," said Azerica. "I have to call her back. The antenna fell out of the phone again and I guess she hung up because of the static."

"Oh, well if your grandmother calls, I need to speak to her so come and get me." With her diva stroll, Candace walked back to her room to finish getting ready for her interview.

Azerica stared at her mother and sighed. *I hope she knows what she's getting herself into*, she thought to herself. *Maybe she's found a new boyfriend and she doesn't want me to know, I just don't believe she's going to an interview for a job dressed like that.*

Azerica was still trying to figure out her mother's weird behavior as she picked up the phone and dialed Trish's number.

"Hello."

"Trish?"

"Yeah, who 'dis?"

"Girl, it's Azerica."

"Oh, hey Azerica! What time are you coming over?" Trish asked smacking loudly.

"Man, I can't come over. Mom's got me watching my little brother and sister 'cause she got a date. You think you can come over here?" Azerica asked.

"I really ain't feel like going anywhere tonight," Trish said, smacking some more. This was exactly why she suggested Azerica spend the night with her Friday. Ms. Christian was a hard woman to work around. "I guess I can come out…But don't you live by Jay?"

"Yeah girl," said Azerica as Trish continued to smack in her ear. "Trish, what are you eating?"

"Sorry, you can hear that? My bad. I'm eating some chicken from Popeye's. Anyways, I'll be over in a few."

"No, don't come yet. Wait about thirty minutes before you leave your house. I don't want Mom to trip," Azerica said.

"Alright, whatever."

"Bye Trish."

"Bye."

-ydn-

"Jason I need to use the phone," Devin said and sat down beside her brother on the brown leather couch their parents just purchased. She loved the way things were coming together. Her mom was able to decorate the way she wanted. Her parent's were blessed with bonuses this year. God was really moving in their lives as a family.

"Jay, did you hear me? I need to use the phone." Devin repeated, a little anxious. She wanted to call Azerica before it got too late.

"Yeah, hold on a minute," Jason said and brushed her off. "So anyways, where you said you'll be tonight? Oh, for real! Yeah girl I'm a come check you out. Yeah, that's right, right next door..."

Devin couldn't wait for him to get off the phone. He was always talking to some female trying to spit game. She couldn't see how he pulled half the girls he did. He was so scrawny and far from being like Kobe Bryant, Jay-Z or some of the other entertainers he looked up to.

"But hey... girl, I'll see you there. Make sure you look just as good tonight as you did today at school. Give me something to look forward to. Yeah, alright. Well my sister gotta use the phone. I'll holla."

"It's about time!" exclaimed Devin. "Was that your new hoochie for the week? You know you really should be more careful. You know all they want from you is sex."

"And what do you think I want from them? A commitment?" Jason smirked. He was too young to think about getting serious with anyone. He knew most of the chickenheads at school just wanted sex. But hey, he didn't care. He was a man. It was about time he got to act like one.

"Jay you know Mom and Dad taught you better than that and even if you haven't been listening to them, you should be listening to Coach Thomas. Didn't he tell you about fast females who just want to have your baby so they can get a paycheck when you get older?" Devin asked.

"Dev you're trippin' it's not that serious. All I'm doing is talking. Nothing else." Jason said and got up.

young, dumb and naive

"Here's the phone," he said and threw it at her. "You need to get a life and grow up."

All Devin could do was stare at him. *God blessed him and gave him the ability to be able to play any sport and he couldn't even think with the right head. His heart always seemed to be in the right place, but he let his talents get in the way of his priorities.*

"God help him," Devin said. It was time to start praying a little harder for him. Hopefully, he'd see it one day.

She picked up the cordless phone and started dialing Azerica's number.

"Hello?"

"Hey Azerica," Devin said. "What are you doing tonight?"

"Oh, I've got to baby-sit. Mom is going out."

"Would you mind if I came over and we could study a little?" Devin asked hopefully. "I thought we could read some more in Romans. I wanted to show you what my dad showed me."

"You know Devin, Mel's dad is supposed to come over and spend time with her and the baby," Azerica said quickly. She didn't feel like reading the Bible with Devin tonight. She had too many other important things to do. "Could we do it another time?"

"Sure, whenever is good for you. Just call me and let me know." Devin tried not to let the disappointment show in her voice, but it did. She couldn't help it.

"Alright. I'll do that," Azerica ignored her tone. "Well I have to go get Chauncey ready for bed. I'll see you tomorrow morning."

"Okay. 'Bye."

"Bye girl," said Azerica.

Not knowing what to do next, Devin just sat there. This was becoming a pattern. She really needed to talk to Azerica about Jay and she wanted to start their Bible study again. They really needed it now. They weren't dealing with the same junior high demons. They were in high school now. But ever since Azerica came back from cheerleader camp this summer, she'd been acting different. She didn't have as much time to spend with Devin and she didn't keep Devin around her new cheerleader friends.

I feel persecuted like Jesus, Devin thought. *I don't see how my own friend can reject me the way she does. It's as if we were never friends. I just don't get it.*

Devin could remember so many times when the two of them did everything together. Azerica had always been her best friend. She was the first person Devin met when she and her family moved to Jacksonville from Ohio. Although she was only five, she knew the Christians would be lifelong friends to her family. At the time it was only Azerica and her mother. Melina was born the next year and before she came, Devin can remember playing house with Azerica and pretending the baby was already there.

"Mommy says my little sister is going to be like this doll," said a six-year-old Azerica.

"How is that?" Devin remembered asking her.

"Because she'll be small and little and you can hold her like this," Azerica pulled her Cabbage Patch Kids doll into her arms and demonstrated how to hold a baby.

Devin laughed to herself thinking about that day. She had never been around a baby until Melina was born. And when Ms. Christian had Melina, no one could tell Devin that Melina wasn't her new sister too. But as Melina got older and started talking, Azerica and Devin used to find secret places to play so she couldn't follow them.

She and Azerica used to do everything together. They always had the same classes and teachers, they were in Girl Scouts, they played softball…they were inseparable and people always thought they were sisters.

Now, no one could even tell they were friends.

I might as well get ready for bed and study on my own, Devin thought to herself. *I don't need anyone else when I have you Lord; you are my one true friend.*

As Devin made her way to the comfort of her room, she passed her parent's room and saw her brother going through their father's cologne. She watched silently as he used a little of *Pure Lavendar* by Azarro.

Devin sighed and continued on to her bedroom. *Any time he uses that, he's meeting some female. I hope he knows what he's doing. I just pray he don't get caught up one day. He wouldn't know what to do.*

Devin opened the door to her room and immediately felt calm and at peace. She quickly closed and locked the door as if her room held a secret she didn't want to share with the rest of the world.

Her eyes got lost in the deep blue surrounding her and she felt as though she were riding on the clouds that floated across her walls. She went to the corner of her room, turned her CD to track 3 and grabbed her spiritual journal to write in. As the sound of waves splashing tantalized her ears, she meditated on the events of the day. She gathered her thoughts so she could focus her prayers and pray specifically for the circumstances surrounding she, her family and her friends. They needed it and she wanted to be prepared for what would come her way tomorrow.

Just as she was finishing her entry for the day, she heard a light tap on her bedroom door, then the sound of the front door closing a few seconds later. Jason was letting her know, he was leaving to meet his girl for the night.

He understood Devin's need to be left alone. In fact, her entire family did. Her bedroom was always open to her family and friends. The only time she ever closed her door was when she wanted time alone for herself or time alone to spend with God. When those times came: she was oblivious to the outside world and didn't communicate with anyone, she had no need to. Out of respect, her family would tap on her door to let her know they were leaving, but other than that, they left her alone.

When she was sure Jason had left and wouldn't return home until later, she left the comfort of her world and entered into the gates of desire and selfishness that was her brother's room. She took note of the place the enemy had inhabited. Physically, the room hadn't changed, but she could sense that something wasn't right. She moved closer to the bed and sat on the floor next to the foot. She grabbed his favorite football and held it tight as if she were holding her brother. Then she began to pray.

Chapter 6

"Would you mind if I touched, if I kissed, if I held you tight in the morning light," whispered Earth, Wind & Fire from the radio station.

"Oh that's my song!" exclaimed Candace and she turned up the volume of her car's radio to sing along. She hated listening to this station, but she had no choice. For some odd reason, her '89 Honda Civic was stuck on V101.5, which played classic old school. Old school, she loved, but 101.5 played the same songs every night at this hour. But every once in a while, they surprised her and played something different. And once every blue moon, they played her favorite old school songs.

"Cause I never ever felt this way in my heart before…" She sang loudly and swayed with the beat. She was trying her best to relieve some of the nervousness she felt from going to this pre-interview, but it really wasn't working. She was very uneasy. *I really can't wait to see Craig again, but I wonder why he wanted me to dress up and meet him at a nice restaurant for an interview, before the interview. The position I'm applying for don't require a degree. I thought I was just going to be admitting patients during the late shift. It just doesn't make sense. I don't know what it is, but whatever it is, I'll have to make sure my nosy daughter doesn't find out. The girl can be just like my mother sometimes.*

"Love has found a way in my heart tonight." The song continued to drown her thoughts, but slowly they came treading back as the song came to an end.

When the soft melody evolved to Computer Love by Zapp and Roger, she snapped back to reality and found herself parked in front of Milano's, Jacksonville's most exquisite Italian restaurant.

Ok. She thought to herself. *He's in there waiting for me. Hopefully he's going to offer me the chance of a lifetime. Lord knows, I really need a good job right now. I can barely afford rent. I just need the money.*

She sighed, glanced in the mirror one last time and made her way to the restaurant's entrance.

It was actually exciting for her to see Craig again. She hadn't spoken to him in almost ten years. She was only joking when she said she hoped he remembered her, but now that she thought about it, she really hoped he did remember. It's been a long while and she's changed a lot. Surely, he's changed a lot too.

He could have a wife and five kids by now. In high school he always said he wanted a big family.

I hope if he is married, his wife doesn't mind that he's out with me, Candace thought. *Or maybe he's been too into his career to have a family.*

Craig didn't waste any time going to college and then medical school after he graduated high school. He was always back and forth between Jacksonville and Tallahassee that no one really believed he was ever enrolled. Their friends always joked and said his parents had enough money to pay the colleges to give him his degrees. They could afford to. Nevertheless, he graduated, came back and redeveloped the health care system in their community.

What did I do? Candace asked herself walking to the entrance. *Got pregnant had a baby, then got pregnant two more times and had two more babies.*

As soon as she entered Milano's foyer, she immediately felt calm and at ease. The soft melodious music danced around her while the dimmed lights teased her eyes. As she waited to be helped, the romantic atmosphere completely enticed her and pacified her mood. She no longer felt anxious like she did when she sat in her car. The restaurant completely changed her frame of mind. As she glanced around the sitting area, she couldn't help but notice the effect the restaurant had on every person in its threshold. Their eyes seemed to be lost in love somewhere between Heaven and Earth. They were completely captivated by each other's words and barely knew anyone else existed.

For a moment, Candace thought she were just as in love. She forgot she was just meeting Craig there for business purposes only. She imagined herself walking over to Craig's table and he pulling out her chair to sit down. With love and tenderness in his voice, he'd ask her how her day was and watch earnestly as she expressed her every thought and emotion from the day's events. He would order white wine for the both of them and a delicious fettuccine dish for them both to eat. While they waited, he would call the musicians over to serenade her and when she wasn't looking, he'd bend down on one knee and ask her to marry him.

"Excuse me, Miss?" someone interrupted her thoughts.

Candace looked up to see who ended her fantasy. "Yes." She replied.

whose "Who's party are you with?" the waiter asked.

"Oh, I'm sorry," Candace said, a little embarrassed of her thoughts. "I'll be joining Dr. Craig Pearson."

"Yes Ma'am, right this way," he said. "Dr. Pearson is waiting for you."

-ydn-

"Azerica! I need my jacket," Melina exclaimed, running crazily through the apartment.

"Shoo, would you wait just a minute. I have to get Chauncey ready."

"But Azerica, he said he'd be here in five minutes and I have to brush my teeth," whined Melina.

"Just go brush your teeth and I'll give you your jacket after that," said Azerica.

"Fine." Melina stomped out of the room.

Azerica watched as her little sister walked into the bathroom and grabbed her Power Puff Girl toothbrush. That girl drove her crazy. She couldn't wait for Greg to come pick her up. When she wasn't talking your head off, she was whining about something. She had her moments when she was happy and silly, but when she really wanted something, all she did was whine.

"Greg I hope you hurry up and get here," Azerica said, just talking to herself.

She placed her baby brother on the changing table in her mother's room and began changing his diaper. The six-month-old was such a happy baby. He rarely cried and when he did, it was because he was hungry or needed to be changed. He had the biggest, brown eyes, long eyelashes and curly black hair. He was dead on his daddy, but he had some of Candace's characteristics. Like Azerica and Melina, he had a decent grade of hair and a cinnamon complexion.

"What are you laughing at?" Azerica asked him, when she heard his soft giggles.

Chauncey looked up at her as if she'd told him a joke and he kept giggling.

I just love my baby brother. Azerica kissed his forehead. *He's so cute. I really don't mind taking care of him sometimes. He's the only person in this house I really like. Don't get me wrong God, I do love my sister, but sometimes I wish Greg could take Mel and we could see her on the weekends.*

"You must have seen your crazy sister running around here looking for her silly Power Puff Girl jacket." Azerica said when he kept smiling.

"Azerica! I still can't find my jacket." Melina came bouncing into the room whining again.

"Mel, wait a second! Don't you see I'm putting Chauncey's clothes on? Wait a minute and I'll get your jacket." Azerica picked up her brother and slid on his navy blue jumpsuit. Still giggling, he sat up and played with his Tigger while Azerica combed through his hair.

"Azerica, he'll be here in a minute."

"Alright." Azerica picked up Chauncey and placed him on the bed beside Melina. "Play with Chauncey while I get your jacket."

Azerica started walking towards the bedroom she shared with her sister when the phone started ringing.

"Hello," she answered abruptly.

"Are you alright Z?" asked Trish. "Sounds like you're babysitting again."

"Yeah, just looking for my sister's jacket. Are you on your way over?"

young, dumb and naive

"I will be in a minute. My mom just left for the club. I just wanted to know what kind of look you wanted."

"It doesn't really matter Trish. I just need something. I'm tired of looking like a baby, no one pays attention to me there. I feel like USG's biggest joke." Azerica complained.

"Naw, you're not the biggest joke, but I'll tell you who is." Trish said trying to reassure her. There was no one at USG who was a bigger dork than this person. People were already starting to talk about her and the first week wasn't over yet.

"Who?" asked Azerica curiously.

"Well, I don't know how close you two are, but Jay's sister." Trish said matter-of-factly.

"Devin?" Azerica asked in shock. "What do they say about her?"

"Yeah, they say she's a real goody-two shoes and she don't mess with anybody. They say she's saving herself for marriage. And can you believe she's never drank anything?"

Azerica stopped looking for Mel's jacket and sat on her bed. Trish wasn't telling her anything she didn't already know, but she wasn't about to tell Trish that. She didn't want Trish to know that she'd never done any of that stuff either. She and Devin have never been to any *real* parties. Besides the wine her mom occasionally kept in the refrigerator, they didn't know anything about alcohol and sex scared her. She and Devin had actually made a pact to stay abstinent and not have sex until they got married. She knew Devin still planned to wait for marriage, but Azerica didn't know anymore.

It can't be that bad to have sex before you get married. So many people do it all the time, it must be OK, she thought to herself while Trish droned on about Devin never smoking weed.

"Trish what time are you coming?" Azerica interrupted.

"I still need to know what kind of look you want. It can be hoochie, sporty, classy...even though classy is BORING," Trish emphasized. "I say, save that until you're 40 or something. We're still young. It's ok to show off our bodies."

"Well, how 'bout sporty? I like tennis skirts and dresses."

Trish shook her head. That's why she was here. To teach the poor lost souls about being young, beautiful and in fashion. "Ok. I guess. I mean, that's a start. You got something sporty you're gonna wear tomorrow?"

"Umm...I was thinking about my Nike tennis dress," Azerica answered.

"Now Z, you wore a tennis skirt Tuesday, you can't do the dress tomorrow. Wait until next Friday to do the dress."

"OK, so what am I supposed to wear?" Azerica asked a little frustrated. This was harder than she expected.

"Z, it's ok. Sporty isn't just athletic clothes. You could wear jumpsuits, short outfits, blue jean clothes...You know, stuff like that." Trish answered. "Don't worry, I'm bringing lots of stuff with me tonight."

"Well, I'll try to have something ready when you get here, I have to finish getting Mel and Chauncey ready, their dad is coming to get them for a little while."

"Oh, that's good. You're little sister is cute, but she don't shut up!" Trish exclaimed.

"Tell me about it. At least you don't have to live with her. Anyways, I'll see you when you get here." Azerica said and hung up the phone.

Wow. Devin is really killing herself. Azerica replayed Trish's words through her mind. *I can't believe she tells people she's a virgin and she won't drink. No wonder Jay didn't want to invite her to Darren's party and that's why he never looked twice at me. He thinks I'm exactly like her. If he wasn't trying to get with Trish, I'd show him I'm different. I guess I just have to chill with Trish more and leave Devin alone for a while. We're on two completely different pages. She's going to end up alone and with very little friends.*

"Azerica! He's here, where's my jacket?" Melina ran into the room.

"Why did you leave Chauncey!" Azerica ran back to her mom's room to get her brother with Melina at her heels, still crying about the Power Puff Girls jacket.

"Azerica my jacket!" Melina screeched.

"Mel, I told you I was getting it. The next time I tell you to watch Chauncey, you stay there until I get back. Never leave him by himself. How many times do we have to tell you that?" Azerica fussed at her sister, grabbed her jacket from the jacket closet and went to answer the door.

"Sorry it took so long Greg. I didn't hear you knocking."

"That's alright Azerica," he said and grabbed Chauncey from her arms. "How's my little man today?"

Still clutching his Tigger, Chauncey just giggled.

"Hey Daddy!" shrieked Melina running around the corner.

"Hey baby doll. I missed you. I see you still have the jacket I got you." It made him proud to see her take care of the things he gave her. That was her connection to him. And he knew she wasn't going to let that jacket get very far out of her sight.

"Yes and she barely lets any of us touch it." Azerica sighed. "Where are you taking them tonight?"

"We're just going to get some ice cream tonight. I won't have them out long. I know how your mother gets." Greg forced a smile. "She's the only woman I know who can hold a grudge for so long. But I promise to have them back soon. I don't want you to get in trouble."

"Thank you Greg, 'cause she would kill me." Azerica said. Her mom had been mad at her all week. She didn't want to make her any angrier.

"How's your dad doing?" He changed the subject in an attempt to lighten Azerica's mood. In the nine years he and Candace were together, he and Azerica did become pretty close. He missed her just as much as he missed his own children.

"He's doing good. I spoke to him the other day. He really hates it there, he said he spends most of his time working out and getting together a game plan for when he gets out."

"Did your mother speak to him too?" Greg asked.

"No, you know how she is. She's still upset with him too," Azerica replied.

"Where exactly did she go?" Greg looked at his watch concerned. He knew she never went out on a school night. And she wasn't much for many changes. Lord, He missed her too, but he couldn't even get her to talk to him.

"She's with a friend, they went to dinner." Azerica told him. She was no fool. *I'm only 14 Greg, but I know you would be out searching for my mother if you knew she was out on a job interview dinner.* She thought. *You'll know the interview is more than a job interview. You'd be chasing her down and threatening whoever she was out with. You're in the military. You're crazy!*

"She'll probably be back in about an hour or so, so please don't go too far and come right back." Azerica said, being careful not to give more information than she should. "Mel needs to be in bed by the time Mom gets home."

"Alright Z, thanks again for letting me see them." Greg said earnestly. He still wasn't satisfied, but he knew Azerica wasn't going to tell him anything more.

"You're welcome." She was going to tease him about coming back for them this weekend, but she knew he would. She didn't have to worry about that.

"We're getting ice cream and you can't have any Azerica." Melina said as she grabbed her dad's hand to walk out the door.

"Like I care. I don't want any Mel." Azerica rolled her neck.

"Come on Mel, stop being mean to your sister. She can have some if she wants to. Do you want us to bring you back anything Azerica?" Greg asked her.

"Naw, I'm fine."

"OK. We'll be back," said Greg and he closed the door behind him.

"Lord thank you for Greg. I wouldn't get a break if it weren't for him." Azerica said to herself. *I wish Mom would get over her issues and let Greg be a father to his kids. Mel and Chauncey don't need me as their second mother. And I don't want to be their mom.*

"Dang it. Trish will be here in a minute," Azerica said and ran into her room. She cleaned up what she could. It was hard to make it look like an adult slept there because of all Melina's stuff, but she threw all the kid stuff under Mel's bed. Then she ran into her mom's room and picked up some of the clothes off her mom's bed. They'd have to do her make-up in there because her mom had a really nice vanity with bright lights.

I might as well turn on the radio and pretend to be at the club since I'm too young to go to the real ones. She pressed the power button on her mom's AIWA stereo system and changed the station to 105.7.

"Pimpjuice, I think its time to let it loose…" Nelly's new song sounded through the speakers.

Azerica danced around and practiced her new walk to the beat, but before she could get it the way she wanted, someone started knocking at her door.

Trish got here kind of fast, she thought and walked to the door to answer it. But instead of Trish, she found Jason. The scent of his cologne overwhelmed her and tantalized her nostrils. He smelled so good! And he looked even better. His yellow complexion became bronze after being in the sun all day at practice. He was wearing his blue and red USG t-shirt and his USG sweatpants with one leg pulled above his calf muscle.

"Hey Jay, you must be looking for Devin. She didn't come over tonight." Azerica got ready to close the door.

"I know," he said nonchalantly, keeping his body in the frame of the door.

For a moment, all she could do was stare at him. *I cannot believe Jay is here at my house and he's not looking for Devin!* Azerica almost passed out. Yeah, she'd known him for years, but they never spent time together alone. She had the biggest crush on him when they were little, but she gave up on that years ago.

"Pop the top and let the sunshine in. On the wood grain let the twinkies spin…"

"You having a party?" He asked when he heard the sound of Trick Daddy coming from the back room. He started singing along and walked inside.

Dumbfounded, she shook her head no. "Actually, I was waiting for Trish to come over."

"Oh, what y'all doing tonight?" Jason played dumb. He headed towards the couch and sat down. *Azerica was pretty attractive for a freshman. She was a little skinny, but she looked good in her cheerleader shirt and shorts.*

"Just chilling." Azerica said, still in shock. She closed the door and went to sit in the chair across from him.

"You want me to go?" He asked, picking up on her vibes. "You act like you don't want me here."

"Naw, you're fine. I just wasn't expecting you and you've never been here to just chill. Usually you just come for Devin."

"Yeah, well, she at home. She's tripping." He said smiling at her. "Y'all don't hang out much anymore, I guess you see how hard she be tripping."

"Yeah," Azerica said, still not sure what was going on.

"Well, Trish is real cool. She's good people. My boys like her and she don't trip like my l'il sis." Jason said earnestly. He was actually glad Azerica was making other friends besides hanging out with just his sister. He always felt like she was missing out on a lot. His sister would never change, he knew. But Azerica still had some potential.

Speechless, Azerica didn't know what else to say. She'd never been alone with Jason before. She never thought he knew she existed. If it weren't for her friendship with Devin, she don't think he would have acknowledged she was alive.

"...I can feel your temperature rise and you can feel my nature too.."

Jason looked into her eyes and started singing the song.

Azerica shifted nervously in her seat. *Ohmigod! He's singing to me! Please Trish get here soon.*

Now she really didn't know what to say to him. Why couldn't the radio keep playing the fast stuff? Things got really tense and she tried to act cool, but she didn't know what to say. Why couldn't she think of something? Anything! She continued to sit in silence while he sang the song. Finally she picked up her VIBE magazine and pretended to look at it. She'd seen it a zillion times before, but one more couldn't hurt especially since she was nervous.

Finally the silence was broken.

"Z. I know you're in there, come open the door." Trish said when she knocked on the door. "Please let me in before the boogie man gets me."

"I'll be back," Azerica laughed and she got up to let Trish in.

Jason just smiled and watched. He knew Azerica had always had a crush on him. He never responded 'cause she used to be just as irritating as his sister. But now she was growing up, she was cool, just a little shy, but she was cool. She had a nice little shape to her. He and his boys always talk about how good she'll look in a few years. Some of them can't wait to make her their baby's momma one day.

"Do you know Jay is here?" Azerica whispered frantically when she opened the door.

"Yeah, you don't mind do you? I asked him to come over." Trish walked inside. That's what's up. He knew what to do. "Hey Jay."

"What's up Trish."

She casually walked to the couch and sat next to him.

Azerica didn't know what to think now. Trish was supposed to be coming to help her with her look, but she invited Jason to *her* house so they could hook up. This wasn't cool. She watched for a few moments while they flirted with each other on the couch. Then she couldn't take it anymore. Trish was cool and all, but she wasn't going to use her for a meeting place so she could hook up with Jay. That don't fly.

"Trish, you can help me with something real quick?" Azerica asked.

"Yeah, sure." Trish got up and winked at Jay.

"Excuse us," Azerica said, irritated. She walked them to the back to her mother's room and closed the door.

"This is a cute apartment Z." Trish said casually.

"Thanks." Azerica glared at her.

"What's wrong?" Trish asked. *Azerica asked me to come over and now she's tripping.*

"Why do you have Jay here when you're supposed to be helping me with my look?" Azerica snapped.

"Azerica," Trish looked at her surprised by the tone in her voice. "He's just chilling. I'm still going to help you. Let me get the stuff I brought with me. Are we going to be in here or in your room?"

"In here," Azerica replied hastily.

"Alright, I'll be right back."

Azerica watched as Trish walked back towards the front. She still couldn't believe what Trish had done. Why would she invite Jason while they were working on something important for her high school career? The least she could have done was have Jay bring a friend with him. That would've been tight.

Azerica let the thought simmer in her mind for a moment, then she got up to get some of her "sporty" clothes from her room.

When she came back she found Trish waiting for her.

"What took you so long?" Trish asked her.

"OK, this is what I have," Azerica slung her clothes on the bed ignoring Trish. "Most of this is what you gave me from the summer and the rest of it is what I had from before. You know, some of my cuter clothes."

"Hmm…some of this could work. You don't have to be sporty all the time."

"Well, what should I wear tomorrow and show me how to do my makeup." Azerica said.

"One thing at a time," laughed Trish. "First try on a few outfits and lets see how they make you look. You know you gotta show off your curves or show a little leg or something."

"Whatchu think about this?" Azerica asked. She was holding up a pair of black capris and a black and white striped baby tee shirt.

Trish stared blankly at the shirt. In her mind, she reviewed different ways to wear the shirt to make it appealing with the black capris Azerica picked out. But nothing worked. Now she knew why Azerica needed her. She really couldn't do it on her own. *I should start my own reality show called High School Makeover*, Trish thought to herself.

"Naw. Let me help you out a little. I'm glad I brought some of my shirts." Trish grabbed her USG cheerleader bag and pulled out some shirts she brought from home. She brought backless shirts, low-cut shirts, tank shirts and sheer shirts.

"I feel like I'm at Charlotte Russe or something," Azerica smiled. It was like Christmas. Her mom wouldn't let her buy clothes like these. "I like this one."

Azerica picked up a blue, low-cut sleeveless shirt that had *spoiled* written across the front in black.

"That's what I was going to tell you to wear." Trish said, happy that some fashion sense was leaking in her brain. "Now, go try it on and yell for me when you're finished. I'll be wit Jay."

Azerica rolled her eyes and closed the bedroom door after her friend so she could change. She was excited about her transformation. Now people won't think of her as an eighth-grader. Maybe they'll finally see her as an attractive young woman and not a really cool freshman. Her new look was the perfect way to start the weekend. Of course she would debut her new look at school tomorrow, but she couldn't wait to show off her new style at Darren's party tomorrow night after USG's football game.

Maybe one of Jay's friends will want to hook up with me. That would be real tight.

"Trish," Azerica opened the bedroom door and called for her friend. She walked over to her mom's long mirror and admired the way the clothes made her look. The capris took the form of her body and the shirt was the perfect tease because it was low-cut. She looked good.

"Trish," Azerica called again when her friend didn't show up. She started to walk towards the front of the apartment to the living room, but before she made it, Trish came walking abruptly around the corner fumbling with the buttons on her shirt.

Azerica didn't say anything, but watched amusingly while her friend tried to act as if nothing were happening.

"Yeah Z, that looks good." Trish said trying not to sound out of breath. "I like the way the capris hug your figure. Girl USG better watch out tomorrow!"

"That's what I said, but that don't help me with Darren's party," said Azerica. "I need something to wear there."

"Girl, you know I got you covered. One thing at a time, please!" she exclaimed.

In another week, Z will be a whole new person and she will have me to thank for it, Trish thought proudly. She turned to her bag and started pulling out more clothes. She had more sheer shirts, low-cut shirts, short shirts, blue jean outfits and shorts.

"Where do you find the time to do all this shopping?" Azerica asked amazed. "'Cause we spend everyday cheering and we sleep on the weekends."

"Oh, girl, most of these were my mother's clothes. She doesn't like to recycle very often, so she gives me what she don't want. I know some of these may be too big for you but all the cute ones should fit you."

Trish's mom bought very small sizes because she wanted her boobs to look bigger than they were. Her philosophy was that if you could get a man to fall in love with your body, you were at the halfway point in making him fall in love with you.

"Was your mom home today?" Azerica asked Trish. She picked out a few shirts she could possible wear to the party.

"Yeah girl, she was with her new boyfriend," Trish rolled her eyes. Another man in love.

"Oh, I called you earlier today and she said you weren't home. I thought you had forgot about me."

"Naw, never. Mom just needed me to run a few errands for her while she tended to her booty call." Trish said nonchalantly.

Azerica stared at Trish as if she'd just told her Jay was gay. She couldn't believe her friend just said that about her mother. *Maybe I'm tripping and Trish is just joking.*

Trish turned and saw the look on Azerica's face and laughed. "Girl, now you know your mom be having booty calls all the time too. It's not just my mom."

"Trish I don't know what your mom does with her spare time, but I **know** where my mom is all the time. She don't have time for that." Azerica said defensively. *I may not always be happy with my mom, but no one's going to talk about her like she's a two-dollar ho.*

"Well, where is she now?" Trish challenged. It was almost nine o'clock on a school night and the woman wasn't home. And she didn't have a job to go to.

Azerica's face felt hot.

Trish's question was like adding gasoline to a fire. She was already concerned about her mother going to a job interview dressed like she had a hot date. Trish wasn't going to know about her mom's career move. She would really know it was a booty call and had nothing to do with a job. Azerica half-believed the story herself, but she couldn't imagine her mother being with a man. Her mom wasn't the type to put her family on hold while she chased a man. Besides that, she was still heart-broken over Greg. She won't admit it, but everyone knows she still loves him.

"She went to her friend Leesa's house." Azerica finally lied.

"Look Azerica. I'm not trying to make you upset," Trish sighed. *I have a lot to teach her.* "Booty calls are a part of life. Mom happens to have them more often than yours. That's fine. And just because I told you she had a booty call doesn't mean that's what she told me it was…"

Azerica sat in silence listening while her friend gave her booty call philosophy. She still couldn't believe Trish was implying her mother was out having sex with some man.

"…I mean every time she sends me out to take care of her bills and stuff, she always tells me she needs her me time. She'll have candles lit and R. Kelly playing, plus wine, grapes and cheese on the dining room table. I mean, come on, I'm not stupid. The only difference between our mothers is that yours handles her business outside of home. That's all."

Azerica was still shocked and amazed. Trish really believed that what she was saying was true. It was obvious you could tell her no different, so Azerica just dropped the subject.

"What did you find for me to wear to Darren's party?" Azerica asked, hoping Trish would change the subject.

"Ok. I have these blue jean shorts and this strapless shirt or this one-piece blue jean short outfit." Trish went back to showcasing her clothes.

The truth hurts, she thought. That was how she felt the first time she found out her mom was having sex all the time.

"I think I'd rather wear the one-piece outfit." Azerica said. "That shirt is a little too much for my coming out. I've got to build up to that."

"Actually Z, that shirt could be perfect. You don't have to build up to it. Just wear it once, let them know who you are and they'll never forget you after that."

"You think so?" Azerica asked.

"Girl, yeah," Trish replied. "Live a little."

"No. I'll stick with the one-piece. I'd feel more comfortable with that."

"You know, you're probably right. You gotta have the confidence to wear this shirt. If you wear it and don't feel comfortable in it, then it's a waste." Trish said while she put the rest of her clothes back in her cheerleader bag. *And that would make me look bad.*

"Well, what about my make-up?" Azerica asked. "I've gotta wear some tomorrow and at the party."

"Will your mom trip about you wearing it to school tomorrow?" Trish asked, remembering how Ms. Christian got upset when she saw Azerica with make-up on when they came back from cheerleader camp. "I mean, you know how she gets sometimes."

Trish is right, Azerica thought. "I know, can we do it in the morning before class?"

"Yeah, where do you want me to meet you?"

"How 'bout the girls locker room since we have to take our things there for the game anyway." Azerica replied.

"That sounds good." Trish zipped her bag. She was ready to go back and chill with Jay some more..

"So what are you and Jay going to do now?"

"He said he'd run home and get a movie if you wanted to watch one," Trish smiled. She wanted to make the most of her time here with Jason. It had to be worthwhile for both of them.

Azerica stared in amazement. Jason never stayed for longer than two seconds at her house and now that Trish is here, she can't get rid of him. She would watch any movie as long as Jay stayed, but she didn't want to be the fifth wheel and Greg would be coming back with Melina and Chauncey soon.

"No thanks Trish, I don't want to get in the way of your pimpjuice," Azerica said smiling. "Although I could probably learn a little."

"Now, you know it ain't like that over here. I know how to handle myself," Trish winked. "And he can call one of his boys over."

"Naw, not tonight. Mel and Chauncey will be back in a minute and you know what her mouth is like. I want to be able to get out the house Saturday."

"Alright, well let me tell Jay we're getting kicked out." Trish said.

It's just as well. Trish couldn't live in a place with so many rules. At times like this she was so happy her mom didn't care about so many silly rules. All these Candace Christian laws, stifled her creativity.

She grabbed her bag and walked towards the front.

Chapter 7

"I'm so glad you were able to join me this evening," Craig whispered into her ear. She looked beautiful in black. The color complimented her short, sleek black hair and gave her a sex appeal he'd always overlooked.

"I'm having a wonderful time," Candace replied sincerely. She swayed with him to the beat of an Italian love song that played softly in the background. The music, the candle lights and the food created the perfect scenery for any romance novel. She felt like a Harlequin queen. If she could keep her eyes closed forever and hold onto this moment, she would.

She couldn't remember the last time she felt this happy and at ease. It had been so long since a man had held her in his arms and meant it. And Craig did a wonderful job. *All he had to do was apply for the position and he could have the job*, she thought. He knew exactly what she needed in order to feel like an appreciated woman. Even if he couldn't save her from life and its consequences, he could momentarily rescue her from the bouts of drama that filled her daily routine.

That wasn't an easy job to fulfill, but he could do it. He always did. Craig had a knack for rescuing her at exactly the moment she needed it.

Candace would never forget how caring he was throughout her pregnancy with Azerica. The lengths he went through to make sure she had everything she needed would stay etched in her memory. *And he didn't have to. I had Jeffrey.* But each time Jeff failed to live up to his responsibility, Craig was there. He never left her side. He was her best friend during that hard episode in her life.

I should've never let my mother talk me out of our friendship, Candace sighed silently. At the time, her mom didn't believe she should have another close male friend. She said Jeffrey was enough and she had to learn to be faithful to him since they wanted to stay together and try to be a family.

That was a big mistake. She lost a friend and gained a headache.

After some years of threats and unpaid child support, she finally saw the light. Jeff was never going to have anything or be anything in life.

Even after she severed their friendship, Craig was still willing to help her get back on her feet. He hooked her up with a job through a friend. She appreciated him so much. It warmed her heart to know he was still willing and able to help her even now after so many years.

"Thank you," Candace looked up into his eyes. She knew the two words could never pay him back for the favors, but that was all she had.

"For?" Craig replied.

"For being such a good friend and always coming to help me no matter what my situation is. You don't know how much I appreciate it."

"Now Candace, you know I've got to always make sure you're doing fine. That's my job. I'm just sorry that it's been this long since we've had the opportunity to get together. I miss the times we shared. No matter what we go through in life, you will always be my friend. I've got to see that you make it through, no matter what." Craig said. Without realizing it, he'd always made that his personal job. He just couldn't help seeing beautiful women in need, especially when he had the resources to make their dreams come true.

Candace was a special case. She always had been and she always will be.

"Candace, I don't mind helping you. I need you in my life." Craig gazed into her eyes.

Candace didn't need to feel the strength of his arms around her. The power and sincerity in his voice was enough to make her feel like a star, like she really was worth something. She had to be floating on air because she couldn't feel her feet touching the ground. She knew everyone else in the room could feel it too and their eyes followed she and this incredible doctor friend of hers across the dance floor.

When the song finally came to an end, the dream dissipated and Craig guided her back to their table where their dessert was waiting.

"You must be a regular in here. They treat you like VIP," Candace commented after Craig helped her with her seat.

"Well, when you're living alone with no female presence you kind of just find your favorite restaurant and make it your home." Craig smiled.

"Surely Milano's isn't your only favorite. I know you must get tired of eating pasta sometimes," said Candace.

"Yeah, that's why I have my favorite Japanese, Thai and Mexican restaurants." He laughed. Candace loved the way his eyes sparkled when he laughed. Tonight, they sparkled fervently like never before. The candle sitting between them seemed to add a deeper affect and a brighter glow to the mystery his eyes possessed.

"Sounds like you have it all figured out doctor," Candace said, bringing her fork to her mouth to take a bite of her dessert.

"All but one thing."

"What's that?" she asked softly.

"You."

Candace felt her cheeks getting hot. She looked down at her plate so that he wouldn't see her blushing. Her little fantasy seemed like it was becoming real, but she didn't think she was ready to handle another relationship. Not this soon anyway.

"Candace, I'm sorry. I didn't embarrass you did I?" He asked, feeling her resistance. "I know your position and where you stand on relationships. I'm not going to push you into anything."

"Thanks. I guess I thought dinner tonight was going to be about business and not so personal. This feels more like a date," Candace looked up nervously. Craig flirting with her was unfamiliar territory.

"Well, I guess you could say it's both," Craig Pearson looked intensely into her eyes. "I do have a business proposition for you though and I hope you'll accept. This could be the answer to your prayers."

Candace choked on her wine; a little shocked at the way he abruptly changed the topic. What could he be talking about? She already knew about working at the hospital.

young, dumb and naive

She glanced at the candle on their table to avoid his eyes. She noticed the light starting to flicker. The dim lights and soft music suddenly began to make her feel a little uneasy. She felt her stomach turning.

"What about the hospital thing?" Candace asked uncertainly, not knowing what type of proposition he wanted to make.

"That you'll have. You can start Monday, but the hours depend on whether or not you want to take me up on this proposition." Craig wanted her to see the bigger picture and establish something more for herself than admitting patients. "We all need a career. And so do you."

Thank you Jesus, Candace thought gratefully. *I really don't deserve this, I didn't even pray about it and you still fixed the problem for me. Thank you Jesus. He's found a career for me!*

"I don't know how you feel about this but you have the potential to make over $500 a week. And this will be extra income for you. Admitting patients will be your regular pay." Craig gently explained it to her, careful not to use the wrong words. He felt like a car salesman selling a lemon to a desperate teen.

"Well, what is it?" Candace's voice sprung from inside her. She felt the excitement running through her blood. She really needed this extra cash, it would make up for what Jeff stopped bringing. And she might be able to go back to nursing school.

Craig pulled a business card from his jacket pocket and grabbed a pen from the table. He scribbled something on the card and slid it over to her. She glanced at the card and was outraged. Before she had a chance to say anything, he cut her off.

"Now Candace, I know you may be a little shocked. But just think about it. Think about how much you could earn and all you have to do is smile and look pretty. Do you know how many women would love to be in your shoes and would love to take this offer? I have women calling me every day trying to get on. I just want you to think about it," Craig preyed on her vulnerabilities.

Think about It? She thought. She wanted to cuss him out. She can't believe he tried her like that! She tried to slide the card back to him, but he pushed it back.

"Please don't say anything. Remember, I just want you to think about it. You may not want to take me up now, but the position will always be there." Craig placed the business card in her palm and closed her hand.

His hands felt hard and rough and his demeanor became almost menacing.

Candace just wanted to throw the card back at him, but she didn't want to do anything to jeopardize her job at the hospital. She really needed to work somewhere. She didn't have enough money to support her family and she couldn't depend on child support alone.

Reluctantly, she held onto the card and placed it inside her purse.

"Yeah, that's good," Craig coaxed her. He knew if he could get her to keep the card, he's sold the product. "Just don't forget where you put it and you can come by tomorrow night to check things out. Don't worry about clothes, we provide everything for you."

Candace reverted her attention back to her dessert and tried hard not to look at him. She was afraid her eyes would tell him everything on her mind and she wasn't ready to give him that piece yet. Maybe once she was secure in her hospital job and she knew she wasn't going anywhere, she would tell Craig where to go and what to do with his little business proposition. She couldn't understand what just happened. One minute, he acts like he wants to be with her and the next minute he's offering her something like this.

"Waiter, can I get the check?" Craig asked, breaking the silence.

Candace took a deep breath and exhaled. She pushed her plate to the side and took one last sip of her wine while Craig took care of the bill.

Any other person would take her silence as a bad sign, but Craig didn't. He saw it as a positive. He knew she was thinking about it. She was thinking hard. She always needed money. She wasn't going to miss an opportunity to make money when she already didn't have any.

"That was a lovely dinner." Craig commented. He tried to keep a conversation going in spite of what he just offered her.

"Yes it was. Thanks for getting me out of the house," Candace responded half-heartedly.

"I would like to get you out of the house quite often," Craig said pulling out her chair for her. "Keep thinking about what we discussed."

Candace looked up at him and smiled as sweetly as possible. His prince charming act was dead.

"I really do have your best interest in mind, Candace. Don't write me off just yet," he said, offering his hand.

Candace casually accepted his assistance and stood to her feet. He led them through the restaurant and towards the front door. The romantic Italian music and candlelit tables that enticed her to welcome the restaurant now made her sick as she walked through. She just wanted to run and get as far away as possible. She felt dirty and she was mad at herself for even believing that Craig was interested in a relationship with her.

If I make it out of this period in my life, I will never let another man get the best of me like Craig just did, she vowed silently.

"You must be tired." Craig tried again to talk to her.

"Why do you say that?" Candace challenged. She glanced at him, but didn't want to hold his gaze for too long.

"You're extremely quiet and I know you like to talk," he chuckled pretending nothing was happening between them.

"I am a little tired, I admit it. Will you walk me to my car?" she asked him hastily and extremely disgusted.

"Sure, where are you parked?" Craig ignored her tone.

She pointed in the direction where her Honda sat waiting for her. Ordinarily, she'd be embarrassed, but right now she didn't care whether or not the ancient white Civic made her look poor.

It did spoil the picturesque scene placed before them, but Craig did that himself when he passed her his business card.

Candace sighed again and tried to focus on what she saw in front of her.

The ripples in the water reflected the silver glow of the moon and stars shining brightly in the sky. The palm trees danced slowly to the rhythm of the wind's melody. Along the coast, couples delighted themselves in the romantic atmosphere of the evening. And sitting in the midst of it all was her raggedy little car; reminding Candace her life would never have a storybook ending.

I do need money, she let the thought sink into her mind.

"Wow!" Craig exclaimed. "You still have this car."

"Yeah, my Honda is real reliable," Candace said trying to convince herself that dependability was the real reason why she held on to this piece of junk. In actuality, she couldn't afford another bill and a new car meant a car payment.

"You know," Craig cleared his throat, taking the opportunity to emphasize his business. "…That if you do decide to take me up on my offer, you would be able to buy practically any new car in the city. It might take you awhile before you started making enough money to get an Escalade, but it's all worth it in the end. You'll feel much better about yourself when you're making the big bucks and can afford to do everything you want to do for Azerica."

Once again, Candace had momentarily gotten lost in the enchantment of the evening and forgot the real reason why Craig wanted to treat her to dinner. Reality came back and hit hard. He could say all day long that she was still his good friend and he was looking out for her best interest, but he only saw her as a money making tool. He didn't care about her reputation, her feelings or her family. He just wanted to use her to bring profit to his world. She was thankful he didn't know anything about her previous relationship and the additions to her family, because if he did know she had two other children to support, he would really press the issue of her starting the next evening.

Craig opened the car door for her and kissed her lightly on the cheek. "Just think about it," he said. "I know it will be good for you."

She sat down behind the wheel and looked up into his eyes, trying to understand his thoughts and actions. She hoped his expression would tell her something that his lips didn't. All she had to do was ask, she knew, but she was scared to open herself up to what she might find out.

"Candace, think about your family and what's best for them." Craig caressed her face with his hand. Then leaned down to kiss her forehead.

In a daze, she nodded her head yes.

"Give me a call tomorrow if you have any questions," he said softly.

"Okay," she responded lightly.

He closed her door and began walking towards his black Mercedes. He felt good. He knew he had her.

Chapter 8

Her ride home from the Southside back to the Westside was a humbling experience. As soon as she got in the car, she turned the volume off on her broken radio. She needed the silence so she could clear her head. The events of the evening replayed over and over in her head. The more she thought about the proposition, the more she realized Craig was using her. He wasn't the same man she befriended all those years ago. He couldn't be. That Craig Pearson would never suggest she make money that way. If she had ever suggested that to him in the past, he would have stopped her from thinking about it and would have even offered her more help. Yet, now that's his number one money scheme for her to get back on her feet.

Letting her mind go blank, Candace continued to ride in silence down Beach Boulevard. There really wasn't much to the scenery but traffic lights and old buildings, but it was calming for her to watch in the late hour. The road wasn't bombarded with traffic like it was during the day. Besides a few cars here and there, she was alone on the long stretch of road.

As she merged onto 95, she couldn't help but notice the city's attractiveness under the pale moon. Downtown Jacksonville was so beautiful at night with its lights shining and reflecting on the St. John's River. But tonight, part of the magic was gone. Every night until about 11 p.m., the bridge that leads to Riverside stays lit up with a neon blue light. Every time she drove by she became enchanted. Many times, she had to stop herself from staring. She couldn't afford the repercussions of not paying attention to the road.

Tonight, she kept her eyes on the road. The downtown scenery wasn't as captivating without the bridge's blue light.

She didn't realize how late it was until after she passed the bridge. She glanced at the clock on the dashboard.

"It's 12:30," she said to herself. "Azerica better have Mel and Chauncey in bed. Hell, Azerica better be in bed."

Thinking about Azerica, Candace was certain her daughter had a field day with no supervision this evening. She had no clue what her child could have done, but she sure wasn't going to put anything past her. All week she'd been acting like she was the only one who existed, always wanting to do what she wanted to do and neglecting her chores. She acted like she couldn't do anything asked of her. But Candace didn't know what the problem was. Azerica could be acting out because her dad is locked up or her new high school status has gone to her head.

High school. Candace dreaded the thought of it. If it weren't for high school she wouldn't be where she was now. *Three kids, no man and no job is not how I envisioned my life to be.*

She always wanted to be a pediatrician. Azerica's birth killed that dream. Now she realized she could have done it during those wasted years before Melina was born.

Well, at least things are starting to look up, she thought. *At least I'll finally be working in a hospital.*

Pulling into Raintree, she started mentally preparing herself for work. Running through her mind, was everything she needed to do to get ready for her job Monday morning. She still needed to find a decent childcare for Chauncey, get an oil change, pay some bills, cancel fall registration for school and buy groceries.

"Am I really ready to go back to work?" Candace asked herself when she opened her front door and saw the mess in her living room. "Azerica obviously did nothing but talk on the phone tonight."

Candace strolled through the apartment and checked in on Mel and Azerica. They both were sleeping hard in the room they shared. Melina was laying on her stomach snoring and Azerica was sleeping with her knees in the air and her hands thrown behind her head.

Closing back their bedroom door, Candace walked to her room and found a sleeping Chauncey sprawled across her bed. She knelt down to kiss his forehead. At the softness of her touch, he shifted in his sleep but then settled back into his deep slumber. Gently, she picked him up and placed him inside the crib next to her bed. Taking a moment to herself, she undressed and put on her nightgown. She started to pick up the novel she was reading, but decided instead to call her best friend Leesa.

"How was your date with the doctor?" Leesa asked as soon as she picked up the phone.

Candace laughed lightly.

"Well, what's up? What happened? You know inquiring minds want to know." She'd been waiting up all night for this moment. She wanted Candace to find a new, better man. And who better than a doctor that was her best friend in high school?

"I don't know where to start," Candace replied. She didn't feel like reliving her emotions, but she knew Leesa didn't ask to be called.

"What's wrong? What happened?" Leesa asked, sensing that something was wrong. "Don't tell me he was a jerk."

"Well, not exactly. But he wasn't the Prince Charming he used to be either." Candace smirked.

"So he didn't give you the job?" Leesa asked concerned. "Why would he ask you out and not give you the job?"

"No, I got the job," Candace reassured her.

"Ok, so he made you pay…" Leesa tried to understand her friend's disposition.

"No, he made sure everything was taken care of."

"Alright then, he's married…"

"No, he's still very single." Candace wished any of those were reasons for why she felt the way she did. She could accept going Dutch or even a married man unhappy with his wife. What she couldn't really accept was his proposition.

"Well, what was the problem?" Leesa asked starting to get frustrated. She hated playing these games with Candace late at night. "The man gave you the job, you didn't pay for the food and he's single. Sounds like he's qualified to be your next baby daddy."

"Sorry, I think I'm going to pass," Candace smirked. "I'm better off with Jeff. He never made me feel like this."

"Candy, what exactly happened? I'm tired of asking you questions."

"Lees, he was the perfect gentlemen the entire night. He was encouraging; he made me feel safe and secure. I felt like I was supposed to be there with him like that forever. I wish I could explain to you what it felt like to have his arms around me while we danced." Candace allowed the image to come rushing back to her. She'd never felt anything like that moment in time. She still longed to feel that way forever.

"Girl, you don't have to say nothing. I feel ya. I feel like that every time Jerome holds me in bed." Leesa interrupted. "And you know how crazy Jerome is."

"Listen to me Leesa!" Candace exclaimed. She kept trying to get her friend to see the picture painted in her head. "It was just his actions, but the mood was perfect. I mean little candles on every table, dimmed lights, and the dance floor and jazz music. I felt like I was falling in love all over again."

"Well what changed that?" Leesa asked. "It sounds like he was perfect. But I know something happened or you wouldn't be acting like this."

"I got the job, of course he hooked me up." Candace said. "That wasn't even the problem. He was all for giving me the job."

"Alright Candy, what's the problem then?" Leesa asked, still not sure what issues her friend really had.

"It's just this thing he wants me to do and I don't know if I can do it," Candace rambled uncertainly, working things out as best as she could in her head. "I mean, he means well and I know he's looking out for my best interest, but there's just no way. I really don't understand how he could ask me to do it."

"Do what!" Leesa interrupted. "Please just tell me Candy. You are driving me crazy and we both have to get up early."

Candace breathed deeply.

Telling Leesa about the proposition may not be the best thing. For some reason, she didn't want her friend to think badly of Craig. *As soon as I tell her, she's going to try her best to keep me from working with him. And I probably shouldn't, but I need to work. My kids need me to.*

"Never mind, Leesa." Candace retracted her statements. "I'm going to go to bed now."

"Oh no, Candy. You can't do that to me. I am your best friend. I know you've got some issues with this man. You need to tell me what's really going on before I come over." Leesa got out of bed and started putting her clothes back on. "I'll be there in about fifteen minutes."

"No, Leesa. Don't come over." Candace tried to keep her friend on the phone.

"Well are you going to tell me what the problem is?"

Candace couldn't tell Leesa about the proposition, but she knew she had to tell her something. She didn't want her coming over and waking everyone up. Leesa never dropped a subject until she got all the information she needed. She'd been like that for as long as Candace had known her.

They'd known each other for about ten years. They were worked together at ADT for years as customer service representatives. That was actually the job Craig hooked her up with after she and Jeffrey broke up. At the time, she was 21 and Leesa was 24. They both were broke, single mothers living alone waiting for child support from two sorry daddies. Even then, Leesa had an ear for information. There was a gay couple in their training class who claimed to be just roommates. Within the first week, Leesa had asked them so many questions that they finally admitted to her they were a couple. The bad thing was she didn't even care if they were or not, she just wanted to know.

The average person would never realize Leesa was a nosy person from the way she asked her questions. They would just think she was concerned about them and their lifestyle.

But I know this is different. She is really concerned about me. Candace reminded herself. *Leesa is a true friend. Not true like I thought Craig was, but a for real true friend.*

Candace breathed deeply again to prepare herself for Leesa's anticipated questions. But before Leesa could even start, Candace decided to stall and recount the events of her evening. She went through every detail from the drive to Milano's to the romantic scenery to the way Craig looked and smiled at her.

"I know all that," Leesa said impatiently. "Now tell me the part I don't know. I still have my clothes on. All I've got to do is put on my shoes."

Leesa hated having to threaten Candace to get her to talk, but she didn't know what else to do. Candace was a grown woman. Leesa shouldn't have to go through this just to figure out what was bothering her.

"What do you mean?" Candace asked nonchalantly, trying to sound like everything was fine. She regretted mentioning the proposition to Leesa. She actually thought Leesa would forget if she took her through the entire date again.

"You know what I'm talking about. Tell me about the business deal." Leesa demanded.

"Oh, yeah." Candace said. "It's really not that big of a deal."

"Not that big of a deal!" she exclaimed. "You were rambling and not making sense and now you act like there's no problem. I'm not stupid. And you know I'm not going to get off the phone 'til you tell me what's going on."

Candace looked over at the clock on her stereo and it blinked 1:12 a.m. If she didn't tell Leesa something, she would never go to sleep because Leesa would be knocking at her door for real.

"Alright Leesa. I was tripping when I first mentioned it to you, but now I feel better about it." Candace lied.

"Well, what is it?" Leesa asked again, not letting Candace avoid the issue.

"You know Craig is a doctor at Memorial Hospital..." Candace began her story.

"Yeah, he works in ER. So what?"

"Lees, you didn't let me finish." Candace said.

"My bad, go ahead." Leesa tried to keep her frustration to herself until Candace got the story out.

"Well he has this entertainment business he's trying to start and he asked me to help him with it." Candace finally said.

It doesn't sound that bad when you put it that way, Candace thought. *I guess that's how I'll start explaining it to everyone.*

"What kind of entertainment business?" Leesa asked cautiously. She didn't trust the vague description. "I know it didn't take you half an hour to tell me that."

"You know, it's like a club and musicians come in and comedians," Candace answered only telling half the story. She didn't even know if what she were saying were true, but it sounded good.

"So what would you be doing?" Leesa questioned in unbelief.

"I'd be helping with the entertainment." Candace said surprised with how confident she sounded.

"Like how?" Leesa challenged.

"Preparing the audience for them and keeping them interested," Candace continued with her story. *And I'm sticking to it.*

"I still think there's something more to the story, but I'll leave you alone for now. I gotta be up early with Isaac in the morning." Leesa gave up the fight. Candace was starting to drain her and give her a headache.

Why? What's wrong?" Candace asked, happy the subject was changing.

"It's not all that deep. I've gotta take him to the doctor for his physical. He hasn't had one in like four years," said Leesa.

"Well you go ahead and get some rest. I've gotta find Chauncey a daycare tomorrow," Candace said.

"Alright then. I'll talk to you tomorrow."

"Alright girl, bye."

Hanging up the phone, Candace sank into her bed and pulled the covers over her head. She hadn't even washed her face, but she didn't care. She just wanted to turn off the lights and go to sleep. The only problem was she wasn't tired. She had too much on her mind to go to sleep. Craig wanted her to meet him there tomorrow night just to see it and see what she would be doing. He said he wanted to introduce her to the others and listen to the way they've been able to finally take care of things for themselves.

Is this his way of saying he's tired of me always running to him for help, Candace asked herself. *The only other time he's helped was when Azerica was four years old. That was ten years ago. I haven't called him for anything since. I wish I knew what made him change. I feel like I found and lost my best friend all in one day.*

She just couldn't figure out his actions. He wasn't the same person he was back then. That's what was really bothering her. One minute he seemed like the perfect gentlemen and someone who was interested in her love then the next minute he's asking her to do something he would never want his sister to do. She didn't understand. She thought there was a time when he considered her like family or at least a really good friend. Now, she didn't know what he thought of her. But he still was her only way out. She didn't have any other options.

Mom would tell me I still have Jesus, but God I wouldn't even know where to start, Candace said still battling with what she felt she had to do and what her mother told her to do. *It's been so long since I've come to you. So much has happened that I don't even know what to say or do. I know I have to start taking care of my family and stop depending on child support or some man to do it. I guess Craig is finally giving me the opportunity to do so. I hate the thought of it, but I don't have another choice. I gotta be responsible now and take better care of my family.*

Still restless and thinking about the near future, Candace rolled over and glanced at her clock. Now it blinked 2:30 a.m.

She knew what the problem was.

She needed to pray, but she felt so ashamed. In the past six months, she'd drifted so far away from God that she didn't know how to get back. Although she wanted to, she knew she couldn't blame Jeffrey for this. It was because of her that she's strayed away from the word. All he did was glorify everything that was wrong. She had gotten too comfortable with what he was doing for her and became caught up in the lifestyle she'd had in high school.

He made her feel carefree again at a time when she was stressed in her relationship with Greg. For some reason, she and Greg weren't on the same page anymore. During the time Jeffrey received his promotion, Greg was going through a career change and his ex-fiancée and daughter were moving back to Jacksonville from Miami. He spent so much time getting them settled in that she, Melina and Chauncey never saw him. She remembered nights spent arguing with him because she was afraid he would reunite with them. His ex-fiancée was so beautiful and she was very insecure at the time because she'd just had Chauncey. She still felt fat and unattractive.

Jeffrey took the time to make sure she and her children were taken care of. With all the extra money he was giving them, she and the girls were dressed in Baby Phat and FUBU and all Chauncey's clothes were coming from J.C. Penney and Belks.

In the time that he spent with her, Jeffrey let her know about his street pharmaceutical job. She let him know she didn't like it, but she loved the money so she didn't say too much about it. Then one night while Azerica was away at cheerleader camp and Mel and Chauncey were sleeping, they sat out on the patio and smoked a few blunts. It felt good to talk to relieve her stress and open up to him. It was like he knew what she needed. All he did was sit and listen to her fuss, whine and complain. But he was there for her when she needed him and that was more than she could say for Greg.

In the midst of their high, they talked about high school and their secret crushes on each other before they knew each other's names. They reminisced about Azerica's birth and their many arguments. Then they apologized to each other for handling things the way they did. Their feelings poured over that night and in the heat of the moment, he was back in her bed. He left real early so Mel wouldn't know he stayed over night. They didn't want her to be confused.

I actually felt guilty about that night for so long, Candace reminded herself. *Then I found out that Greg was with his ex-fiancée that same night. He still tries to tell me he didn't sleep with her, but I'm not stupid. He spent way too much time with her and she made sure to reclaim her territory when she first met me.*

Ughh!! You need to go to sleep! Candace screamed to herself.

young, dumb and naive

Scared to even look at the time, she pulled the covers back over her head and closed her eyes. She forced herself to clear her mind and go to sleep. She needed her rest for everything she had to do tomorrow.

"You know God," she said silently, realizing she was just as messed up now than she had ever been. "I still need you. I just don't know how to get back to you."

Chapter 9

"So Z, what's the plan for tonight?" Trish asked Azerica in the locker room before class started. "You still staying over?"

"Yeah girl, of course," Azerica replied throwing her cheerleader bag in the locker she shared with Trish. "Tonight is going to be so much fun."

"But the fun starts now." Trish said and closed the locker door.

"What are you talking about?" Azerica asked confused. "Where's your make-up? You gotta do my face, remember?"

Azerica turned to look at herself in the mirror and was pleased. She felt so good about herself today. Today really felt like a new day. For the first time, she didn't look like a baby. She actually looked like she was in high school, with much thanks to Trish. The blue, low-cut *spoiled* shirt she brought to Azerica complimented her figure and looked good with the black capris. Azerica made sure to use her mother's wave iron this morning to give herself an edge and complete the look she was going for.

And she achieved it.

She actually turned some heads this morning when she walked onto campus. She didn't really pay attention to who they were, but she felt their stares. It felt so good to be noticed.

"Trish I need some make-up to be complete," Azerica posed dramatically as if she were going to fall off the bench.

"Oh yeah. I got it," said Trish, very happy that Azerica felt good about herself today. She was really going to feel good by the end of the day. They were about to have the best time of their freshmen lives.

Trish re-opened the locker and grabbed her make-up bag from inside. She pulled out foundation, mascara, eye shadow and lipstick for Azerica.

"But like I was saying, we're not going to class today." Trish said returning to her subject. "Sit right here."

"What about the pep rally fourth period?" Azerica asked while Trish started covering her face with foundation.

"We'll be back for that." Trish reassured her. "Believe me, I know we can't afford to get in trouble today. So don't worry about that. That ain't happening to these two cheerleaders."

"Well what are we doing?" Azerica asked anxiously. She started breathing a little funny. She hated surprises that could get them in trouble.

"We'll be chilling with Jay and Darren wherever they decide to go. We're skipping with them. Is that cool with you?" She couldn't wait to be alone with Jay again. She hadn't seen him since that night at Azerica's earlier in the week. Except for after practice, but that never counted because they were always too busy trying to get home and relax.

"Well aren't you going to say anything?" Trish asked Azerica.

Not knowing what to say Azerica shrugged her shoulders as if to say okay. She'd never skipped a class before but she didn't want to tell Trish that. She tried to act nonchalant. She had a dozen questions but was too scared to ask them because she didn't want to sound like a fresh, scared fish.

"Azerica don't you at least want to know why Darren is skipping with us?" Trish asked breaking the silence.

"Why?" Azerica asked. Now that Trish mentioned it, she did want to know. They really didn't know Darren very well except that he was the star senior quarterback. And from what she knew, all the females had a crush on him.

"'Cause he likes you!"

"Are you serious?" Azerica asked in complete shock. She almost fell over in her seat. "How do you know that?"

"Jason told me he be asking questions about you all the time," Trish said. "Jay said he been asking about you since he saw you at one of the practices over the summer."

"Me?" Azerica still couldn't believe it. She knew who Darren was, but never realized that he thought twice about her. She met him for the first time during the summer when she came back from cheerleader camp, but they never conversed. The most they ever did was pass each other, smile and say hey.

"I don't believe you," Azerica said in disbelief. "I'm the girl that's looked like a baby all week and you're telling me that he's liked me since the summer! What did I look like then?"

"All that matters is that he likes you," Trish said pointing at her. "He ain't thinking about anyone else according to Jay."

All Azerica could say was, "Wow."

"Z do you know what this means?" Trish continued. She was ecstatic that her friend had a fine love interest too. They could double date.

"No, what?" Azerica asked.

"Girl, you pulled a senior and you weren't trying. You did better than me. Do you know how many seniors alone are in love with Darren and he won't talk to them?" Trish rambled. "He can have any girl that he wants at USG and he wants to get with you. And now you don't have to worry about talking to one of his brother's friends."

"Yeah, I gotta little pimpjuice in me too." Azerica joked. "Maybe you need to take some lessons from me."

She reviewed herself in the mirror, going over every detail and decided she was happy with everything. She knew she had to look really really really good today. She would be spending her morning with Darren Lewis: the senior football star.

I wish I could scream right now, Azerica thought. This was more exciting to her than joining USG's varsity cheerleading squad.

"But for real, I don't know what you did, but you got something in your blood that Mr. Lewis likes." Trish continued. "But you know he and Makeisha used to talk."

"For real?" Azerica said nonchalantly. "For how long?"

"For a short minute, but sometimes she acts like she still like him," Trish warned. "You might want to be careful."

"How can you tell?" Azerica asked but not really caring. It didn't really matter to her how Makeisha felt about Darren. He liked Azerica now.

young, dumb and naive

"I know you see the way she be acting around him on the field," Trish responded.

"No, I don't pay attention to either of them. Should I start?" Azerica wondered.

"Yeah, if you don't want Makeisha watching you all the time," Trish said as if Azerica were crazy. The rumors Trish heard about Makeisha weren't pretty and she didn't want Azerica to have to deal with the trick. "But don't worry about it today. Today's our fun day."

"Alright," Azerica said not sure what to think now. She'd never had an issue with Makeisha and she really didn't want to start having one now. She'd only known her since the summer.

Makeisha Wright was a senior and the head cheerleader at USG. Makeisha was cool. Azerica didn't always know how to talk to her, but she was cool. Makeisha could be a little intimidating at times because she seemed so perfect. She was intelligent and pretty. All the guys liked her because she was thick and all the females loved her clothes.

"Don't she have a boyfriend?" Azerica asked trying to feel at ease.

"I think she's talking to some college guy, but Nikia told me Darren and Makeisha were each other's firsts," said Trish. "And you know how that goes."

"Yeah," Azerica said lightly.

Not really! She screamed in her head. She'd never had sex before. She had no clue what people were talking about when they referred to people as being each other's firsts. *How does it go exactly?* She wanted to ask, but she didn't want to be embarrassed.

She and Trish had never talked about the sex thing before and whether or not the other were still a virgin, but she wasn't ready to bring up that subject now. If she said one thing about being a virgin, everyone in her circle would find out. And if Darren found out her secret, he wouldn't want to talk to her anymore.

I don't want to lose his attention. I didn't put in all this work to change myself for nothing, she thought. Besides that, she was starting like him. But pushed deep in the back of her mind was the question she avoided asking herself. Was she really ready to have sex and give her virginity away to Darren?

Trish finished applying eye shadow and mascara to Azerica's eyes. She handed her some lip gloss and a tube of lipstick. "Put this on and tell me what you think."

Azerica walked to the floor-length mirror pleased with what she saw. The foundation Trish used hid almost all of her freckles. The eye shadow and mascara accentuated her eyes and gave her a somewhat mysterious look.

"Did I tell you my dad called the other day?" Azerica asked hoping they wouldn't talk about sex anymore today.

"Yeah, I forgot he was locked up. How's he doing?" Trish asked casually. She felt close to Azerica because they had a few things in common.

"He's alright. All we did was sit and talk. I told him about cheerleading and school and block scheduling," Azerica answered. "He's not happy. I can't wait 'til he's out and I can see him again."

"Why don't you go visit him?" Trish asked.

"I don't have a way to get there and I'm not sure if I want to see him that way, you know. I don't want to leave there and my memory of him be one of him in jail," Azerica rationalized. "I want my last memory of him to be the night I came home from camp."

"I guess," said Trish. It really didn't matter to her. A memory was a memory. You "You know, my sperm donor is in prison in New York."

Azerica laughed. "Your sperm donor?"

"Yeah girl. He made a deposit and left," Trish said matter-of-factly. "You know, it was a hit and run. That's what my mom tells me anyway. But I met him later. They got back together and broke up so many times before we moved to Florida."

"I'm sorry," said Azerica not really knowing how to respond to her friend.

"Don't apologize, it ain't your fault. He's just a sorry ass nigga." Trish's eyes glazed over.

"Well why is he locked up?" Azerica asked becoming curious.

"Rape charges, assault and battery and something else. I don't remember." Trish answered, her voice fading. She pushed the thought of him to the way back of her mind. She didn't want any memories of the past to resurface.

Not knowing what else to say, Azerica finished applying the lipstick and handed the tube back to Trish. She wanted to encourage her friend, but she couldn't find any words to encourage her.

Trish instantly grew distant and silent. Some things she tried so hard to forget, but they kept coming back no matter what she did. She wanted to erase the hurt and pain and forget she'd ever experienced them. *Not today*, she forced her mind to say. *You're not coming back ever again.*

Trish blinked the quickly forming tears away, but she couldn't blink away the memories of waking up in the middle of the night to her dad feeling on her and forcing himself on top of her. She couldn't blink away the force he used to enter her or the way he gagged her to keep her from screaming.

She blinked her eyes once more, but couldn't prevent the tear that escaped.

Noticing the quick change in Trish, Azerica reached and grabbed her hand. "Are you ok?"

Trish took a deep breath and sighed. "I'm fine."

Azerica hadn't known Trish for very long, but she knew her well enough to know something serious was bothering her and it had something to do with her dad. Why Trish tried to act like it was nothing, Azerica didn't know. She just didn't want to press the issue and make Trish even more upset.

Azerica watched in silence as Trish casually put her make-up bag away. The unusual droopiness in her friend's actions contrasted greatly with the bright, vivid colors of USG's gym locker room. The crisp color in the blue walls and red lockers were not enough to drive away Trish's overcast mood.

Before Azerica had a chance to say anything else, the first bell rang warning them they had five minutes to get to class.

"Oh Lord!" Exclaimed Trish breaking free from her daze. "We gotta hurry. They want us to meet them in the senior parking lot and I still gotta go to my locker."

Trish slammed shut the door to their locker in the locker room, grabbed Azerica's arm and rushed out the door. Exiting the gym, they brushed past students headed to class. They quickly turned sharp corners almost running into a few teachers. Some of their friends tried to stop them to talk, but Trish and Azerica sped by barely managing to say hello. They stopped only once to speak to their cheerleading coach who just wanted to remind them of the cheers they were to do at the pep rally. As soon as she finished her mini-refresher course, the second bell rang letting them know they had only one minute to get to class.

"Why did she have to talk so long?" Trish asked. She was already back to herself. "I don't have time to go to my locker now."

"Why not? It's right there," Azerica nodded her head in the direction of the freshmen hallway.

"'Cause if we don't get outside now, we'll never be able to leave the building to skip with them," said Trish anxiously trying to get outside without any teachers noticing them.

"What did you have in your locker anyway?" Azerica asked following close behind her.

"I wanted to grab a few rubbers just in case something went down, but I guess Jay and Darren will have it covered. If not, won't be none available to them."

Goodness. Azerica thought. *Am I ready for today? Help me God.*

This could be the day she became a woman. She never imagined it would happen so early in her life, but she had to prepare herself. She was scared, but she tried to tell herself it was better now than later. She needed to get some experience somehow. She still didn't know how to kiss.

Well, there was the time she kind of kissed this guy named Mike, but that was just on the lips. Neither of them knew what they were doing so they sat with their lips joined, their mouths opened and their tongues immobile. Azerica could flirt and talk a good game, but she'd never done anything before in her life.

What am I getting myself into? Azerica asked herself as she climbed in the front seat of Darren Lewis' silver Nissan Sentra.

"Hey girl," Darren said smiling when she closed the car door.

"Hey," she greeted, smiling shyly.

Alright, so he is fine, she said to herself. *At least he looks good.*

But that didn't mean she wanted to sleep with him. But she didn't want to look like a baby to him either. She was lucky to be chilling with him today. He didn't spend his time with just anybody.

Darren gazed over at her.

Azerica looked at him shyly and then turned her head towards the road. He made her extremely nervous.

"You know, Z. I been waiting all summer for this," Darren squeezed her hand.

"For what?"

"For some time with you." Darren said. "You're not an easy person to get to. I can get scholarships to UF, FSU and Texas A&M, but it took me this long to get you in my car."

Azerica blushed.

"So what did you decide?" Jason interrupted them.

"Texas A&M." Darren said. "I'm happy 'cause it's outta state and my parents are happy 'cause it's a historically black college. They don't want me to go to a white school 'cause they say I need a deeper sense of black culture. All I wanna do is play football so I can get to the NFL."

"Must be nice," Trish sighed, leaning close to his ear. "Why don't we get married and I come with you to Texas? I always wanted to be a football player's wife."

Darren laughed at her. "Are you crazy girl? I ain't getting married. Especially not to you Trish. You alright and all, but you ain't Beyonce. You gotta another ten years before you get there."

Trish slumped back in her seat close to Jason. *Seniors always thought they knew everything.* She was finer than Beyonce already. And besides, Beyonce couldn't do half of what she could do.

"That's alright. I ain't wanna marry you anyways. I got Jason. At least he's got green eyes," Trish retorted. "Me and Jason's gonna get married one day, right Jay."

Darren smirked. "Are you going to let her plan your future?"

"No comment," Jason shrugged his shoulders. "I wanna get some tonight."

Trish smiled. "At least you got some sense."

What am I doing here! Azerica screamed inside. This was too much for her. This was the first time she'd ever heard Jason talk about sex and she's known him since she was five years old. She felt like a child peeking through her fingers to watch the sex scenes in a movie. Was this all juniors and seniors did? Talk about having sex.

"So what do y'all wanna do?" Darren asked them, glancing in his rearview mirror at Jason and Trish and then turning to Azerica.

Azerica waited silently for Trish and Jason to respond.

"Dog, it don't matter 'long as we get back for the pep rally." Jason replied. He didn't want to get in trouble for being late.

"Well, I don't know 'bout y'all but I'm hungry. Can we go get some food?" Trish asked, rubbing her stomach. "I'll be calling up the Martians in a second."

"That's cool," Darren agreed. "You alright with that Z?"

"Yeah, I'm a little hungry too." Azerica replied.

"Where we going?" Darren looked at Azerica and asked, trying to get her involved in the conversation. She hadn't said a word other than hey since she got in his car.

"Can we go to Denny's?" Trish asked before Azerica could say anything.

"Alright," Darren said without taking his eyes off of Azerica. "There's one on Lex Av."

As soon as he answered Trish, Azerica turned her head, glad to get away from his eyes. She felt a little strange every time he looked at her. She didn't know why he made her so uncomfortable, but she never wanted to hold his gaze that long. He was charming and handsome with a brown complexion, a baldhead and a goatee, but his dark brown eyes seemed menacing to her. They kind of smirked at her as if he knew something that she didn't know. They were real intense, but kind of playful at the same time. Azerica didn't get it. She just knew she didn't like the combination.

Goodness, it would be horrible if I got caught by the school and Mom for skipping, Azerica changed her own subject. She didn't mean to think about that, but she saw so many old Honda Civics on Lex Av today.

My life would really be over if Mom found out, she allowed herself to acknowledge. The more she thought about it, the more she realized she should've stayed in school. She would have experienced no trouble there. *Lord, what have I done?*

"I have a question for you," Darren said breaking her thought process.

Azerica looked at him.

"Aren't you going to ask what it is?" Darren teased.

Azerica smiled at him. "Well, that's what I'm waiting for. What is it?"

"Why is it that Trish is so loud and obnoxious and you are quiet and sweet? How did you get a friend like her? You must have found her on the side of the road or something," Darren said.

"Hey, I heard that!" Trish exclaimed.

Azerica laughed.

She eased up a little as Darren continued to pry into her life a little deeper. He asked her questions about cheering, her family, her hobbies and her friendship with Trish.

"Trish found me at cheerleader camp over the summer," Azerica smiled. "She was like a lost puppy and followed me home."

"Are you sure she wasn't a stray dog?" Darren asked ignoring the evil looks Trish tried to give him in the back.

"I'm positive." Azerica replied. "She's actually a great friend."

young, dumb and naive

Azerica told him she met Trish at cheerleader camp and they'd been like best friends ever since. She told him a little bit about her mom, sister and brother, but she mentioned nothing about her dad. Not that it was a secret or anything. Azerica would never deny it if anyone asked her. She just didn't want to broadcast the fact that he was in prison. She wished she could forget about it and pretend that he was in another country working for a few years. But since he was from Jacksonville, that lie would never work. He knew too many people in Jacksonville that knew the truth.

Now that Darren liked her, she didn't want to mention it and have him think badly of her because her dad was locked up. If he did know about it, he did a good job of avoiding that subject.

"Thanks for letting me get in your head a little," Darren smiled at her.

"You're welcome." Azerica's eyes twinkled.

Darren couldn't believe how innocent she seemed. He glanced over at her several times during the drive and tried to read her demeanor, but he couldn't. He'd never pursued anyone like her before. She would be a challenge. He might have to talk to his brother about this one.

When they pulled into the parking lot at Denny's, Darren turned once more to look at her. She tried not to look back at him, but their eyes locked again. Azerica felt her stomach flutter. The same intensity that scared her before, still made her uneasy.

"We're here already?" Jason asked disappointed. He wasn't ready to take his hands off Trish.

"Yeah," said Darren disengaging himself from Azerica to look in the back at Jason and Trish.

"Let's eat!" Trish exclaimed, scurrying to get out of the car.

Azerica watched the three of them spring from the car and head towards the entrance. She took a deep breath and casually followed them in.

Lord, she silently prayed, *please don't let my mom or any of her friends be in here today.* Azerica quickly scanned the restaurant looking for any adult that she and her mom might know. But she didn't see anyone.

"Thank God," she said softly so no one heard her. She could feel her heart pounding through her throat every time she turned her head. *If this is what it feels like to skip, I think I'm just going to stay in school next time.*

"We got this place on lock." Trish turned around to face her. "Do you see how many people from USG are in here?"

It was like being at a party and chilling with the most popular people. Trish loved every part of it. There was nothing like it. She could feel the haters cutting their eyes at her and the nobodies wishing they could be her. *One day, you can be like me*, she wished she could tell them.

Trish grabbed Azerica's arm and strutted behind Darren and Jason. She made sure to twist a little harder for her own entertainment.

"It's all in the walk," Trish leaned over and whispered to Azerica when Darren and Jason stopped to talk to a few of the football players.

"Huh?" Azerica asked. She walked just fine. It wasn't like she was clumsy and tripped over herself all the time. "What do you mean?"

"You know, the infamous walk. The walk that makes all the guys turn their heads and follow you," Trish whispered. "There's more to it than just the clothes Azerica. That's just a basic. You need a walk too. You know, with a little twist while you walk."

There was too much to learn! Azerica screamed to herself. It was becoming too hard to be noticed. She had to have the look, the clothes and now the walk. What was next? The legs. How far did she want to go to be popular?

All the way, she answered herself. It felt too good for people to notice her and wonder who she was. She liked the attention she was getting from her peers even if it was because she was with Darren and Jay. At least no one was bumping into her and knocking her over. If she could maintain this on her own, she would be happy.

"Darren who you got wit you?" asked one of the other senior football players at another table.

"Z and Trish. They both cheerleaders. Don't you ever see them on the field?" Darren asked him.

"Naw. I think I would'a noticed any new fine cheerleaders," the guy winked at Azerica and Trish.

Azerica stole a glance at Trish and they both laughed.

Yes, it finally felt good to be noticed.

When the waitress was finally able to get them through the crowd, she ended up seating them at a booth near the entrance. Trish bounced in next to Jason leaving Azerica to slide in next to Darren.

"I love Denny's," Trish said excitedly. "I always get the American Slam. It's my favorite. I could eat breakfast for dinner..."

"I really don't eat here that often," Azerica said, trying hard to remember the last time she did go out to eat with her family.

"Girl, you don't know what you're missing," Trish said. "I mean if all else fails, you always have Denny's."

"Or Waffle House," Darren interjected.

"Or Famous Amos," added Jason.

"Denny's ain't the only late night restaurant Trish. You act like you don't ever leave Lex Av. There's more to Jacksonville than Denny's." Darren teased. "But I guess you wouldn't know that since you don't have a car."

Trish cut her eyes at him. "And I don't care because I only want Denny's anyway."

"But didn't they get sued for racism?" Azerica asked.

"Discrimination." Darren smiled and stared deep into her eyes.

"Trish, why you wanna support a restaurant that don't like black people?" Jason turned and asked her.

"They didn't do that to me." Trish quickly defended Denny's. "And don't you see all the black people they have working in here? How many black people work at Waffle House and Famous Amos?"

"Who cares? I'm ready to order," Jason cut her off. "Waitress!"

"Why is your friend so rude," Trish asked Darren. "He cut me off and didn't even answer my question."

"Just order your food Trish," Jason said after he told the waitress what he wanted.

"I want the American Slam with a large apple juice," Trish told her.

"I'll have the same," Azerica said when it was her turn.

"Lady, I'm hungry. I want whatever's going to give me a lot of meat." Darren flirted with her.

"How 'bout the Lumberjack Slam," the waitress smiled at him. "You get ham, bacon, sausage, eggs along with pancakes hash browns or grits."

"I can work with that." Darren inched closer to Azerica.

"Do you want hash browns or grits?" the waitress asked.

"Grits." Darren placed his hand on Azerica's knee.

"What about to drink?"

"Some O.J." Darren winked at Azerica. "O.J. keeps the doctor away."

"Your orders will be right out." The waitress walked away.

"Azerica you're going to love the American Slam. It's just so good. I've never had anything like it before," Trish started rambling again.

"Trish leave the girl alone. Just 'cause she don't eat here everyday don't mean she's never had the breakfast before." Jason said. "You make it sound like she's from Mexico or something."

"No, there are Denny's in Mexico," Trish said matter-of-factly.

"How do you know?" Jason questioned her in disbelief.

"Go to dennys.com when you get online again." Trish answered. "I bet you don't see Waffle House or Famous Amos in any other countries."

"So you been to the website," Darren moved his hand up towards Azerica's thigh. "You must really love this restaurant."

"Girl, you've got issues," Azerica concentrated on getting her words out.

Darren's hand roamed up and down her thighs and he kept talking as if nothing were happening. Remembering what Trish said about not acting like a baby, Azerica let him continue. She had to show him she was more than just a silly freshman. But deep down, she didn't like it. She hated it. She wished it would stop. Each time she got the nerve to push his hand away, Trish's words drowned her conscience.

Azerica felt helpless as if she didn't have a say in the matter. And she really didn't according to her new friend. That's why Azerica trusted her to change her image. Trish said she had to be a certain way and Darren was proving that to be true.

Even still, it made her uncomfortable. She felt like a piece of meat and she was surprised that no one noticed her frowning while they ate and talked. Not even her new best friend noticed the change in her attitude.

"Z, look. He is so fine!" Trish exclaimed, pointing at the cash register. "I'd make his dreams come true."

Azerica nodded in agreement, too ashamed to speak.

"Hey isn't that that doctor?" Jason asked.

"Where?" Darren asked, trying to see through the crowd.

"At the register," said Jason.

"Oh, yeah dog. We gotta check him out next Friday." Darren said smiling.

"What for? What does he do?" Trish pried. They weren't leaving her out. If there was a party she wanted to go too.

"He got 'dis strip joint downtown that my brother be talking 'bout," Darren replied. "He said it's hot. It changed the game."

"Y'all are too young to get in. Why are you trying to go?" Trish asked.

"Age ain't nothing when you're brother is security. He'll let us in. He already promised me VIP," Darren boasted.

"Dog, I can't wait," said Jason.

"Man you won't know what to do wit all that ass shaking in front of you. It ain't nothing like these young girls you be messing with," said Darren.

Jason laughed. He probably wouldn't know what to do, but he'd try it. He didn't care. A woman was a woman.

young, dumb and naive

"You know you can't pull no thick twenty-something wit booty," Darren continued. "That takes some game."

"Man, you don't know what I got," Jason said confidently. "I got more game than you think."

"Naw, but I know what I got and it'll take you some time to develop it, but that's what I'm here for," said Darren smiling. He'd love to see Jason get with an older chick.

"Well what are we here for if you just like older women," Trish interrupted mad. "Take us back to school. We can find some other guys to spend our time with."

"Damn shorty, we just talking. If we didn't want to be with you we wouldn't have asked you to come," Darren responded, placing his hand back on Azerica's thigh to confirm what he said was true.

"Y'all ready to go?" Jason asked when he'd noticed they'd stopped eating a while ago.

"Yeah," said Azerica. She couldn't wait to get from under Darren's hand and get back in the car. At least she knew he'd keep his hands on the wheel in the car.

"Are you guys paying for this 'cause we ain't got no money," Trish said to Darren and Jason.

"Yes, Trish. We got this," Darren answered, tired of all Trish's questions. He was glad Jason was with her. She'd get on his nerves after awhile. "We wouldn't bring you here if we couldn't pay for it. Chivalry ain't dead."

"What's chivalry?" Trish asked.

Darren sighed and shook his head. He paid his bill and guided them outside.

In the parking lot, he and Jason stopped to look at a black Mercedes sitting next to the Sentra. It was sleek and shining black. The windows were tinted so dark they couldn't see inside. When a man unlocked and opened the car door to get out, the guys jumped back scared.

"Sorry, fellas. Didn't mean to scare you. I saw you admiring the car," the doctor said.

"Yeah, she's tight," said Jason.

"Would you guys like to take a closer look? Come on. You can sit inside," the doctor invited. "Take your time. I'm in no rush."

He turned and smiled at Trish and Azerica.

They smiled back in admiration. He was a nice-looking older black man. He was so fine. They stood, wishing they were older so they could have a chance to be with him.

"Thanks man," Darren said getting out of the car.

"No problem," said the doctor as he climbed back into his car.

"Yeah man, thanks," said Jason. "My name is Jason and that's Darren, Trish and Azerica."

"Hello," the doctor turned to greet them. "I'm Dr. Craig Pearson."

Azerica watched silently as he continued to talk.

"What school do you guys go to?" He asked them.

"USG," They all said in unison and then laughed.

"And you must be the infamous Darren Lewis." Dr. Pearson shook his hand. "What schools are you interested in?"

"Texas A&M is my only choice," Darren responded. "I wanna get up outta this town. I got family in Texas too so it's cool."

"Good choice, but don't depend on the NFL. Get yourself a good education while you're there so you have something to fall back on. You don't want to fit the black athlete stereotype." Dr. Pearson advised. "Too many young blacks go pro and don't know anything about anything else. It stays very obvious so America don't treat them with respect. If you go to college, get the respect that you deserve."

"I never thought about it like that," Darren said thankfully. "I did want to be a doctor when I was little. I guess I can major in that while I'm at Texas A&M."

"Good choice." Dr. Pearson smiled and glanced at Azerica. "But I am a little biased. Listen. I don't want to hold you kids up anymore, but Darren when it's time for you to work in the field, look me up and call me. I can get you an internship at Memorial Hospital."

"Thanks Doctor. I'll remember that," Darren shook his hand.

"Well kids, I'll see you around," Dr. Pearson climbed back into his car and gave Azerica one last look before he closed the door and pulled off.

"Did you know him?" Trish turned to ask her. "He kept looking at you."

"I know, but I don't think I know him." Azerica replied. But there was no mistaking. There was definitely something about his voice that was so familiar to her. Azerica didn't know what it was. It was a like a voice from the past, but she didn't know from where.

Darren walked up behind them and spread his arms over both their shoulders, guiding them back towards his Sentra.

"Well it's time to ride," he said. "I gotta run home and check some stuff for the party tonight."

"Sounds cool," said Azerica anxious to get back in the car. She still wasn't sure where she knew Dr. Pearson from, but she hoped he wasn't one of her mom's friends checking up on her. She reached for the door handle to the front seat to get in and felt someone come up behind her.

"Now what makes you think you can sit up here again," said Jason, pretending to push her out the way.

"Jay!" she exclaimed and laughed.

"Girl, I'm just messing with you," he laughed with her. "Trish is crazy, but she don't drive me that crazy. But I'll let you know when she does."

"Z, you grew up with Jay, right?" Darren asked her when they were all in the car.

"Yeah, you could say that." She responded nervously and glanced back at him. She hoped he wouldn't mention Devin.

"Then you know that nigga ain't got no sense," he chuckled. "That's why he's my dog. You gotta be a crazy ass to be young and be around me."

"Man, stop all that talking and get to your house, we gotta make sure things are straight for tonight." Jason said. "Your moms left this morning, right?"

"Yeah, Jay. Her flight was at nine and my pops won't be back from visiting his sister 'til Sunday. Nigga we straight."

young, dumb and naive

"Well, where you stay at?" Trish asked curiously.

"Just watch the rode," said Darren sarcastically. He liked playing with Trish. She fell for everything.

"Naw, Negro. Where you got us going?" Trish smiled.

"Riverside." Darren said and winked at Azerica.

Azerica just shook her head and enjoyed the ride. They took Lex Av to Cassat and then turned onto Edgewood. As soon as he drove into the entrance to Jacksonville's Historic Riverside, he made a right and pulled into a long driveway. The house was quaint and beautiful. It was plantation style with big windows and a long porch. The setting made Azerica feel as though she were with an authentic American. She knew she was American too, but everything anyone related to Americanism was represented with his home. His family even had a swinging tire hanging from the only tree in the front yard.

"I thought only rich white people lived out here," said Trish when Darren parked the car. "I didn't know black people could afford to live out here."

"You don't get out much do you?" Darren asked her. "Ain't many of us out here, but niggas live here too."

"Your parents must be rich," she said in awe. She didn't know black people could live like this. She felt like she was at a circus or something. This was the first time she'd ever been to a rich friend's house.

"They financially stable," Darren responded. "Not rich. I hate when people say that. To me rich is when my moms don't have to work and I can have any car I want and not pay for insurance."

"Shoot, this is rich to me. What you're talking about is Bill Gates rich and he's a millionaire." Trish gave her definition.

"Well, what do they do?" Azerica asked, trying to get them off the rich thing.

"Dog, I bet you feel like you on 106th & Park," Jason laughed. "Mr. Celebrity being drilled with questions by two really nosy reporters."

Darren laughed. "I don't care."

"Well, we're waiting," Trish stopped walking and put her hand on her hip.

"Girl come on," Azerica grabbed her arm. She really didn't want to know that bad.

"Ladies, if you must know. My dad is a lawyer and my mom owns her own beauty salon. We've only lived here about four years. We used to live in a dinghy house on Lennox, but Dad saved his money from working as a mechanic and bought this house. He really started making money as a lawyer about four years ago."

" That's it and you have all this!" Trish exclaimed. His dad bought rich before he was even rich.

"Yeah, Mom always worked as a hair stylist and made mad money on the side but Dad bought her salon for her last year," Darren said. He was proud of his parents. They worked hard to get where they were.

"Well show us the house," Trish demanded. She had to see what it was like in a huge home that black people owned.

Darren agreed to a little mini-tour. He showed them every room but his parents' master bedroom because it was sacred and even he and his brother never enter it unless they really need to. His parents' bedroom was on one end of the house and he and his brother's rooms were on the other end. Darren's room was done in black and white decor. He had black furniture, a 19-inch TV and VCR, a Playstation 2 and a black futon sitting on a furry white rug in the corner of the room.

Azerica was utterly impressed. She felt like she knew so much about the Lewis' from just being in their home. She adored everything about the house from the layout of the rooms to the colors that decorated them to the pictures of his family members hanging in the halls.

When they finished the tour, Darren took them to the family room and turned on the wide-screen, flat TV to BET. Cita's World was on and they sat down to watch videos.

"Hell, I forgot to do something," Darren said jumping up from the chair he sat down in.

"Well," said Trish. His outburst made him look crazy.

young, dumb and naive

"What time do we need to be back at school?" Azerica asked Trish and Jason. She could feel herself getting paranoid again. *What if the school called her house and told her mom she wasn't at school today?*

"You sound scary," Jason teased her. "We promise nothing will happen to you."

"Naw, I'm not worried about that," Azerica lied. "I just need to go to my locker before we gotta be on the field."

"Well, I think Coach wanted all the cheerleaders to meet in the gym at 1:00," Trish said.

"So we need to leave here in about an hour and a half 'cause it's already 11:20," Azerica said, working out the details in her mind.

"I'll be right back," Jason said and got up.

"Dang, what's their problem?" Azerica asked, hoping they would decide it was time to go back and they'd all get in the car.

"You know they getting ready for the party tonight. It's going to be off the hook!" Trish exclaimed. "And I don't know of any other freshmen coming besides us."

"You better not say that too loud. Remember you don't want them to know," Azerica teased her.

"Shut up girl!" Trish said, acting like she was going to throw a pillow at her.

Azerica laughed.

"Trish," Jason said walking back into the room. "I wanna show you something, come here."

"Girl, I'll be right back," Trish said, smiling really big. "The man has summoned."

"Yeah, whatever," Azerica smiled.

Azerica watched Trish trot out of the room following behind Jay. They had some weird connection that she didn't really understand. She just shrugged it off and left it alone. She wasn't sure if she even wanted to know what their connection was. It might be too much for her virgin ears.

While Cita took a break, Azerica flipped through the channels looking for something else to entertain her until someone came back. The only shows that flooded the television were talk shows and court shows. And she couldn't stand any of them. They all got on her nerves. She finally settled on Cartoon Express and was watching the Smurfs when Darren came back and sat beside her.

"You like the Smurfs?" he asked sitting down on the couch beside her.

"Yeah, they're my favorite cartoon."

"Wow, you look like you'd like the Jetsons or something," he said trying to pick at her.

"I like them too, but the Smurfs are my favorite," she smiled.

"Which Smurf do you like the best," he asked her.

"Smurfette," she replied.

"Hmm," he said mischievously. "I bet I can tell you why she's your favorite."

"Why?" she challenged. She could handle flirting with him with his hands in his own lap.

"'Cause she got more sex than any of them," he said.

"I didn't think about that," said Azerica starting to feel a little uncomfortable again. *Did he always think about sex?*

"Well, just think about it. Now, she's the only female in a village with nuttin' but men and you know men, they got needs. I bet they was horny all the time," Darren said "I would've been in line right with the other Smurfs."

"You're killing my cartoon," said Azerica and she turned it back to BET.

"I don't see nothing wrong wit a little bump 'n' grind..." sang R. Kelly.

Lord, why does this always happen to me? Azerica asked remembering when she was sitting alone with Jason at her house and some freaky slow song came on the radio. She felt Darren itch closer to her. Then his hand found its way back to her thigh. She sat there almost scared to move and terrified to look in his eyes. He moved his hand up her thigh and over her hips to right below her breast and brought her closer to him.

young, dumb and naive

As soon as she was pressed against him, she felt his hand travel back down her body towards her middle. Finding the courage, she took her hand and moved him away. He brought his lips to hers and started kissing her. Then his hand began to travel south again. For the second time, she swayed him. He kissed her harder and deeper. Instead of going back down, his hand moved up inside her shirt. He played with her breasts and tried to undo her bra, but Azerica moved his hand once again.

"Let's go back to my room," he whispered in her ear.

Azerica had no clue what to do or how to react. She allowed him to stand her up and she followed his lead to the back to his room. Inside, he turned the radio on 101.5 and closed and locked the door. She had no idea where Trish and Jason were, but she had a feeling they were somewhere in the house doing the same thing. He sat her on the bed and commenced to doing what he was doing when they were sitting on the couch, yet this time she didn't stop him.

She wasn't as uncomfortable as before. She was actually starting to get used to the intense rubbing of his hands across her thighs. And part of her enjoyed feeling him touch her.

After about 15 minutes of him kissing her and his hands gliding over her, they were interrupted by a knock at the door.

"Darren," said Jason on the other side.

"What?" he asked a little irritated.

"Where they at?" Jason asked.

"They should be in the top drawer, you don't see them?" Darren tried to brush him off.

"Naw, negro, ain't nothing there," said Jason. "We ain't got a lot of time. Come show me."

Darren turned his attention back towards Azerica and kissed her hard. He laid on top of her and pressed his body against hers.

"Darren," said Jason knocking again. "Are you coming?"

"I'll be right back," Darren told Azerica sliding off of her. He straightened up his clothes, walked to the door and went outside.

"Jay, man, follow me," he said. "I'll show you where they are."

Azerica watched them walk down the hall and around the corner. She didn't know what they were looking for or what Jason needed so badly, but it must have been important. She could hear them rummaging around in the other room not being able to find what they needed.

"I don't know what he did with them," Azerica heard Darren say. "Let me look in here."

She heard them walk into the bathroom and open and close cabinet drawers. After about five minutes, they still hadn't found them. Then she heard Darren tell Jason he was out of gas and he better keep it safe. Jason was a little upset and told Darren that's why he had wanted to go to the store before they came over. But Darren reminded them they still had tonight.

Azerica couldn't help but laugh to herself when she heard them fussing. They argued like an old married couple. When Darren walked in and saw her smiling, she told him she thought they were funny.

"Oh, you think we're funny?" He asked her and kissed her leg.

"Yeah, y'all got issues," she said, beginning to feel more comfortable around him.

"Naw, he's just a horny little negro. I still got a lot to teach him," Darren said.

Azerica laughed.

"I don't want to talk about him anymore, let's talk about you," said Darren, sitting up beside her.

"Okay," said Azerica cautiously. "I thought you found out everything you wanted to know earlier in the car."

"I can never know too much," he said. "Tell me this. How many boyfriends have you had?"

"A few," Azerica said thinking back to past relationships she'd had. None of them really counted, but she didn't want to tell Darren that. She rarely saw her first one and the second one acted like he was scared of her, so they barely even talked.

"You don't have one now?" Darren asked, trying to sound surprised.

"No," she responded.

"Why not, you're beautiful."

Azerica just smiled. He made her feel good about herself.

"I know. You needed a nigga like me to step in 'cause all those boys around you don't know what they're doing. I understand, you ain't gotta tell me," Darren said smiling. "That's always the case. They're too young to appreciate you."

Azerica laughed again. If only that was it. She just couldn't attract anyone. No one even knew she existed ever since she came to high school.

"They were too young to know how to satisfy you. I bet they didn't even know how to kiss you the right way," Darren said, trying to feel her out. He needed to know what to do to get her to a new plateau in her life.

"You don't have a girlfriend?" Azerica asked trying to change the subject. Her face was hot. She couldn't handle that kind of pressure over something she's never done before.

"Naw, I don't keep females like that," Darren replied. "They just get irritating and controlling. I wasn't going to marry any of them chickenheads but they used to trip like they owned me or something."

"That's crazy," said Azerica, really unsure of what to say back to him.

"I did learn a lot from them though," he said earnestly and gazing into her eyes.

"Like what?" Azerica asked.

"Let me show you," he requested.

Without saying yes or no, Darren proceeded to kiss her anyway. She was real curious to find out what he learned from other females that he could show her, but she wasn't sure if she really wanted or needed to know. She knew that if she didn't make up her mind soon, she was going to find out anyway because Darren wasn't going to stop. He kept touching her, kissing her and pressing against her.

Azerica had never felt these kinds of emotions before. She didn't know how she was supposed to feel or how she was supposed to respond, but she knew she liked it. It felt good. Darren was doing everything that made her body feel good, yet she still didn't know whether or not she liked him. It was hard for her to believe this was her first week at USG and already someone was interested in her and it wasn't just anybody, it was Darren Lewis. He was one of the most popular guys at USG and he was a local athletic star. She was just a plain jane who still had much to learn and experience. She was cute, but she hadn't fully developed into what she would be and he was still sweating her.

Darren was still kissing her and he started trailing from her lips downward. The lower he went, the more her body tensed up. As he started to pass her navel, he was interrupted by a knock at his door.

"Hey y'all, we gotta get back to school," Trish said banging on the door. "So put your clothes back on and let's go!"

"Yeah the pep rally starts in 20 minutes," said Jason.

Azerica and Darren quickly got up and readjusted their clothes. They met Trish and Jason in the family room and the four of them rushed out the house and back to the car. They did not need to be late for the pep rally. If they were, and they got caught for skipping, Darren and Jason wouldn't be playing tonight and Azerica and Trish wouldn't be cheering. Darren sped back to Lex Av and made the 15-minute trip in eight minutes. As soon as they pulled into the senior parking lot, they ran inside the building. Over the intercom, they heard the announcement for all football players, cheerleaders and band members to meet in the gym.

"I'm glad we left when we did," said Azerica forgetting about what just happened at Darren's house.

"Okay!" Trish exclaimed. "We would've been running laps forever."

When she didn't hear them talking, Azerica turned to look for Darren and Jason. They were walking a few feet behind them as if they all didn't just skip together. Azerica shook her head and kept walking. It didn't really matter anyway Darren was with her and wanted to be with her. As far as she was concerned, no other female mattered.

"Time to get ready for this pep rally," said Trish, interrupting Azerica's thoughts.

They walked through the double doors leading to the gym and then to the right to the girls' locker room where they had begun their morning.

Chapter 10

"Chauncey, please stop crying," begged Candace to her six-month-old baby.

She was trying to get him up and ready so they could find a daycare for him, but he was so fussy that he didn't want to do anything. Normally he woke up bright and early, but this morning he slept until after 10. Then when he did get up, she had to fight with him to get him to eat.

"Baby, are you getting sick?" Candace asked him and pulled him close to her. She held him in her arms and rocked him until his crying softened to a whine.

She sat with him in her arms and comforted him. They watched *The Price Is Right* until he calmed down. When he stopped whining, she got up to run the bath water so the two of them could take a bath and begin their day. The bath water always made him happy and he laughed and played while he splashed water all over the place.

"You silly boy, is that all you wanted?" She cooed to him. "All it took was a little bit of water to make you happy."

Chauncey looked at her and giggled.

"I still think you might be catching something though," she said feeling his forehead for a temperature.

They didn't spend much more time in the water. Candace didn't want him to get cold and get sick for real, plus the floor had almost more water on it than there was in the tub. She dried him off first and then sat him on the toilet seat while she attempted to dry herself off. She watched him as he sat there laughing and playing with his Blues Clues toy. He was such a happy baby and it upset Candace when he wasn't smiling. Any time things seemed like they were going all wrong, she could watch him for a few minutes and feel at ease all over again.

"Alright, let's go put our clothes on," she said picking him up. She was careful not to slide on the water that drenched her tiled floor.

Lugging her baby on her hips, she walked back to her room and sat him on the bed. She threw on her pajamas until she finished dressing him. She wanted him to look

young, dumb and naive

cute today. They both had to look good because she didn't have enough money to pay for a full week of daycare up front. She hoped she could find a decent place that didn't require advance payments. If she couldn't, she'd just have to beg her mom to come stay with her until she got her first paycheck. It would take a lot to convince her mom to come, but she would need it. That would probably be the best thing for her financially, unless she decided to take the second job Craig offered her.

Thinking about the proposition opened her mind up to a whole new set of problems. She still couldn't believe Craig would do that to her and be serious. But then again, he was a man, she shouldn't be surprised.

Candace lost herself in thought, reliving the events of the previous evening. She was so deep in thought that she didn't realize the phone had been ringing until she heard the answering machine pick up.

"Hi Candace. It's Craig. I just wanted to call and see how you were doing today and see if you wanted to have lunch this afternoon. Give me a call back on my cell. The number is 877-4821. Talk to you later. 'Bye."

Candace shook her head.

Think about him and he calls, she thought to herself. *I must be a little psychic.*

She looked down at Chauncey in his blue Tigger jumpsuit she'd bought from Wal-mart. She wanted her baby to look good, but not too good. She couldn't dress him in the JC Penney or Belks clothes she'd just gotten for him. She didn't want the daycare people to think she had some money.

"Chauncey," she said, looking at him. "Do I call him back or leave it alone?"

He just looked at her blankly in response. She really didn't expect him to answer, but a smile or a frown would have helped.

She toiled with the question while she got dressed. No matter what, she knew she needed to talk to him. Whether or not she went with the proposition, she still needed him to secure her job at the hospital. He said she had it and it would start Monday, but she had no clue where she was supposed to go. She hadn't even filled out an application and she didn't have any real medical experience. Since she would only be admitting patients, she wasn't real worried about experience. She'd probably have to learn the hospital's database program or something, but that should be no problem, she'd always been a quick learner when it came to computers.

I just have to get the job first, she thought to herself.

"Okay Chauncey, you were no help, but I'll call him anyway," said Candace after she glanced in the mirror at herself. She was wearing a pair of dirty denim jeans and a sleeveless white shirt. She tried not to appear like she had money, but then she wanted to dress a little attractive just in case she decided to have lunch with Craig.

Pleased with her appearance, she sat down on the bed next to Chauncey and picked up the phone on her dresser. She started dialing the numbers, got nervous and then hung up.

"Now why are you doing this?" she asked herself. "You've known him for years and it ain't like you're going on a date with him. You've gotta ask him about the job."

But she knew why she was nervous. She still didn't have an answer to his business deal and she still had to tell him about Chauncey and Melina. He still thought Azerica was her only child.

She picked up Chauncey and put him on her lap, then started dialing the number again.

"Hello," he answered on the first ring.

"Hi Craig," she said.

"Candace, I've been waiting for you to call me back," he said. "Do you want to have lunch?"

"That's fine, but someone will be coming with us." Candace told him.

"Your baby?" Craig asked her as if he could read her mind.

"Yeah, how did you know?" Candace asked him a little surprised.

"I saw the car seat in your car when we were leaving Milano's last night," he replied.

"Now I feel foolish," she said.

"Why?" Craig asked her.

"I almost thought I was keeping something from you until now, but I see I can't get anything past you," she joked.

"Yeah, that's what they all say," he laughed.

"Before we can meet you, I've got to try and find a daycare for him. What time did you want to meet?" Candace asked.

"Well, actually I was going to pick you up," he replied.

"Oh, okay. Well I should be finished in a few hours. Can you pick me up at 2?" She asked him.

"That would be perfect."

"Oh, and Craig," she said lightly.

"Yes, Candace," he said.

"I have something else to tell you."

"What's that?"

"I also have an 8-year-old daughter," she told him reluctantly.

"And I bet she's lovely just like her mother and her older sister," said Craig. "Make sure you bring some pictures. I see we're going to have a lot to talk about."

"Well, no meal with you is ever boring anyway Mr. Pearson," Candace smiled.

"That would be Dr. Pearson, ma'am," he joked. "Get it right."

"Make sure you call me before you come so I can give you directions to where I live," Candace told him.

"Candy dear, you act as if I'm not from Jacksonville. I know you're on the Westside, but where on the Westside?" Craig asked.

"I'm sorry, I forgot you were a native," she laughed. "Anyways, I live in Raintree off of Lincoln Boulevard. The apartment number is 16."

"Alright. I know where that is. I'll call when I'm on the way," he said. "Good luck with the daycare thing."

"Thanks," she said and hung up the phone.

Candace hugged and kissed Chauncey. She felt better now that she'd told Craig about her other two children. Although he'd probably sweat her about working the other job now, she didn't really care because she wasn't hiding anything from him anymore. He had been such a great friend to her she didn't want to betray his trust in any way. Especially not after the things he'd done for her to see her through her major financial struggles. She started thinking about the cost of living for she and her kids and her mind began telling her Craig's suggestion may be a good idea until she started receiving child support from Greg. It always took so long for the military to process that stuff. She filed it a month ago and still hadn't received anything yet.

Don't they realize he has two children that have to eat, she asked herself getting up from the bed. *Obviously military kids are not a priority.*

"Chauncey, they don't ever want to do anything," she said. She didn't understand the system and why it took so long to go through the child support office. She never went through this mess with Jeff, but he never had any money to go after. *That sorry negro. I'm glad he's locked up. He might as well be in for back child support. Good for nothing, mom told me to be careful with him and I didn't listen.*

Now, she wished she'd heeded her mom's warnings. Her mom always said to be careful of older guys because they all wanted the same things. *She told me not to trust them because they didn't think like me. She said they never thought with the right head. Man, I wish she would've explained that to me then.*

As if her thinking conjured up another person, the phone rang.

"Hello," Candace answered without checking the caller ID.

"Hey baby, how is everything?" Sheryl asked on the other end.

"Mom why didn't you make me listen to you when I was in high school?" Candace whined. "You told me not to talk any older guys 'cause they thought with the wrong head and I didn't listen."

"Honey child, by that time you'd made up your mind. I couldn't change it and I couldn't lock you up in chains. What else was I supposed to do? You wanted to know what it was like to be older and you found out," Sheryl answered concerned. "Is Azerica putting you through this now?"

Candace smacked her lips. "No, she better not be Mom. I would tie her up in chains. She wouldn't be able to see the moon light."

Sheryl laughed. "Baby, she is a teenager now. She may not be boy crazy yet, but she'll get there. And when she does, you can't keep her locked up. She will find a way out. Believe me, you did. Try to keep her close and make sure you get to know all her friends. And please make sure she keeps God in the center of her life. If it weren't for Jesus she wouldn't be here anyway. And I know that child is saved. Make sure her spirit man keeps growing."

"Yes Mom," Candace felt like she was getting scolded.

"Now have you found a job yet?" Sheryl moved on to the next topic on her list to discuss with her daughter. "I know we spoke just the other day, but God can work miracles darling."

"I did have an interview last night," Candace was happy to give her some good news. "It's at Memorial Hospital admitting patients. I start Monday morning."

"That's wonderful!" Sheryl exclaimed. "Girl, didn't I tell you God could work miracles. Sounds like you've been spending some time with him praying and praising."

"Yeah," Candace tried to avoid lying to her mother. "I have to find a daycare for Chauncey today since you won't come up here. And I don't have any money to pay any fees up front."

"I keep trying to tell you, you can't always depend on me Candace. You are a grown woman now. Stop making excuses. Stop living in the past. And stop regretting having sex with Jeff. You can't change what happened. And you've gotten a beautiful daughter out of that. And now you've got two beautiful daughters and a handsome baby boy." Sheryl tried to encourage her.

Candace did this to her every time she called. She always threw a pity party and wanted sympathy from her mother. After giving it up to God, Sheryl was finally able to stop worrying and watch Him work.

"Mom, I am a single mother. The cost of living is much higher than when I was small and you just had me. You didn't have any other children." Candace pleaded her case.

"Dear, if it's really that hard, get some assistance from the government. They will give you what you can't afford. You'll get food stamps and they'll pay for child care and my grandbabies will have a better health insurance." Sheryl offered the suggestions Mr. Henry discussed with her.

"Mom, I am not getting welfare. I am not a welfare person. I start my job Monday and I am going to have money. I will just find me a good daycare that doesn't charge anything up front," Candace sighed. She couldn't believe her mom suggested she get welfare. What did she look like?

"Dear, you know what's best for you," Sheryl sighed. "All I can say is keep praying, praising and tithing."

"Yeah, Mom. I will. I have to go now," Candace rushed her mom off the phone.

"Tell my grandbabies I love them."

"I will. 'Bye Mom." Candace said and hung up the phone. Life would be beautiful if she could just get her mom to come up and help her, but she just wouldn't do it. It was almost like her mom was being brainwashed into answering no every time Candace asked for help.

But no time to think about that now, Candace glanced at the clock sitting on her dresser and shook her head in disbelief. It was telling her the time was 12:30, but she didn't believe it. There's no way it could be that late already. They'd just gotten out of the tub maybe 20 minutes ago. She looked for her watch to get a second opinion and her watch said 12:32. She quickly slid on her shoes to walk out the door when the phone rang.

"Now who could that be?" She asked aloud still carrying Chauncey on her hip.

She walked to the caller ID and saw Greg's name and number.

"What the hell is he calling me for?" She asked. I wasn't thinking about him. "He is wasting his time, I am not answering that phone. If he needs to tell me something, he can leave a message."

Not thinking anything else of it, she walked out the door and to her car. She placed Chauncey in his car seat in the back and pulled out.

He is not going to get to me today, she thought, forgetting all about her mom's phone call. For the first time in her life, she'd started trying to do things on her own, for herself, for her children. She didn't want him back in their lives. She told him not to ever call her again. She didn't know what his problem was. She knew he sometimes called Azerica when she wasn't home, but he knows Azerica is at school right now. Why he was trying to talk to her, she didn't know. She hoped her answering machine would suffice because that was the closest thing he was going to get to having another conversation with her.

She was seething and the jerky movements of her driving made it obvious.

She turned up the volume on her radio and calmed down a little when she heard *When Will I See You Smile Again* by Bell Biv Devoe playing.

"Chauncey, that used to be one of Mommy's favorite songs," she said, smiling at him. He sat in his car seat playing with his Winnie-the-Pooh, oblivious to his mother's erratic mood swings.

Candace traveled down Lex Av hoping to find a daycare that was close and easily accessible for she and Azerica. She had actually passed by quite a few good ones, but didn't feel like stopping. She just didn't want to hear anyone tell her she needed to pay a deposit and the cost of the first week up front. She knew she didn't have that kind of money right now. That was out of her budget until she could start work Monday unless she started working with Craig tonight. Who knows what she could make in one night there. He talked as if she could make enough to pay her rent within a few hours.

I kind of need that, Candace admitted only to herself.

She was still trying to decide if that was something she wanted to do. She had no clue. All she knew was that she was broke and tired of depending on child support for comfort when four months ago her life was so easy. Jeffrey showered her with so much money that she could stay home with Chauncey all day and attend class in the evening.

But like every other time in his life, he found a way to mess up.

Men seemed to always fail her when she needed them the most. Had Greg been what he was supposed to be to her, she wouldn't have needed Jeffrey's money and if Jeffrey had learned responsibility in the first place, she would never be in this situation. And now that someone wants to help her, she doesn't want to do it. She should be grateful she could fall back on Craig and he would be there to help her.

She was so enveloped in her thoughts that she didn't realize she'd driven by another daycare until she passed it. She made a U-turn at the next light and drove back.

She pulled into the parking lot to My Little Angels Daycare and said a silent prayer, asking God to bless her. Before she got out the car, she checked her appearance and then double-checked Chauncey to make sure he was presentable too. Then she picked him up and carried him inside.

Before she could make it completely inside the door, a small, plump black lady grabbed the door and held it open for her. She was really dark with loose, greasy curls sitting on top of her head. The lady wore a bright green shirt with faded blue sweatpants and a pair of worn out Nikes. She spoke quickly, running words together in a way that made her seem as if she could fluently speak another language.

"Thank you," Candace said to the woman as she walked inside the daycare.

"N'prolem buh you 'on't wanna go in'ere," the lady said to her, then continued on in the conversation with herself.

Candace watched dumfounded as the short, stout woman quickly waddled towards the bus stop, muttering something she didn't completely understand.

"That's just geechy baby," Candace laughed when she turned and saw Chauncey's puzzled expression and his eyes following the woman. "She's from deep in the cut in Jacksonville and she don't know how to talk."

She watched as Chauncey gave the lady one last flustered look and turn his attention back to playing with his bear. She didn't blame him. Jacksonville's backwoods people seemed like such foreigners sometimes. She didn't want to seem stereotypical, but from what she knew, the majority of them were from the Northside.

Still standing at the entrance, Candace held Chauncey closer and observed the scene before her. This would be his first time ever going to a daycare and she wanted to make sure everything was right for him. So far, she was impressed with what she saw. There seemed to be at least one worker per five babies or children. The room was separated into two parts: the left side of the room was filled with tables, chairs and highchairs for eating; the right side of the room had toys and instruction materials. But no matter where they were, all the children appeared to be having fun.

They sat in the midst of a beautifully painted garden. In the top right corner of the center wall, shone a yellow sun with rays extending through to the surrounding walls. The sky surrounding its brightness was a deep shade of blue that hummed serenity. Peeking up from the grass painted a few feet below the skyline were flowers of all types: roses, lilies, daffodils, chrysanthemums...anything you could think of, they were there. The carpet was even the same color of green as the grass painted on the walls and there were even artificial flowers set up in the four corners of the room.

"Chauncey, this is your daycare. I can see it," Candace said excitedly. She knew she would have no problem dropping him off here every morning before work. She was completely comfortable with everything and she hadn't even spoken to anyone yet.

"Good afternoon, how can I help you?" said one of the workers, walking up to Candace.

"I'm fine, thanks." Candace replied sweetly.

"Is there anything I can help you with today?"

"I'm looking for a daycare for my baby for Monday," Candace told her.

"Ahh, and he's about six months, right?"

"Yes, that's right." Candace was impressed by her guestimate.

"Well, would this be Monday through Friday, morning 'til afternoon?" the worker asked her, gathering the information she needed to determine if they had room for him.

"Yes ma'am, but I'm not exactly sure of the hours yet. I wanted to see what I needed to do to get him enrolled and ready for Monday," Candace said.

"No, problem. I can help you. Walk with me to the desk," the lady said, leading her towards through the center of the room and to the back office.

The small office seemed raggedy and small compared to the spacious, bright room set aside for the children and babies. It was unorganized and a little junky. Candace watched as the skinny daycare lady rummaged through papers on top of the desk to find what she needed.

"You can have a seat," the lady told her. "Please excuse the mess. We just moved offices today. The office used to be in the front and now it's back here."

Candace smiled.

"There is some paper work that I need you to fill out. We have a medical release form, a procedures form and a few others. I've stapled them together in this packet for you," the woman handed her the small packet.

Candace listened as the woman continued to explain the company's policies and procedures. The woman spoke as if she'd started the business herself. She was a Spanish woman about 5'4'' and had long curly brown hair. She wore gold-rimmed glasses that fell a little below the bridge of her nose. She had on a pair of khakis, a red T-shirt and a blue apron that had My Little Angels inscribed in silver thread above the breast pocket.

"The rate for a six month old per week is $160," the woman said.

"That sounds okay," Candace replied slowly. She hoped she could afford it when she started work Monday. *Dang, I am going to have to work with Craig at the club to pay for daycare. It's going to be over five hundred dollars a month.*

"Yes and the deposit is also $160."

"Now when must the deposit be paid?" Candace really wanted Chauncey in this daycare. She didn't care what it cost.

"Upon completion of the paper work, or the first day the child begins," she responded.

"Alright," Candace said, a little disappointed. She didn't have the money to afford the deposit right now, but she knew this was exactly where she wanted her baby to be. She loved the atmosphere.

"Now ma'am, if you'd like, you can take home the packet, fill it out and bring it back with the deposit on Monday," the daycare worker said.

"I think I will do that," Candace said, a little relieved. Now she had to find a way to get the money.

"Now don't forget, the spots fill up quickly and we only have five available," the skinny lady reminded her.

"Thank you, I won't forget," said Candace getting up from her seat.

"And remember, if you have any other questions you can give me a call. Here's my number," the woman said as she handed her a business card.

Merlina Salinas, Candace read the card to herself.

"Thank you for your time," said Candace.

She shook her hand and walked back to the front to the entrance. She had absolutely no clue what she would do now. She had to start work Monday, but she had no one to leave Chauncey with. Leesa worked during the day and had her own child to worry with. Azerica would be in school and she knew her mother wouldn't come down for that day to help out.

"Chauncey, all she would do is tell me to pray about it again," Candace said, putting her child back into his car seat.

"What to do?" she asked herself.

She turned her radio off so she could ride in silence.

Think, Candace, think, she told herself. *I don't have anyone who will give me the money. Mom will say pray. Jeffrey's in jail. I refuse to talk to Greg and Craig will tell me I can start with him at any time. But I guess that's what I'll have to do. I made my own bed, now I've got to lay in it. Only I can make things better. Mom's right. I can't depend on people to bail me out all the time.*

Thinking about the time, she glanced at the clock to see if she had time to stop at another daycare. She wanted to see if she was able to find one that didn't require a deposit, but she decided not to stop anywhere else when she saw how late it was. School would be out soon and Azerica had a game tonight. She and Craig would have to be finished with their meal by four so she could pick Melina up from school.

"Chauncey, it's 1:30 already. We need to get home, we've got a lunch date today," Candace tried to ease her mind of the millions of thoughts running through it so she could focus on being hungry and eating with Craig.

After about ten more minutes of driving, Candace turned into Raintree. She parked in front of her building, grabbed Chauncey and went inside. She placed him in his walker and turned the television on to her favorite soap opera, The Bold and the Beautiful. She really didn't enjoy watching it anymore since they'd killed Taylor's character, but it still was entertaining. She couldn't help but watch it, she almost felt as if she knew the characters personally since she'd been watching the show for so long.

When the program went to a commercial, Candace reached for the phone to call Craig. She dialed his cell phone number and waited a few rings before he answered.

"Hello, Dr. Pearson," he answered.

"Craig, hey. I'm ready whenever you are," Candace told him.

"Sounds good, I'll be there as soon as I finish up. Give me about 15 minutes." Craig responded.

"That works. I'll see you when you get here," she said.

She clicked the cordless phone off and went into her bedroom to change. Although she wanted to be casual, she didn't want to wear her dirty denim jeans and sleeveless white shirt to lunch with Craig. There was no telling where he'd take her. She pulled a pair of boot cut jeans from her closet and threw on a black halter-top. She grabbed her black sandals and went back to the front to finish watching her show. Chauncey was still in his walker strolling around.

"Hey baby, did you miss me?" Candace asked him, planting a kiss on his forehead. "Of course you did, I'm your mommy."

Chauncey giggled and laughed harder when she tickled him.

"We won't change you for this date," she told him after she picked him up and checked his clothes. "I didn't have you looking too homely today."

She sat back on the couch, while he collapsed in her arms and got comfortable. They finished watching The Bold and the Beautiful together and were about to fall asleep when there was a knock at her door. Not wanting to disturb her baby, Candace slowly and carefully got up from where she was sitting with Chauncey still in her arms and she walked to the door to let Craig in.

"I'm sorry," he said when she opened the door. "Did I wake you?"

"No, we were watching TV. Chauncey started to doze off a little right before you came," she replied.

"Would you like to stay here and I can pick something up to eat?" Craig asked.

"You wouldn't mind?" Candace asked. "I really don't want to disturb him. And Craig I promise he's not a cranky baby."

"It's not a problem," he laughed and squeezed her arm. "I'll grab something and bring it right back. I really don't mind Candace."

"Thank you Craig. Chauncey's he's been a little tired all day. He would probably be fine if we did go out, but I'd rather stay in and let him sleep," Candace explained. "Life is so much easier that way."

"No need to go into detail. Just tell me what you want to eat and I'll go get it and bring it back," Craig told her.

"You know Craig, I just want you to surprise me," she responded.

"Alright Candy, I'll be right back," he said and kissed her cheek.

He walked back out the door and down the stairs to his black Mercedes. She watched him exit Raintree and drive off towards Lex Av. She didn't know why, but she felt excited like a teenager who was dating someone for the first time. Craig didn't exactly give her goose bumps or butterflies, but it was kind of exciting for her to be in anticipation over a new love.

She carried a dozing Chauncey ~~to the back~~ to her room and laid him down to sleep. She crawled in bed beside him and lay there until she was sure he was sleeping. When his breathing got heavier she made sure he had cover and was secure in the center of her bed. She turned the radio on to 101.5 and turned the volume down to where the music was playing softly. She then went to her vanity and sprayed on more of her Victoria's Secret body spray. Her favorite scent was Secret Crush, but she ran out of it. She was trying to use the rest of Endless Love before she purchased any more.

Before she had a chance to sit down and turn on the television in the living room, there was a knock at her door.

"That was fast," she told Craig when she opened the door.

"I thought I was taking a long time," he responded. "I wanted to give you some extra time."

"I guess I was so busy putting Chauncey down that I didn't realize how much time had passed." Candace said. Time had been getting away from her all day.

She motioned for Craig to come in and she closed the door. She directed him to the kitchen table and they sat down in her sunny, yellow kitchen.

"What would you like to drink?" she asked him.

"What do you have?" Craig enjoyed the servitude from Candace. She'd never been the type to wait on any man. He smiled discreetly, happy to see this new change in her.

"Well, I can get you some Sprite or Kool-Aid," Candace suggested. "I haven't been to the store yet."

"Sprite will be fine," he said. "I'm not picky."

Candace got drinks for the two of them and joined him at the table. He had already taken the food out of the bag and placed the Styrofoam containers in front of them. She wasn't sure what she had, but the aroma was enough to win her over.

"What are we having?" she asked, her stomach started growling before she could even sit down.

"I'm not telling." He teased.

"Why not?" Candace laughed. She loved surprises.

"You told me to surprise you and that's what I've done."

"Oh, goodness," she teased. "I'm afraid to see what's in here."

"Just open it up, it won't be that bad," he grabbed her hand to reassure her. "I promise."

Candace opened the lid to her container and inside she found a chicken gyro and some fries. The gyro was huge and greasy with lots of cheese, grilled onions, lettuce and tomatoes. She smiled because she knew the meal could have come from only one place and she hadn't been there to eat in years.

"I haven't been to the Snackshack in forever!" Candace exclaimed. "I didn't know the restaurant was still open and you had time to drive all the way to Lennox and come back before I could even look up to see how long you were gone."

Craig laughed.

"I remember when we used to skip school and eat there," Candace continued to talk. "They had the best breakfast and you got a lot of food too. I wonder if it's still the same? Oh well, but anyways, their lunches are good too. Do you remember the pep rally we had your senior year and we all met there and ate breakfast during homeroom? That was so much fun."

In the middle of chewing, Craig smiled. He swallowed the remainder of the food in his mouth and took a drink of his Sprite. Then he said, "It's funny how history repeats itself."

Reaching for her fries, Candace stopped and looked at him. "What do you mean?"

"You know, the times change and the people change, but the young always experience the same things that people from previous generations do," Craig continued. "There's never anything new under the sun."

"Huh?" Candace asked, staring at him puzzled. She could have swore they were just reminiscing about their high school days at Lee and how much they enjoyed skipping school and eating at the Snackshack. Why in the world was he getting philosophical on her now?

"I met Azerica this morning at Denny's," Craig ignored her puzzled look. "She didn't know who I was, but I knew who she was. She's beautiful just like her mother. But anyways, I know USG has a big game tonight and a pep rally today. When you mentioned our outing that day, I remembered that we had a pep rally that afternoon because we were playing Ed White that night. It's funny the way history repeats itself."

"You saw **my** child at Denny's this morning?" Candace asked, a little bass and lots of attitude poured through her voice. "What time was that?"

"Candace." Craig tried to say her name sternly to discourage her from getting upset. It worked when they were in high school, but the look in her eyes at this moment, told him that stopped working when she had children of her own.

"No, tell me what time you saw her there and who was she with," Candace demanded. "**My** daughter was supposed to be at school."

"I guess it was about 11:00 this morning," he replied softly. Then Craig described the other cheerleader and the two football players who were with her.

"So you're telling me **my** daughter was with two football players and her little cheerleader friend?" Candace repeated back. She wanted to make sure she had the story straight so Azerica couldn't deny anything. "And they were at Denny's at 11:00?"

Craig couldn't avoid giving her the answers she wanted, so he tried to talk slowly and quietly to calm Candace down.

"Yes, Candace." Craig tried to deepen his voice to add to the effect. He grabbed her hand and stroked it. "Let her live a little and have some fun. She's in high school now. She's 14 and she's got a new social world with boys that she likes. And the ones she was with wouldn't harm anyone. I know the oldest one's family."

"Craig I could really care less if their families were millionaires. She has no business skipping school with older boys. Don't you know what happens when teenagers with raging hormones are alone?" Candace asked him as if he spoke another language. "You were a teenager at one time. Don't tell me you don't remember."

"Don't you think you're overreacting?" Craig questioned her actions.

young, dumb and naive

"No. I don't. And I am so sorry that you feel like I am, but **I** am her parent. **I** know what it's like to be young and stupid. I am not about to let her ruin her life the way my mom let me ruin mine." Candace exploded. What right did he have to tell her she was overreacting? He didn't have any children.

"Candace, all I'm saying is that just because they skipped, doesn't mean they are all having sex together." Craig pointed out to her. "They were eating breakfast at Denny's. And besides, Azerica's a good kid with a good head on her shoulders. I don't think she'd just go and have sex with anybody."

"Craig, I don't care what you're saying. I know my daughter. You just met her again today. You don't know what I've gone through with her. Whether or not she'd have sex, I don't really know, but I do know I don't want her to be tempted. All teenagers are curious. You were. Jeff was. I was and that's how Azerica was born." Candace continued to argue. She knew he didn't understand what she was saying. He had it easy all his life.

"Candace don't take away her teenage years." Craig warned. "You don't want her to rebel and have sex anyway. Talk to her before you discipline her. I see too many teenagers come to the hospital pregnant because they rebelled against their parents."

Candace continued fussing and ignored what Craig just told her.

"If the child wants to be fast, she can be fast at home and take care of Chauncey all night after school. All this skipping school mess is telling me that she wants to spend her free time with her little boyfriend." Candace stared him down, forgetting to blink.

Tired of playing her game, Craig stayed quiet. She was furious and he wasn't going to say anything else about it.

"I'm not going to be responsible for her stupidity. So since she thinks she can be grown and chill with some older boy who just wants to hit it, she can take care of my baby and see what it's like to have that responsibility before she's able to vote."

Candace took a deep breath to try and calm her nerves. She didn't like getting this upset, but she knew where this was going. Craig didn't see it. He didn't have any kids. But she knew her daughter and this was way out of Azerica's character.

young, dumb and naive

Candace didn't know what had gotten into her daughter lately. She had never skipped class before. And whatever she did do, she did with Devin before or after class. Her child could not afford the time away from class to miss out on something she could be learning. She had to maintain a 3.5 grade point average in order to cheer. That's the only reason why she let Azerica cheer in the first place, because she knew USG expected a lot of them academically. Now it seems, her daughter's priorities were in the wrong place.

"You know, I can just undo this at any time," Candace said to herself, letting her rage show through once more.

"What do you mean?" Craig asked softly, trying to use his tone as a way to coax her back to tranquility since reasoning wouldn't work.

"She takes for granted everything she's been blessed with, all she has to do is go to school," Candace fussed. "If she can't go to class, then she can't be a cheerleader. It's as simple as that. I'll take her off the squad."

"Candace I wasn't trying to get her in trouble," Craig said quietly, still trying to use his voice to keep her calm. He would never have mentioned it if he'd known Candace would act like this.

"I know, but that's not going to help her get off the hook," Candace replied. "You just don't understand what she puts me through at home. She is so selfish. She knows how much I'm struggling to take care of them and she's never home to help me. Every time I ask her to do something she complains. I practically have to threaten her to get her to do anything."

Candace shook her head and tried to eat the rest of her gyro.

"You know, I remember seeing the two of you together ten years ago at The Landing. She was just a little girl then, but you two were so happy," Craig said, watching her as she played with her food.

"Yeah," Candace smiled, remembering those times. "That was before puberty when she was a normal child. You don't know this Azerica."

"Candy, don't say that. She's still a normal child," Craig reminded her. "She's adjusting to the hormones in her body. This is all normal for a girl her age."

Candace rolled her eyes. "And now you're going to remind me of the changes I went through at her age. Save it. I already know."

"What's the real problem?" Craig was tired of playing this game.

"What do you mean?" Candace asked him surprised.

"I know it isn't just Azerica. What's really going on with you?" Craig stared at her.

Silence stared at them both for minutes.

"Money is my problem Craig. I can't afford anything. I don't have anything and I have my kids to think about. Things have never been this bad and I don't know what to do." Candace poured out her heart.

Craig listened. He didn't have to mention his business venture to her again. He had her. She was desperate and really needed money. All he had to do now was stay in her corner and be a friend.

"If you think about it Candy, you were in the same position then that you are now, the only difference is you have two other children and child support money. Back then it was just you and Azerica and Jeff couldn't afford to buy you a Whopper once a week," he said trying to show her how far she's come since then.

"Things are much harder for me right now, I never expected it to get like this. I mean my life six months ago was easy compared to now," Candace wished she could go back in time.

"What's so different?" Craig asked curiously.

"Chauncey was just born, but other than that, Jeff was finally giving me money. I mean he was doing over and above his call of duty. You know, he was trying to make up for all that lost time," she replied. "He gave me so much money that I could go to school and I didn't have to work. But now all that's changed."

"Well, where is he now? What happened to the money?" Craig inquired.

Feeling too ashamed to answer, Candace tried to change the subject. "I should've known this was going to happen. Jeff doesn't know what responsible means. To him it's doing what you can when you want to. Dumby me knew that. I guess I had to be taught the same lesson. I should've known it wasn't going to last, but I didn't think about what might happen in the end. All I saw was the money."

"Candace, you still didn't answer my question," said Craig, trying to piece together the puzzle. "Where was he getting the money?"

Candace sighed and then searched Craig's face, pleading him with her eyes not to make her rehash that story.

But it didn't work.

"Candace, I don't know what you're so scared of. I'm not going to think different of you because of something that happened with him," Craig said encouraging her to talk. "We've been friends since high school. There is nothing you could say or do that will make me end our friendship."

Candace sighed again and rubbed her eyes with her right hand. She just wanted to close that chapter in her life and move on, but she could see that Craig would not let that to happen so easily.

"He was selling drugs," Candace said shortly.

"And you allowed him to continue seeing Azerica and come over?" Craig asked, surprised that she would risk her family's security for drug money.

"I didn't know it at first. He had started working at Wal-mart as a manager and I thought he was actually making decent money. I had no idea he was giving me drug money," Candace said defensively.

"Well, how did you find out?" Craig pried deeper.

She really didn't want to tell him that she found a dime bag in Jeff's car one day and then asked him for a joint. Craig drank, but he was against drugs. He hated them and what they do to people. His oldest brother died from a heroin overdose and his drug usage started with smoking a little weed. Ever since then, Craig had been a strong advocate for any anti-drug program that entered the public school system. She remembered when they were in high school and the way he treated her when he found out she had tried smoking weed. He fussed at her for days. She didn't want to go through that again, especially since she was a mother now. He really wouldn't let her hear the end of it.

"Candace," he said breaking the silence. "I'm still waiting to know how you found out."

She looked at him and said, "I found a dime bag in Jeff's car one day when he came to bring me some money."

"In his car!" Craig exclaimed. "He didn't have enough class to leave it at home? Do you know what would've happened if you had decided to go for a ride with him and the cops pulled him over while you were in the car? Candace, you could've gone to jail also."

"But that didn't happen," Candace reminded him. Now he sounded like her mother. *Lord, he's making it sound bigger than what it was.*

"I know, but you've got to be more responsible as a parent. You have three impressionable children. Whatever it is that you do affects them and their lives. Candy, you've got to think about them at all times. You can't put yourself in situations that could jeopardize your life. What would happen to them if something were to happen to you?" Craig asked not believing he was having this conversation with her.

"I know," Candace sighed. "I know."

"Well, don't you think it's time you act like you know?" Craig asked, still upset.

Candace couldn't say anything. She knew he was right. She sulked back in her chair as if she were a child being scolded by her father. *Now this is the Craig I know,* she thought. *This is the same Craig from high school. I don't know who it was the other night that offered me a job at his business. Whoever it was, it wasn't this Craig.*

Like she remembered, her high school friend Craig cared about her and how she treated herself. Her high school friend Craig recognized how "impressionable" her kids were and realized what she brought into her life affected them.

He probably didn't realize it, but he basically sat and told her not to take him up on his business venture. In all honesty, she knew that would be something that would affect she, Azerica, Melina and Chauncey. All Candace could think about was how Azerica would look when she found out. Luckily, Mel and Chauncey were too young to understand the nature of the business, but Azerica's world would be shattered. She couldn't imagine what Azerica would say or what her friends would say when they found out.

"Thanks for your help and concern," Candace said genuinely. She finally felt at peace with herself for wanting to turn him down on his offer. "That's why I always come to you for help. You seem to always know exactly what I need."

"You're welcome, I'm glad you feel comfortable enough to impose your life on me," Craig said smiling.

"You're silly," Candace laughed.

She got up from where she was sitting to throw away the Styrofoam containers. She didn't have very many friends, but she was happy to have Craig. He was a wonderful friend. She glanced at the time on her way back to the table and noticed it was 3:58.

"Mr. Pearson I've enjoyed my lunch with you this afternoon, but I need to wake Chauncey and pick Melina up from her Girl Scouts meeting," Candace started to feel a little better about the things happening in her life.

"I've enjoyed myself also. Thank you for having me," he smiled and hugged her.

"You know, I still haven't forgotten about Azerica. I'm going to go straighten her out. You thought you were slick in getting my mind off of it, but I remember," she said, getting upset all over again. "That child has a lot to learn. And I don't want her to learn the hard way."

"Well, it never hurt to try and get her off the hook," he laughed. "But I had an ulterior motive. I was curious to know how deep your relationship with Jeff was."

"Well, it ain't like that and never will be again," she assured him. Jeff wasn't going to trick her into thinking he was responsible again.

"What are your plans for this evening?" Craig asked her.

young, dumb and naive

"I don't have any," she replied, forgetting about touring his club. "Are you trying to take me out?"

"I want you to meet me somewhere," Craig said and he pulled a card from his back pants pocket.

Candace grabbed the card and looked it over. It was the same card he used to introduce her to his business. The name, address and phone number were all on it along with his business logo. As soon as she realized what he was inviting her to and why, she felt her heart drop. All the shit he was talking about being more responsible for her kids and how they are affected by her actions was bull. He didn't care. Every free moment he got to throw his proposition in her face, that's what he did.

I should've never told him anything, Candace was mad at herself for being so stupid. *It was all a game. I was vulnerable and he took advantage of me. Now he knows I really need the money. And all I am thinking about is the money.*

Yet no matter how upset she was at this moment, she still didn't want to speak out and tell him how she felt. She was afraid if she said something that made him mad, he wouldn't help her and she really did need him. And now, she couldn't decide whether or not his proposition was really something she needed to be doing. Just a second ago, she knew it wasn't and now she second-guessed herself. Over and over her mind kept telling her she needed the money, but her heart told her she couldn't do what he was asking her to do because it wasn't right.

"When you come," Craig said, taking for granted that she would come and join him. "Make sure you wear something sexy and in layers. We won't put you on the spot tonight, but I want you to get used to the scene and the atmosphere."

Candace quietly walked Craig to the door and stuffed the card in her jeans pocket wishing she could forget about it altogether. She opened the door for him and forced herself to smile as he was walking out.

"Candy, I'll see you tonight," Craig said and kissed her lightly on the cheek.

Candace closed the door and went to sit on the couch. She needed money, but was she ready to compromise herself to make it? She felt like she had to meet him tonight, she couldn't tell him no because she still hadn't started working at the hospital. And she didn't have the money for Chauncey's daycare.

"I have no options," she said, frustrated with herself.

The only thing she could do was call her mom back and beg her to come up for a week until she got settled at work. She picked up the phone and dialed her mother's number in Orlando. The phone rang five times before she reached her mother's voicemail. Candace left her a long, detailed message whining into the phone and letting her know how things were going.

When she hung up the phone she sat there a few minutes longer before she walked to the back to wake Chauncey. Then she put him inside the car and drove off to talk to Azerica and then to pick up Melina.

-ydn-

Azerica could still feel the energy from the pep rally as she and the other cheerleaders prepared themselves for the bus ride to Ed White. The game didn't start for another four hours, but their cheerleader coach expected them to stay after school and practice for a few hours and then they always ate dinner at Barnhill's and after that they traveled back to the school to ride the bus with the football players to the game.

This was the first time Azerica ever experienced this ritual and so far, it's been a wonderful first experience.

Everyone seemed ready for the game tonight; they all had a lot of school spirit that fueled the cheerleaders and the football players. She was sure Jay and Darren were ready for tonight's challenge. And she couldn't wait for Darren's party afterwards. She loved high school!

She finished changing into her practice clothes and went onto the field to meet Trish. She and the other cheerleaders were at the 300-track marker stretching their legs.

She skipped over to join them, ecstatic to be part of the group. Besides Trish, she was the only other freshman on the squad. There were a few sophomores, but most everyone were juniors and seniors.

They all had a lot in common. They talked excitedly about Darren's party and who they thought he wanted to holla at. She dared not tell them about the time she spent with him today. She still wasn't sure whether or not she liked him. She knew she liked the attention.

When Trish started to mention their breakfast this morning, she nudged her to quiet her. If she and Darren did get together, she wanted it to be a surprise. She didn't want anyone to be prepared for it.

She laughed when they started talking about Jay and the way Trish scooped him up the first day. And Trish was basking in her victory, letting them know she's got the juice.

"Azerica," someone said interrupting the conversation. "Isn't that your mom driving up?"

Oh, Lord, she thought. *What could that woman want now?*

"Yeah, that's her," Azerica said nervously, not knowing what to expect. "I'll be right back. Let me see what's up."

Azerica got up from stretching and walked over to her mom's car parked outside the fence. She could tell from the way her mom looked that she was upset. *Lord, what did I do now?* Azerica asked.

When she walked up to the old Civic, she opened the passenger door and climbed inside. Chauncey was in his car seat half-asleep.

"Where's Mel?" Azerica asked casually.

Candace rolled her eyes. "She's at her Girl Scouts meeting. I haven't picked her up yet."

"Oh," said Azerica. She waited for her mom's rampage to begin. It has happened so often lately that Azerica had it timed down to the second. In her head she could see the ten second clock begin and at the moment it struck zero, that's when her mom started.

"Where were you this morning?" Candace asked, trying to keep her voice low and her temper under control.

"I was at home and then I came to school," Azerica replied. She knew where this was going. Somehow her mom found out that she had skipped school this morning.

As best as she could, Azerica tried to act as nonchalant as possible, but it wasn't working and her mom could tell. Every time Azerica had to lie about her whereabouts to stay out of trouble, she became very defensive and distant. She answered her mother's questions briefly, giving no details. She stayed quiet and stared out the window, making it a point not to look her mother in the eyes.

"Do you think I'm stupid?" Candace asked her.

"No," Azerica responded lightly, watching the other cheerleaders finish their stretches and practice a few new cheers for tonight.

"Well, why do you keep lying to me? Don't you understand that I will always find out the truth?" Candace said. "No matter where you are or what you are doing, someone out there knows me and that someone will tell me what you're doing."

Azerica couldn't believe the way her mother was acting over something as small as this. She knew her mom did the same things when she was in school, but she always acted like she was a perfect angel. She wanted to say something, but she held back. She didn't want to escalate the argument in the school parking lot. She didn't want to be embarrassed by her mom's rage, not while the others were around. She knew they could see them from where they were, but they couldn't hear anything.

Thank God.

"Are you listening to me?" Candace asked her.

"Yes," Azerica snapped back.

"You know what. That attitude of yours is going to keep you in trouble this year. I don't know what the problem is, but you need to fix it. Because if you don't, you won't be cheering again," said Candace.

Azerica didn't have to look at her to know her mother's neck was moving back and forth. She could sense it and she could feel the fury in her mother's eyes.

"I'm just going to tell you this one time. I better not hear about you skipping school again. You are here to get your education. You can't afford to miss any classes because you have to keep your GPA up. If you can skip school, than you don't need to be cheering," she said.

"What does that mean?" Azerica turned and asked her mother.

"Do I need to make it more simple?" Candace asked, mocking her. "Child, that means that if you skip another class, you've retired as a cheerleader because you will start spending your nights at home with Mel and Chauncey."

"You can't do that," Azerica said, expressing her indifference.

"Why can't I?" Candace said as if Azerica started speaking another language.

"Everything is paid for and we won't get any money back for turning the stuff in." Azerica tried to remind her how much they invested because her mom hated wasting money.

"Azerica, I don't care. I'm the one who paid for it. I'm the one who let you do it. If I decide to take you out of it, I will." Candace retorted.

Azerica sighed.

"You can make all the faces you want, and when you have a child, you can do whatever you please. But you are my daughter and I have control. You are going to do as I say." Candace reminded her.

Tired of listening to her mother, Azerica grabbed the door handle and started to push open the door to get out of the car. She didn't want to hear anything else her mom had to say. She planned to have fun tonight and get away from all this drama that connected her life with her mother's.

Before she could get both feet outside the car door, her mother broke the silence and started talking again.

"You have to come straight home after the game tonight," Candace demanded. "I have another business meeting to go to and you've got to watch Mel and Chauncey."

"Mom you always do this to me!" Azerica exclaimed. "I told you I was going to spend the night with Trish tonight."

"Well my dear, your family comes before your friends and I need you at home tonight. Leesa or someone will be there until you come back. Make sure you come straight home afterwards," Candace said sternly.

"Why do you always find ways to ruin my life?" Azerica asked. She wasn't ready to lose this battle. This was her night to shine. She couldn't miss out on Darren's party or staying all night with Trish.

"I'm not ruining your life dear, I control it. Now get out my car and I'll see you when I get home."

Realizing that she would never get her way, Azerica proceeded to get out the car. Trying to regain her spirit, she walked back to the field to rejoin the other cheerleaders who barely seemed to notice she had been missing. It was a good thing their coach, Ms. Richardson, didn't require them to be there, or she would have been in trouble. Then everyone would have known she was gone.

Oh well, it didn't matter anyway. Pretty soon she'd be able to come and go as she pleased. She just had to wait for her mom to realize she wasn't a baby anymore.

Until the time came, she had to do what she could to still be able to go out and have fun with her friends. Somehow, she had to come up with a way to get out of baby-sitting tonight. The last thing she wanted to do was admit to Trish that she got in trouble for going to Denny's this morning, and now she has to go right home after the game. There was no way she was going through that. Trish already thought it was crazy that she had a curfew.

Before Azerica could make it through the fence that separated the field and track from the bleachers, she saw the figure of a girl running to catch up with her.

After staring for a moment, Azerica realized it was Devin.

Oh, God, she thought to herself. *Not now. I can't deal with my mom and then deal with her.*

But after realizing Devin wasn't going to go away either, Azerica decided to walk over to her to see what she wanted.

Azerica rushed towards Devin to meet her. They met beside the storage building for sports equipment. Noticing that they were still in view of the other cheerleaders, Azerica guided them towards the center of the building so no one could see them. After what Trish told her about Devin's reputation, Azerica didn't want anyone to see her talking to Devin.

"Hey Devin," Azerica said trying to sound happy see her.

"Hey girl! It looks like everyone is getting ready for the game," commented Devin brightly. "I was actually looking for Jay but then I saw you and decided to say hi. We haven't seen each other in a while."

"I know, this cheerleading thing keeps me pretty busy," Azerica said, staring off.

"Well, since I've joined the newspaper, I've been pretty busy too," Devin said, happy that she had something more in her life. "I still can't believe the way God worked that out for me. I am so happy. And you know, when I went to see my guidance counselor and have the classes switched, she said there was just one opening left."

"Wow," Azerica said, still trying to coat her voice with excitement.

"Yeah, so I'll be working at the game tonight," said Devin, waving her camera. "They gave me a press pass so I can get in free. They want me to take pictures and get a few comments from the people. They said I'm in training since I've never had any journalism classes."

"That's good, I'm glad things are working out for you," Azerica forced a smile.

"Well, what are you doing tonight? I thought maybe we could watch a movie after the game or something. Mom gave me her Blockbuster card and she said she'd take me to get a movie after the game." Devin knew the answer, but she asked anyway. She was still praying for Azerica. Maybe God had answered her prayers already.

"I can't do anything," Azerica said sadly. This time it was the truth. "I'm stuck watching Mel and Chauncey tonight."

"Oh, well, if you want, I can help you and we can do something else," Devin suggested. "I haven't seen Mel and Chauncey in so long. And that's a shame considering we live in the same complex."

Azerica faked a laugh. "Yeah. I know."

"I can help you if you want. I don't mind." Devin said again.

Still not sure what she was going to do to get out of baby-sitting, Azerica decided it wouldn't be a bad idea to let Devin help her. Devin could help her get to the party. Even if she just made an appearance and left, she'd be happy. She just wanted to make it there. Trish, Darren and Jay all expected her to be there.

"If you want to come over and help me, that's cool," Azerica finally said. "My mom's friend Leesa will be waiting for us. She's going to be watching them until we get there."

"So do you want me to meet you there after the game or do you have a ride?" Devin asked excitedly. It seemed as though God were answering her prayers and she was so happy to be getting her friend back.

"You can meet me there. My friend Trish will take me home," Azerica replied. Honestly, she wasn't sure how she'd get there, but she didn't want to kill whatever opportunities she might have to get to the party.

"Alright, well I'll see you at the game." Devin said uncertainly. She didn't understand why Azerica would still take another ride. "Well, I've got to prepare myself for this newspaper thing."

"Alright then," said Azerica as Devin walked back towards the building.

That's great, Azerica thought to herself. *Mel and Chauncey love Devin and even if I didn't make it back in time, she'd stay with them until me or Mom got home and she'll go straight there after the game. Now I can go to the party for a few hours and then go home. When I get there, I'll just tell Devin my ride left me and I had to wait for another one.*

With her plan in place, Azerica felt at ease again. She silently thanked God and joined the rest of the cheerleaders. They had just finished practicing two new cheers and now they were going to work on their dance routine. Azerica hopped in her spot next to Trish and started dancing when the music blared through the small speakers of Makeisha Wright's Sony boom box.

young, dumb and naive

Chapter 11

Sitting at the center of the table, Azerica was tripping because she was at Golden Corral with Darren Lewis, Jay Christian, Makeisha Wright, Nikia Walker, Robert Allen, Ka'tina Harris, Twanny McDonald and of course Trish and the rest of the football players and cheerleaders. But everyone seated with her at the two long tables joined together, were juniors and seniors. That is, except for she and Trish, yet everyone included them in their conversations as if she and Trish had been at USG since their freshmen years.

Darren, Makeisha, Nikia and Robert who sat across from her, were all seniors. Makeisha was crowned Miss USG at the end of her junior year. She and Darren dated on and off last year, according to Trish, but Makeisha started talking to a college sophomore at the University of North Florida.

Nikia Walker was Makeisha's best friend. The two of them were Jacksonville natives and had practically known each other since birth. They attended all the same schools and were always involved in the same activities. Nikia didn't have as much school spirit as Makeisha, but she was college-minded and ready to enter into the next phase of life. She had no clue what she wanted to study. She just wanted to get out of her parents' house.

They were both cute. They had thin, short black hair. Makeisha usually kept hers in braids and Nikia always did candy curls or waves. Makeisha had real defined features. Her mother was from Jamaica and her father was from Texas. She had slanted dark brown eyes and her complexion was a deep-bronzed brown. She was about 5'4'' and thick. All the guys in Azerica's freshman class fell at her feet and the freshman girls all wanted to be like her. She seemed perfect. She had the cutest clothes, a college boyfriend, excellent grades and a wonderful personality.

Nikia was her less-serious counterpart. She didn't keep herself as polished as Makeisha, but she wore nice clothes also. She was 5'5'' and her skin was beautiful and creamy like peanut butter. She was thin and her body was toned and muscular from years of cheerleading and gymnastics. Naturally her eyes were brown, but she wore green disposable contacts. She always says she has an image she has to uphold. Her goal is to be a professional video girl.

"Have y'all seen the new Jay-Z video?" Nikia asked.

Knowing what she was going to say next, everyone at their table ignored her.

"I know y'all negroes hear me," she said flabbergasted. "That's alright. When y'all want to come to my LA home and chill and partake of some of my video money, I'm gonna say, 'Do you remember that time we ate at Golden Corral? Well, I think it's time you found another duck.'"

Makeisha laughed. "Girl you know we're playing. We know you gonna be the biggest video girl in Hip Hop."

"Now see, that's why you my girl. You got my back," said Nikia, hi-fiving her friend. "Now the rest of y'all just need to go to hell 'cause you just be hating on my dream."

Nikia pretended to turn her back on them and finish her plate.

"Oh, come on now Nikia. You know we love your talent. I plan on hiring you to dance in some of my videos," teased Robert Allen, sitting to the right of Nikia.

Robert was also a senior. He transferred to USG from Orange Park High School to play football. The team often picked at him for his experience in O.P. Orange Park is a small, residential community that lies on the outskirts of Jacksonville. The area attracts numerous families because of its location and convenience. Blanding Boulevard travels from Jacksonville to Orange Park and you can find anything on Blanding once you've made it out of Duval County.

Robert's family moved to Florida from Atlanta, Georgia. His family chose to live in Orange Park because his father heard the schools were better there. But once his dad realized Robert's football potential, he decided to transfer Robert from OPHS to USG. Robert was happy to come to USG. He said Orange Park was too fake for him. He said it was booji and almost like going to school in Beverly Hills. The black student population acted more thugged out than what they really were. The Asians tried to maintain a certain sense of ghetto. The Hispanics were just as bad as the blacks and the whites were either preppy, gothic or mini-me Eminems.

Robert's stories had them cracking up for hours. He played like he was a quiet, unsociable geek, but Robert was a closet class clown. Azerica didn't really become acquainted with him until after summer camp.

When she and the other cheerleaders came back from camp, they spent all day on the field practicing cheers and routines. While they were slaving in the sun, the football players were usually imprisoned to Coach Walker and his strenuous practices. Although the cheerleaders started practice hours after the football players, they all finished at the same time. Before going home, Azerica would join Trish, Jay, Robert, Makeisha, Darren and the others to Dairy Queen for ice cream.

That was when she had her freedom. But that was also when Trish was the only one interested in befriending her.

And that was when Azerica's mom was happy because she was getting money. Now that she's broke, Azerica can't do anything.

Disengaging herself from the chatter around her, Azerica started planning out her evening in her head. She knew Devin would be there for her, but she couldn't figure out whether or not to go to the party first and then go home, or actually meet Devin at home and then leave for the party.

Either way it would be difficult.

"...I think Z is."

"What?" Azerica asked, not sure who it was that mentioned her name.

"Nothing," said Ka'tina Harris. "Makeisha was just trying to figure out who the baby was at the table."

"Oh," Azerica replied, not sure of what to say next.

"The worst part about being the baby is you got to fight with your parents to be able to do anything," Ka'tina continued to talk. "I mean, can you believe my mom wouldn't let me hang out with anyone who was two years older than me. And I couldn't talk to any guys. Not even on the phone, it was like she was scared we would have sex."

Azerica could relate. Her mom was tripping now, but she was surprised Ka'tina had been so restricted. She could do practically anything now. She always knew where the party was and she was quick to use her fake ID to get into the Stadium Club or T-Birds. Since her parents bought her a 2001 Honda Civic for her 17th birthday this past summer, she's been everywhere.

Ka'tina was 5'5'' with chocolate-brown skin. She had dark brown eyes and short eyelashes. She kept her eyebrows arched slick and her hair slicked straight. Her straight black bob was highlighted blonde. She had dimples that showed only when she smiled and her eyes always glowed mischievously.

"You know, I'm thinking about giving myself bangs and redoing my highlights to make them red. What do you think?" Ka'tina asked everyone at the table.

"Your hair is your hair," said Darren, eating his food and trying not to pay a lot of attention to her. He didn't care what she did.

Ka'tina just rolled her eyes at him and waited for a response from anyone else at their table.

"I like the blonde, why red?" Trish asked her.

"She's trying to be like Kelly Rowland," said Twanny McDonald, Ka'tina's first cousin.

"Oh, and you don't look like Nelly with that bandanna 'round your head and the Band-Aid on your cheek," Ka'tina snapped back.

"Now you know Tre'von cut me this morning," Twanny said, speaking of Ka'tina's little brother. "That l'il nigga is dangerous. I thought he was Jason chasing me down the hall."

Twanny and Ka'tina's mothers were sisters. They were from Virginia but moved to Florida as soon as the youngest, Ka'tina's mom, turned 18. They started working and roomed together until Patrice, Ka'tina's mom married a few years later. Although she wasn't married, Stephanie, Twanny's mother, became pregnant shortly after she discovered her sister was pregnant with Ka'tina. She never mentioned where she met Twanny's dad or even how long they'd been seeing each other. No one ever saw her with him and the family was certain that he didn't exist. They often tease her and say a sperm bank donated the sperm that helped her create Twanny.

Born a few months apart, Twanny and Ka'tina grew up together and acted more like brother and sister than first cousins. They shared an unbreakable bond that grew stronger as they grew older. Their family ran deep and within the past five years they had gone through so much that only they truly understood what the other was thinking. Sometimes they got in a slump and would talk to no one, but each other.

Azerica had only known them for a few months, but she witnessed the slump a few weeks ago at practice. All she knew was that cheerleader practice was going well and the football players were doing okay, but as soon as practice was over Ka'tina and Twanny left without saying 'bye to anyone. They got in her red Civic and drove off as if they were heroes going to rescue someone from a dangerous situation. Azerica didn't know what was really going on, she just admired the bond they shared.

"Anyways, Darren, you got everything ready for your party tonight?" Ka'tina asked. "You know I got some more moves I wanna practice."

Darren laughed. "Yeah, my brother's gonna have it hooked up for us."

"Everybody going?" Makeisha asked everyone at the table.

"Of course, why would we miss it?" Trish asked.

"Just wanted to make sure **everyone** was going to be there," Makeisha said and glanced at Azerica. "USG athletes support each other."

"We got her covered, Momma Wright," Trish said and winked at Makeisha.

"Well, y'all, I know the food is good and all, but we gotta go," Nikia said reminding them of the time.

"Damn, the game starts in a few hours," said Jay, breaking his silence. He'd been buried in his food during the conversations.

"Your food must have been good, 'cause you ain't talk to nobody the whole time you were here," Trish said to him as they all stood and prepared to leave.

"I gotta eat to live," Jay said smiling.

"Depends on what you're eating," Trish flirted back.

"You know, my ears are too young for this," Azerica said playfully and walked ahead of them. She caught up with Darren, Makeisha and Nikia, who were all avidly discussing USG's winning strategy for this year.

It didn't take her long to realize she felt at home with the cheerleaders and the football players. They made her high school transition much easier. The guys didn't really care, but the cheerleaders always tried to look out for her and make sure she was able to do whatever it was they were doing. She appreciated their concern.

-ydn-

Thank you Lord, Devin said to herself.

She got up from where she was kneeling, her meeting place with God. She had to thank Him for this week and the opportunities presented to her. She never imagined she could literally walk into the newsroom and be part of the writing staff in just a day. Nor did she believe they would give her an assignment within the first week. But here she was, getting ready for the game and preparing herself to take pictures and get quotes from the fans.

She had to admit though, not everything in her life was wonderful.

This entire week at school was great except she'd completely lost her companionship with Azerica. She didn't know or understand what was going, but Azerica had completely changed. Devin noticed a slight change in her after cheerleader camp, but it became very noticeable this first week at school. Devin was no longer in her circle of friends and Azerica's new friends call her Z. She's started dressing more trendy and sexy, and she looks older, more mature now.

She could only pray that God would watch over her and draw her back to Him. When that happens, she knew she and Jesus would be waiting for her as if nothing ever happened.

"I guess that's why I have peace with this whole thing," Devin said, half talking to herself and half talking to God. "I mean, she's my friend, my sister in Christ. She's struggling right now, but she'll be back. All I can do is sit and wait for her. No need in getting upset."

And she could be closer than I thought, Devin remembered back to their conversation after school today. *Azerica either is trying to be my friend again or she's using me.*

She didn't want to believe Azerica would use her, but she had a feeling that Azerica probably wasn't trying to be her friend again.

I don't want to think about that right now. I'll pray for the best.

Devin walked over to her dresser and combed through her hair. She made sure her outfit reflected, cute, comfort and school-spirit. She had on a pair of blue jean capris and a USG tee shirt with her brother's number on it. Satisfied with her clothes, she went to her closet and pulled out her blue and gray Air Force One's. Then she returned to the mirror for one last look.

Still not finished talking to God she continued her conversation.

"And you know God, I'm not stupid. I know about Darren's party tonight and I know they asked Azerica to come. She wants me to help her baby-sit, so she can leave and go to the party. But you know I love Mel and Chauncey as if they were my brother and sister so I have no problem with it. That'll give me time with them to share some Bible stories and watch some movies. But Lord, if it be your will, please let her heart be convicted. Please let her see the road she's taking is wrong. Please strengthen our friendship once again."

But either way, Devin would be fine. She loved spending time with Mel. She was so bright and full of energy. She reminded Devin of a sponge, soaking up every ounce of information. She picked up on everything quick. If Devin were a vengeful person, she could use Mel to find out whatever she wanted. But the God in her would never let her do that. She resented the fact that she learned of Jeff's arrest through Melina. Melina had a big mouth and didn't know when to not share the information she knew.

That day was awkward for everyone. Devin remembered waiting for Azerica to come home from practice and being bombarded with questions from Melina. She wanted to know why the police arrested people for having weed and not the people who smoked it all the time.

She kept talking about her dad and how he never smoked anything, he just had another woman. Finally, Devin cut her off and asked her what was going on. As Melina finished telling her story of Jeffrey being arrested for having weed, Azerica walked into the room. She was upset, but it wasn't her first time hearing the story. She barely said hi to Devin that day. Devin remembered telling her they could study another day, she hugged Azerica and then left.

"God, I know I should've prayed with her. I felt it in my spirit, but I didn't. Please forgive me," Devin pleaded. "I prayed for her on my way home. I know that's not the same though."

Devin grabbed her camera bag and some money and walked into the kitchen where she found her mom cooking a fast dinner.

"Mom, what are you cooking?" she asked her.

"Nothing big, just some fried fish. Are you hungry?" Lauren Roberts asked her daughter.

"Yeah, I guess so," Devin replied.

She watched her mom add a few more pieces to the fryer. Sometimes Devin would sit and watch her mom in amazement. Her mom was like a combination of Clair Huxtable, Martha Stewart and June Cleaver. She could do everything. She didn't have the career that Clair had, but she was a workingwoman. She always had decorative ideas that turned their three-bedroom apartment into a comfortable home. She kept inventory on everyone in the house and knew exactly what everyone had scheduled at all times.

Besides that, she had time to work and time for herself and time set aside to spend with God.

"Mom, how do you do it?" Devin asked her after making herself a plate of food.

"What do you mean?"

"I mean you do everything and make time for everyone and still stay happy," Devin responded. "I admire that."

She watched her mom smile.

"You know my maker," she answered. "It isn't easy, but I give everything up to Him and he helps me and directs my path."

Devin couldn't imagine life without her mom. Her mom was absolutely wonderful in her eyes. She had a glowing personality and a beautiful spirit. Naturally, she was beautiful. She had honey-colored skin and hazel green eyes. She was from the old school and kept her straight, honey brown hair long. She called herself staying fashionable by keeping blonde highlights in her mane. If her face weren't so round, she would look like a younger version of Vanessa L. Williams.

"What time do you need to leave for the game?" Lauren asked, preparing plates for she and her husband.

"When I finish eating, if you don't mind taking me," said Devin. "I know it's just across the street."

"That's not a problem dear." Lauren waved her hand and smiled. "Will you be riding home with me and Dad?"

"Yeah, I think Jay and his friends are doing something afterwards," Devin replied.

"Okay, well, I'll be right back." Lauren took off her blue apron and put it inside the drawer.

"You're not going to eat anything?" Devin asked her.

"No, I'm going to wait for your father to come home. Then we'll eat and go on to the game," Lauren answered.

"Okay," Devin said and watched her mom walk to the back towards her bedroom.

Chapter 12

"Lees, what time will you be here?" Candace asked.

"As soon as I can get there," Leesa responded. "Isaac's been driving me crazy since he decided to tryout for basketball this season."

"Football season just started," Candace said confused. "He's got time before basketball starts."

"I know, but he thinks he's the next Kobe Bryant. He said he wants to make sure his game is tight," Leesa said laughing. "I got some overtime on this check, so I'm going to take him to the mall and get him some Air Force Ones."

"Oh, well is he going to the game?"

"I think so. He said something about that and a party," Leesa said. "I don't care, as long as he's home by 2."

"Let Azerica try that, I'd kill her," Candace said.

"Yeah, but she ain't a 16-year-old boy. It's different, she's just 14."

"I know. But anyways, I'll see you when you get here, I gotta get the kids together and get myself ready," said Candace.

"Alright, girl. 'Bye."

Candace hung up the phone and maneuvered her way past Mel and Chauncey who were sprawled out on the living room floor. He was playing with his Winnie-the Pools and she was playing with her dolls. She kept trying to make him hold Pooh like a baby, but he kept making faces at her and jerking Pooh back from her.

"Mel, leave him alone," Candace finally said when Chauncey started to act like he was going to cry.

"But Mom, he's not doing it right, you said we were supposed to hold our babies like this and he won't do it," Melina whined in her tattle-tell voice.

Candace stopped what she was doing and gave Melina the look.

"Stop." Candace commanded.

"Fine," Melina responded and went back to playing with her babies.

Candace walked into the kitchen to get some dinner ready for them. They always had easy finger foods on Fridays or they went to McDonald's. Candace didn't have time for Ronald today, so she pulled out some corn dogs and waffle fries from her freezer. She placed them on a pan and put them in the oven. Then she walked back to her room to find something to wear to the club tonight. Craig suggested she dress in layers, but she refused to do that. She was not some showgirl or some high-class hoe.

To help her relax and calm her nerves, Candace turned on her radio. She jumped when *In da club* by 50 Cent came blaring through. She quickly turned the volume down and turned the dial to 101.5 where *September* by Earth, Wind and Fire played.

She turned the volume up and danced around her bedroom and over to her closet. She forgot about Craig and his suggestions. She really just wanted to find an outfit that wouldn't make her standout drastically. She scrambled through every corner of her closet and after about 20 minutes, she decided on an outfit that she'd borrowed from Leesa about two weeks ago.

"She won't mind if I wear this," Candace said laying the outfit on her bed. It was a club outfit Leesa let her hold. The shirt was a half-shirt that tied behind her neck and also midway behind her back. The shiny, gold shirt was cut low to the peak of her breasts. Sometimes, she grew self-conscious of her body when she wore the shirt because she felt as though everyone were staring at her. When she and Leesa went to Jim's Place the week before, all she could think about were roaming eyes following her breasts. The black pants Leesa let her borrow didn't make it any better because they were tight and revealed her booty. Wanting to avoid that headache, Candace decided to wear her short blue jean skirt instead of the pants. Although the skirt had a split in the front middle, she didn't mind. She'd rather show off her legs than her butt.

"Mom!" Melina cried, running into her room.

"What's wrong?" Candace asked sounding concerned.

"You forgot about our food!"

"Oh, shit!" Candace said, running into the kitchen. When she got to the stove, the corn dogs and french fries were deeply blackened. She turned the oven off and threw away the food.

"So what are we going to eat now?" Melina asked.

Candace ignored her and rummaged through her refrigerator for something else quick and easy.

"You know, we could always go to McDonald's. It's just up the street," Melina suggested. "And we can order from the dollar menu 'cause it's cheap."

Shutting the refrigerator door, Candace turned around and faced her daughter.

"You know kid, you've got a point," she said. There were times she couldn't stand Melina's know-it-all mouth, but during times like today, Candace loved the way her mind worked. "Let mommy finish getting ready and we'll go. Just watch Chauncey while I'm in the shower."

Candace kissed Melina's forehead and returned to her room. The gold shirt was on her bed, but she had to find the blue jean skirt. She didn't remember seeing it in her closet and she couldn't remember the last time she wore it, but she searched through her dirty clothes pile anyway. She found the skirt at the bottom of the pile wrinkled and damp because it had been under a wet towel.

Oh, well, she thought. *No one will know. It'll probably smell like smoke and sweat. They'll never know my skirt was dirty.*

Candace threw it on her bed to iron it. She plugged up the iron and set it next to her bed. Then she walked over to her dresser and grabbed her Caress body spray and sprayed it down. As soon as the iron heated up, she spread her skirt across the bed and glided the iron over it until all the wrinkles were gone.

Candace was ten years old when her grandmother taught her how to iron on the bed. She remembered spending the night with her grandparents and wanting to iron her clothes the next day because they were so wrinkled. She asked her grandmother for the iron and ironing board and her grandmother told her she didn't need the ironing board. She said to just use the bed. When Candace didn't understand what she meant, her grandmother walked over to the bed and carefully laid out Candace's clothes. Then she skillfully ironed out the wrinkles.

Ever since that day, Candace always ironed on the bed unless she had to iron a ton of clothes or a collared shirt.

Perfect. Candace lifted the skirt up to her nose to make sure it smelled clean and then put it with the gold shirt.

Before she could undress and hop into the shower, the phone rang.

"Hello," she answered.

"Hi dear. I saw you called me earlier," said the familiar voice of her mother. "I didn't listen to the message yet. I just went ahead and called you back. What's going on?"

"Oh, hi Mom," Candace said a little relieved her mom called. "Everything is going fine. I got the job at the hospital admitting patients. I start Monday and I think I'll be making $9 an hour."

"Oh that's wonderful!" Sheryl exclaimed through the phone. "See what prayer can do! We were just talking about a job the other day and you got an interview yesterday and you already start working Monday. If that ain't God, I don't know what is."

"I'm excited," Candace responded, trying her best to make the pitch in her voice match her mothers. She wished she could share her happiness without her mother shouting Jesus all the time.

"What's wrong, you don't sound that excited?" Sheryl pried. She couldn't rejoice if her daughter didn't rejoice.

"Mom I just don't know what I'm going to do about daycare. I told you the other day if I started working, I'd need a daycare for Chauncey and I can't afford it." Candace started complaining.

"Well, did you even look for one?" Sheryl asked. *Lord please get her through this trial quickly or give me the patience to see her through.*

"I did and it's a really good one. I loved everything about it. The atmosphere is nice and the people are wonderful. It's called My Little Angels, I think." Candace stopped complaining. "But they want $160 the day he starts and another $160 at the end of the week."

"All that money? What's the first $160 for?" Sheryl was astonished.

"The deposit." Candace said, hoping her mom would help her now since she saw how much progress she's made.

"That sounds very expensive. But I guess it's because he's still an infant." Sheryl sighed. "I never imagined childcare would get this bad. But the times have changed. I thank God it wasn't like that when you were small."

"Mom, please can you come up next week? I can't do this without you," Candace begged. If her mom would come, she wouldn't have to meet Craig tonight and she could stay home with her children.

"No dear, I can't." Sheryl hated giving her the bad news, but she wasn't sure if Candace had learned to be responsible yet.

"Why not?" Candace protested. "It's just for one week. I don't see what the problem is. I'm really trying and you can't do anything to help me."

"I'm sorry Candace. I've made other commitments next week. I can't get out of them," Sheryl lied. *Lord forgive me, but it's for her own good.*

"Alright Mom. Well I have to go now," Candace didn't want to talk to her anymore.

"I love you Dear. Don't forget to thank God for the job. Just pray and trust Him for another miracle. He'll make a way to get childcare for you. If He did it once, He'll do it again." Sheryl said confidently. "One day you'll listen and believe."

"Mom, I really have to go get ready for Azerica's game now," Candace tried to cut her off.

"Oh, she's finally cheering for the high school. Give her a kiss for me," said Sheryl, excited for her first grandbaby.

"I will," said Candace shortly.

"I'm going to let you go now." Sheryl said. "Call me later and tell me how things are."

"'Bye Mom." Candace said. If she couldn't depend on her own mother to save her from this madness, who could she depend on? Of course, God is what her mom would say. But she really didn't have time for that anymore. Candace always thought God used people to help others through trials. But apparently, her mom wasn't getting it.

Whatever, she thought to herself and got in the shower. *If she ruined her life, it would be her mother's fault again, with or without prayer.*

-ydn-

"'Bye Mom," said Devin as she climbed out of her mother's blue Toyota Camry. "Thank you for dropping me off."

She was excited to be at the game. There was something about football season and the energy from the fans that made her love the game. No matter what their differences, the fans always came together on Friday nights to support USG's football team. It was almost as if they all came into agreement in prayer before the game even started. Whatever sparked their enthusiasm, Devin prayed it continued.

Devin loaded her Kodak 35mm camera with new film as she made her way to the entrance. When the man asked for her ticket, she lifted up her press pass and he let her walk through. The game hadn't quite started, so Devin walked onto the field to take pictures of the teams practicing. She saw her brother, Darren, Robert and a few others playing around. When they saw her walk up, they started showing off, telling her they needed cameos in the school paper. She laughed at them and kept taking pictures.

Jason's friends have always been like brothers to her. They seemed to protect her and look after her. She was proud to be at USG with them and belong to something they were apart of. With Azerica cheering and her brother playing football, Devin was afraid

young, dumb and naive

she wouldn't find an activity to participate in. Now that she had the school paper, she felt positioned.

Finished with her snapshots of the teams, she walked towards the track to where the cheerleaders were and started taking shots of them. Azerica barely said hello to her, but Devin didn't care. She was there to perform a duty and so was Azerica.

After almost thirty minutes of action shots, Devin walked to the stands and found her parents sitting near the top row, directly in front of USG's cheerleaders. She went up to join them for the game.

As soon as the buzzer roared to indicate the start of the game, the fans jumped to their feet and screamed.

Once again, Devin was awestruck by the energy pouring from the crowded stands to the players on the field. The football team fed off the energy and pushed themselves harder. Any time the Soldiers grabbed hold of that momentum it was hard for their opponent to regain control. Even though Lee's Generals were just as good as USG, they didn't have the fan base to carry them on. They lost their drive and slipped behind in the second quarter. By half time, they were down 24 to 36.

After watching Lee's dance team perform to *Number 1* by Nelly, Devin left her seat to interview some of the fans about the game. When she finished, she walked to the concession booth to get a drink and saw Azerica and some of the cheerleaders getting snacks. As she got closer to them, she could almost feel Azerica trying to ignore her. But as soon as Trish saw Devin, she called her over.

"Take a picture," Trish stuck out her butt to pose. "I love taking pictures. You can never get enough of the cheerleaders' pictures in the paper."

Devin laughed. "I left the camera in the stands. I finished the roll except for a few shots. I'm saving those for the win."

"True," said Azerica, finally acknowledging Devin's presence.

"Girl, your brother is the shit!" Trish exclaimed. "You saw how he outran all dem niggas on Lee?"

Trish pretended to run and dodge invisible people running after her.

"Yeah, he's alright. Don't blow up his head. His ego is big enough already without the compliments," Devin laughed. "Anymore compliments will make him feel like he's Michael Vick or somebody."

"Girl your brother is fine, it don't matter. He can be Michael Vick, Donovan Darius, Tracy McGrady, Chris Rock…well, not Chris Rock. Chris Rock is ugly. But you're brother is real fine." Trish gawked. "His sexy self can take me anywhere."

"I'm sure you're not the first to feel that way," Devin said, not sure how to respond.

"But I will be the one to get him," Trish said confidently. She had skills to make a college man chase her.

"Well, I need to go back and get my camera. The game's about to start back. I'll talk to you later Trish." Devin said, after she noticed Azerica had turned to speak to one of the other cheerleaders.

I can't understand what Azerica's problem is, Devin thought to herself, momentarily forgetting about her prayer. *If her new friend Trish can talk to me, why can't she? How can she treat me this way and still expect me to be willing to help her baby-sit?*

Because she knows I'll do it, Devin answered her own question. *But God I know you'll bless me in the end.*

Devin climbed the bleacher stairs to her seat and found her parents anxiously waiting for the second half to begin.

"Mom, do you mind if I help Azerica baby-sit tonight?" Devin asked her mom as she sat down next to her parents.

"No, that's fine." her mom said, happy to see them hanging out again. "That will be good for you, I know the two of you haven't really spent time with each other in a while. And I'm glad you're getting out of the house."

Devin wanted to tell her mother about her inhibitions. But before she had the chance to respond, the buzzer roared to prepare them for the second half.

Out of nowhere, ran blobs of blue and gray from the visitor's locker room.

Devin didn't know what had happened in Lee's locker room during half time, but whatever it was, it got the Generals crunk and they worked to close the gap in the score. The game was tied during the entire fourth quarter and Devin was actually scared USG might lose. That is until her brother scored a touchdown with two minutes remaining.

USG fans exploded, jumping to their feet. They quickly sat down when Lee's number 15 ran the ball towards the other end of the field. No one could stop him. Then out of nowhere Darren came running up and slammed him to the ground. USG fans rose to their feet cheering again. They watched anxiously as USG stopped Lee's run and intercepted the ball.

When the buzzer sounded to let everyone know the game was over, Devin was already standing on the track waiting to take pictures of her peers. They were ecstatic over their 52 to 45 victory.

"Are you ready?" Lauren Roberts walked over and asked her.

"I think so. I finished my roll," Devin replied.

"Do you want to see if Azerica needs a ride," Devin's mother asked her.

Devin glanced to where Azerica was celebrating with Trish. In her heart Devin knew that if she asked her, Azerica would tell her no and she'd meet her there. Not wanting to be lied to, Devin responded, "No, she has a ride. I'll see her at her house."

Chapter 13

"Thanks for having dinner with me before going to the club. I hate working on an empty stomach. The smoke makes me sick when I'm hungry." Craig said to Candace as he paid the check at Ruby Tuesdays.

"No problem," Candace replied feeling like she was floating on air. "I needed those glasses of wine."

"You're not nervous are you?" Craig asked, guiding her out the door.

"Naw. I'm just checking it out, right?"

Craig laughed. "Of course, nothing more. Not tonight anyway, unless you feel lead to work. Which, I don't have a problem with. Making money is a beautiful thing."

Candace sighed and stared at the scenery that lay before her. Downtown Jacksonville was very attractive at night. The city government had really been working to clean it up and it showed. The newly built condos stood high in the sky, the bridge that connected Riverside to the Southside shone bright blue, and from where she was standing at The Landing, she could see it all.

"It's beautiful tonight," Craig commented. "Would you like to walk before we go?"

Candace nodded.

When she was younger, her most favorite thing to do was come to The Landing with her mother. It was a beautiful tourist attraction for Jacksonville. It sat on the St. John's River and consisted of a mini-mall and several restaurants. She and her mom spent countless Saturday afternoons window-shopping. When they grew weary, they would take a seat at one of the park benches that faced the river. She missed those times with her mother. As she got older, she spent less and less time with her. And now that her mom lived in Orlando, she really didn't see much of her.

"You know I really miss my mom." Candace reached for Craig's hand for consolation.

"When was the last time you talked to her?" Craig held her hand tightly.

young, dumb and naive

"Today." She responded.

"Okay..." said Craig, not really understanding. "You've got to help me out a little Candace."

"I mean, we don't spend time together like we used, you know? We used to walk up and down the Riverwalk when I was a little jit. We'd admire the boats, watch the birds and even watch the water to see the fish jumping across the river," Candace's mind wandered to those memories. "Now we only talk on the phone. She doesn't come back to Jacksonville very often. And when she is here, she's fussing and complaining about me not going to church anymore."

"Why don't you take the kids and go visit her some weekend?" Craig suggested.

"Well, I hadn't been able to afford anything Mr. Pearson. Remember, I start work with you Monday?" Candace smiled thankfully. She hadn't worked since she was pregnant with Chauncey.

"Yeah, that's right." He said. "And perhaps two jobs."

All he needed was a few more women on board and he would have the beautiful staff that he'd imagined. Candace was a piece of the puzzle that was missing. He couldn't wait to get her there so she could see it. He knew that whatever misgivings she had would vanish as soon as she walked inside. The place was magical and she needed some magic in her life.

"Let's head out to the club. I'm sure they're waiting for me," Craig said.

Reluctantly, Candace stood up in agreement. If she didn't go now while she had a buzz, she would probably never go. Part of her dreaded what was coming next, but the intoxicated Candace couldn't wait to get there so she could get another drink. She needed to numb her conscience while she was there, otherwise she wouldn't be able to sleep tonight.

Craig walked her to the passenger side of a black Ford Explorer and opened the car door for Candace to get in. Then he climbed into the driver seat, and they drove alongside the St. John's River. They stopped at a building that wasn't even five minutes from The Landing.

For a strip club, the building was nice. Craig had purchased one of the older, rundown buildings along the water and remodeled it. The building now had this Apollo Theatre-type feel. Candace had to admit it was clean. Emerging from the top of the building was a long sign that read Eternity. Eternity was spelled out in bright white flashing lights. To the right of the sign was a booth that looked like an admission booth for a movie theater from the 1930s.

A young black woman wearing an extremely short, loose-fitting shimmering silver dress sat inside it taking money from patrons entering the club. As soon as they paid, the two security guards standing in front of the entrance, opened the doublewide wooden doors to let them in. The guards even looked classic. They wore black slacks and white collared shirts with black bow ties.

Candace almost felt as if she were VIP coming to a very respectable place. She couldn't believe how classy the place seemed. She almost couldn't wait to see what it looked like inside.

Craig parked the car and walked to the passenger side to let her out. Automatically she reached to grab his hand, but he was already walking towards a small door to the side of the building. She rushed to catch up with him.

"This place is pretty impressive," she said.

"Yeah, it's one of a kind," Craig said half-heartedly. "Though it's not worth bragging about yet."

Feeling the tension, Candace quickly and quietly followed him inside. Just as she imagined, the place was gorgeous. The tiled black floors glowed with silver glitter. The walls were midnight blue with glow-in-the-dark stars and moons covering them. The tables and chairs were silver with black tops and black cushions. The stage was T-shaped with two silver poles at all three ends. To the left of the stage was the bar. A black woman wearing a black negligee with a black bow tie around her neck served the drinks. The DJ was situated in the back of the room in an enclosed sound room. He was the most casually dressed person there, wearing a nice, black short-sleeved shirt and black slacks.

"Sit here." Craig commanded when they got to the bar.

"Heaven, give her a martini," Craig said to the woman bartender. He laid his jacket across the seat next to Candace and briskly walked to the center of the stage.

"Good evening," he said. "I just wanted to personally welcome all of you to Eternity. Like always we've got nothing but the best for you, along with some new additions. But all beautiful luscious girls ready to meet your needs. For your private dances and peep shows, you can go to one of the many rooms available directly outside this door. Now sit tight and let the ladies work their magic. Thank you for coming out."

As soon as Craig stepped off the stage, the DJ started playing *Feeling on Your Booty* by R. Kelly. The men cheered when a group of four women came out to do their routine to the song.

Candace expected to see four flabby women with stretch marks dance, but instead four beautiful women in elegant lingerie performed gracefully with ease. She really wished she could be one of them. They all looked like Victoria Secret models. She would come in and dress up every night to perform if she knew she would look like that.

They definitely weren't strippers. They were more like Las Vegas showgirls without the extra costumes. The men barely even touched them.

"What exactly is it that you want me to do?" Candace asked Craig when he took his seat next to her. Excitement had rushed through her twenty times over. She would start tonight if he'd let her.

Craig laughed. It was funny to see the attitude wash away once she walked into Eternity. All the women he interviewed were like that. They all assumed his club was a dirty strip club just like the other ones. As if he didn't have any class. He couldn't stand fat, ugly strippers any more than the next man. He was an up and coming doctor with a reputation to uphold. He had class and he loved beautiful women. That's why he changed the stripper game with Eternity. One day he would franchise and open up others around the state.

"I'm glad to see you're opening your mind to the position. There really is no pressure, though. I don't expect you to start dancing right away." Craig explained.

"But I'd like to start," Candace reassured him. "I think so anyway. It's not as bad as I thought it would be."

Candace turned back to the show and watched as they finished the routine and another set of women came to the stage. They were just as beautiful as the first four. And a few of them kept all their lingerie on. They didn't strip. Doing the kind of dancing they were doing would not make her feel like a whore at all. She could come home from work every morning with a guiltless conscience.

"I do want you to get to know Heaven and come up with your own club name. For the time being, you'll be helping her tend bar." Craig brought her attention back to him. "It doesn't seem like it at the moment, but the place will be packed in about 20 minutes with men all wanting to escape from life. They'll need drinks and Heaven isn't always able to get to them all in time."

"Oh." Candace said, confident that she could do anything here.

After seeing the expression on her face, Craig laughed again and ordered her another martini. "Drink up," he said, noticing that she still seemed a little nervous even though she was excited.

Candace nodded her head and surveyed the room. So many men were there from all walks of life. She saw young men, older men, retired men, black men, white men, thugs and even some who looked like business professionals. They were all enjoying the show and howled when one of the dancers shed a piece of her clothes.

I can't lose any of my clothes, she told herself. *I won't put myself through the embarrassment of seeing someone I know watch me dance naked. I'll just be like some of the other women and dance with all my lingerie on.*

Candace paid close attention to the men's reactions, especially the classy business ones. Every time the dancers came near, they couldn't wait to put money in their bikinis and fondle them. Candace couldn't tell whether or not the dancers minded the groping, all she could see were the 20's and 50's and the 100-dollar bills protruding through their costumes. She would give anything to be one of them at that moment. That was exactly

young, dumb and naive

the kind of money she needed. She could easily make the $160 she needed by Monday for Chauncey's daycare.

"What would I have to do to be up there?" Candace turned to Craig and asked.

Craig chuckled.

"I'm serious Craig. I need what they're getting." Candace slurred her words and almost spilled her drink on herself.

Craig smiled at her. He'd finally won the game. "No rush. I just want you to watch tonight. We'll figure something out for next time."

-ydn-

"Azerica!" Trish shouted from the field. "Come on. Let's go. We gotta go change."

Rushing to catch up with her friend, Azerica quickly walked across the field to where Trish was waiting for her. The game had been over for about half an hour, but everyone was still there trying to figure out how they were going to get to Darren's party.

Azerica had gotten stuck talking to Ka'tina and Twanny who were arguing over what they were going to do first. And the only reason Azerica went to talk to them was to see if she and Trish could get a ride with them, but it didn't work because they had no clue what they were doing anyway.

"Who you was talking to?" Trish asked, a little irritated that she had to wait. She hated waiting for people when she had some place to be.

"Twanny and Ka'tina, they tripping. They don't know what they're doing." Azerica said amused. She didn't notice the aggravation in Trish's voice. "They must never know what they're doing. I always see them act like this."

"Well you shoulda known better than to wait around for them," Trish made herself respond nicely. "Anyhow, Darren said he's taking us to his house. But I told him we had to change first."

"So where are we changing?" Azerica asked curiously. They didn't have very many options and Trish was walking away from everything nearby.

"Girl, the locker room, a bathroom, somewhere." Trish said shortly. "Just follow me."

Unsure of where Trish was going, Azerica followed behind her across the field to the side where the away teams always sat. Below the bleachers was a small door hidden behind shrubs and trees.

When Trish reached for the knob, Azerica was a little afraid because she had no clue where they were going or what was behind that door. Quietly she followed Trish inside. Relief trickled down her spine when Trish turned on the lights and standing in front of them were to restroom stalls.

"How did you find this place?" Azerica asked amazed to see it existed.

Trish winked at her coyly. "You know, Jay and I come here before practice sometimes. He can't get enough of me."

Azerica rolled her eyes.

"I'm for real. He be talking 'bout other chicks and hoes he be wit who can't do nothing for him. He said he gets tired of showing them how. He said he's glad he got me because them other females drive him crazy. I told him I know they can't handle a real man like I can. Mom always say make sure your man is satisfied so he always comes back for more."

"She told you that?" Azerica asked astonished. She'd never heard of anything like that before in her life.

"Yeah, girl. And I watch the way her men react. You can tell who gets the koochie coupons 'cause those be the ones that call all the time and buy me stuff." Trish boasted. She loved her life sometimes. "I just don't like the arrogant men that come over and act like their doing my mom a favor. I mean come on, if she weren't helping them out, they wouldn't be leaving their wives every night."

Deep down, Trish knew she didn't really feel that way. She'd become so accustomed to covering for her mom that it was natural to brag about the special treatment.

"Well, what about your mom?" Azerica soaked everything in. She'd learned more about Trish in the past week than she'd learned all summer.

"Oh, they give her money to go shopping or they pay our bills. Whatever she's got, I hope it's in my genes 'cause I wanna be like her for real. Mom really don't need to work. I don't want to have to work either," Trish said. "Unless it's a hobby. Mom just works sometimes to have a little extra money."

Boy am I sheltered, Azerica thought while Trish carried on. Everything that came out of Trish's mouth lately shocked her for days. She never imagined people thought the way Trish did. It wasn't biblically correct or even politically correct. But Azerica knew God still loved them. Her Christian friends would probably judge them and say Trish and her mom needed prayer. Azerica agreed, but she also thought it was cool that they didn't have a normal life.

Azerica commenced to get dressed. She reached into her duffel bag and grabbed the one-piece blue jean outfit she was wearing to the party. She enjoyed this transformation from little 9th grader to upcoming diva.

"Girl, you look good," said Trish, taking a break from talking. "You shoulda wore the other outfit though, but I know you wasn't ready for it yet. Anyhow, you ready to go find your man!"

Azerica blushed. "He is not my man, only my hoe."

"Now, you sound like me!" Trish laughed and tugged Azerica out of the restroom. "Let's go Hoochie!"

Together they bounced out of the restroom and to the senior parking lot to find Darren. They walked through gobs of people standing around next to running cars and loud music. They heard Darren's car in the core of the crowd bumping *Get Low* by L'il Jon and the Eastside Boyz.

Thinking they may have taken too long, Azerica was almost afraid to see him. As they walked up to his car, they saw him standing with Jay, some seniors and a few guys that had graduated last year.

Darren looked at her, winked and waved them over to get into the car.

"Alright man, make sure you come through. I know my brother would want to see you," Darren said to the USG alumni. "We trying to get crunk tonight since my folks are out of town."

Jay turned to Trish and Azerica while Darren finished handling some business. "Ladies I hope you don't mind riding in the back, Darren and I got some stuff to do before we get to his house and I need to be in the front."

"We don't mind." Azerica said, happy that she was going.

"…Touch your toes. Get low!" Trish danced up behind Darren and smacked his butt. "To the window. To wall!"

Darren ignored her and started talking to Jason. "You leaving your car here?"

"Yeah, I can come back and get it. We need to take this ride together." Jason climbed into the car.

Trish danced into the back seat and Azerica climbed in behind her.

"Alright then, let's go." Darren said and drove off.

The first stop was at Winn-Dixie on McDuff Avenue. Only Jason got out then. Trish and Azerica didn't know what he possibly needed from Winn-Dixie at 11:30 at night, and they really didn't care as long as they got to the party. When Jason got back in the car five minutes later he didn't have anything with him.

"What did you have to get?" Trish asked curiously.

"Some gum," Jason turned back and smiled at Trish. He had plans for her tonight and he wasn't going to take any chances.

"Where we going," Trish asked five minutes later, noticing they were driving towards the Northside and not Riverside. "You don't live this way."

"Don't worry, we'll get you there," Darren replied. "I have to pick up something for my brother at his friend's house."

"Who's at your house with all them people?" Trish questioned him.

"You one nosy chick," Darren laughed and turned to Jason. "You sure you can handle her? She sound like she feisty."

Jason laughed. "I got her. She ain't that feisty."

"Alright y'all, I know I'm nosy, but where we going?" Trish asked yet again. She was a little scary about driving through the ghetto after dark. Homeless people and crackheads always walked up to the car windows.

"We gotta ride to Beaver real quick. It a take just a minute," Darren finally answered her question. "Why? Are you scared?"

"No. I was just wondering what we were doing." Trish lied and put on her seatbelt.

Ten minutes later, they were at their destination on Beaver Street. Darren pulled up in front of this old creepy-looking shack and got out. The place looked condemned with grass climbing up the fence and crawling onto the sidewalk. Without streetlights, the place really looked like it belonged in a scary movie.

Just as soon as he walked in, Darren walked out.

And they were on their way to Riverside.

Jason and Darren were eerily quiet the entire ride back. They seemed to be in deep thought over something. Each time Trish asked them a question, they both took turns giving her one-word answers.

"I am so glad we made it to your house Darren!" Trish exclaimed when they finally pulled into his driveway. "I was gonna tell you to take me home. I almost didn't wanna party."

Darren didn't acknowledge her comment. He climbed out of the car and maneuvered passed the crowd walking into his home.

"What's wrong with him?" Trish asked Jason.

"He alright. I don't know. Let's go inside," Jason brushed her off. "Z you alright?"

"Yeah," she responded, wondering if she'd made the right decision. She didn't want to be at a party when her man was tripping. She could've stayed home babysitting with Devin or something. *Well, the party was still better than that under the circumstances*, she decided. *I hope Devin made it there alright.*

The house was full inside. There were a lot of people from USG but most everyone else were friends of Darren's older brother. They were drinking and smoking weed and black and milds. The house was beginning to cloud over from all the smoke. Yet no one noticed or no one cared because the music was crunk. No one was standing still, and if they were, they were working game.

Jason walked them to the kitchen to get drinks. Underneath the counter was a huge cooler with Smirnoff Ice, Sky Blue and Coronas. They each grabbed something to drink and began walking through the crowd to talk to friends. Twanny and Ka'tina finally made it and had everyone cracking up over their most recent adventure from the field to McDonald's to Darren's house. Makeisha and Nikia were there, but they were over in a corner talking to Darren's older brother and his friends.

"What happened to Darren?" Azerica asked Jason after an hour of dancing and talking to Twanny and Ka'tina. She needed to find him to take her home in an hour so she wouldn't feel completely bad about tricking Devin into babysitting.

"I think he's in the back," Jason said, taking a swig of his third Corona. "Why don't you go check on him?"

Almost reluctantly, Azerica grabbed her Smirnoff Ice and walked towards Darren's room. Just as she was about to walk down the hallway, she heard someone say, "Psssst." She turned her head to the right and saw Darren talking to his brother. She heard his brother say, "That's the one." Then they walked over to where she was standing.

"Hey, girl. Are you having a good time?" Darren asked and pulled her close to him. He grabbed her waste and caressed her side.

"Yeah, it's fun," Azerica replied, allowing herself to be handled like a doll. She liked the attention. It felt good for a guy to hold her close. She almost felt complete.

"You like Smirnoff?" Darren's brother asked her.

"Yeah." Azerica flashed her half-empty bottle in front of him.

"I almost didn't buy any 'cause I didn't think it was strong enough," he chuckled. "I need hard liquor, but Darren reminded me that rookie can't handle the stuff."

"Well, I'm glad you bought it." Azerica said. "It's just right for me."

"Let me get you another one, that one has been open for too long," Darren's brother grabbed her half-empty drink and smiled.

Azerica laughed and willingly gave it up. "Good looking out."

"He's trying to be Mr. Host," Darren said, laughing at his brother stroll off.

"That's okay. He's nice. I can't believe he's going to get me another one and I didn't even finish that one. And you know, Trish was the one who drank most of that. She said she just wanted to be reminded of how it tasted," Azerica rambled to him.

"What was she drinking?" Darren asked her.

"Sky Blue, but I didn't like how it tasted. It was too something. I don't know, but I like the Smirnoff better." Azerica opened up. "Are you hot?"

Darren laughed. He could tell it was the first time she'd ever had any alcohol.

"No, I'm fine." Darren smiled.

Noticing that he didn't have a bottle in his hand, Azerica asked him why he wasn't drinking.

"My brother's bringing back a Sky Blue for me," he said. "That was my drink last year. I made my brother buy me a case every weekend and me and Robert would chill and drink every time my parents went out of town."

"Oh." Azerica barely paid attention to what he said. "Well I'm going to go dance while I wait for him. Are you coming?"

"Sure." Darren said and followed her into the next room. He couldn't wait until she was completely gone. They were going to have fun. Everything about her said virgin and he hadn't been with one in years. It would feel good to break her in to the real world.

Darren danced up behind her and kept his front close to her back. After only a few minutes, Darren's brother came up to them and gave them their drinks.

"Thank you, I was thirsty." Azerica said and began drinking fast.

The few sips she'd taken from the other bottle had gotten her blood warm and made her thirst for this one. When she brought the bottle above her head to take a drink, she vaguely noticed something white floating and fizzle away. She didn't pay attention to it. It could have been a piece of fuzz that fell off when she turned her bottle up.

I guess I've digested fuzz before, Azerica kept on dancing with Darren. She tried to keep up with his fast rhythm and grinding, but kept losing her balance.

"Dee," a deep voice called to Darren.

"What?" Darren responded, agitated that someone had broken his concentration.

"I need you to go get me some more rope," his brother appeared.

"Now?" Darren asked in disbelief. "I just came back from there."

"Yeah, now. We don't have any and my boy over there needs some," his brother said, nodding in the corner at some dude dancing with a high school chick.

"You know I hate going out there," Darren contested.

"Dee, I ain't got time for this. Take the keys and get outta here." Darren's brother demanded.

"Alright," Darren gave in. He didn't have a choice. He was alone with his brother until his parents came back Sunday. "Azerica come with me."

Azerica shrugged her shoulders okay and followed him out the door.

"Let me get another Smirnoff before we leave," she said. She couldn't believe she was still thirsty. She'd drunk one and a half Smirnoffs already and she didn't even drink all of the first one.

"I'll get it. Meet me outside." Darren quickly walked towards the kitchen. He wanted to get this run over with so he could come back and concentrate more on his mission: Project take Azerica's virginity.

"Okay," she said and walked outside to his car. She was starting to feel a little weird and off balanced. Somewhere inside, she knew she shouldn't drink anymore Smirnoff, but she needed it. She was so thirsty from all that dancing.

Darren handed her another bottle and they both climbed into his car.

"Where are we going?" She squinted her eyes to ask him.

"To get some rope," Darren kept his eyes on the road.

"More rope. Who needs rope right now?" Azerica questioned. She just couldn't understand what they were going to do with all that rope right now.

"One of his boys I guess. I don't know. I'm just following orders," Darren said. He drove them out of Riverside and back to Beaver Street.

"You know this ain't a store," Azerica placed her hand over her head when she saw the same shabby house.

"I know, but they got the rope." He started to open his door.

"Oh. Well, can I wait in here?" Azerica closed her eyes. "My head's starting to feel crazy."

"Like how?" He asked, concerned. She looked like she had a headache.

"I can't explain it, but something ain't right." Azerica's voice grew softer.

"It'll be fine," Darren coaxed her. He leaned close to her and kissed her.

Something about his kiss this evening was different. She felt it travel through her body. It left a memorable trace that replayed hundreds of times during the five minutes he was inside getting the rope. By the time he got back in the car, the memory of the kiss was so powerful that she didn't notice that he didn't have a line of rope with him. He kissed her again and this time she asked if they could be alone somewhere before going back to the party.

"Yeah, I know a place near the water," Darren said excited. *It worked. My brother was right. I should've listened to him years ago.*

He drove the car back towards Riverside and passed the exit he needed to get home. He drove to Ortega and pulled into Ortega Park. Without lamps, the only thing they could see were trees and the reflection of the moon against the water. The view was horrible, but Azerica barely noticed. She felt as if she were becoming groggier with time. With the car parked and Jaheim crooning through the CD player, Azerica was ready for whatever it was that was about to happen.

"Thanks for coming wit me," Darren started feeling over her body. "My brother's an asshole sometimes. He wants what he wants now."

Azerica looked at him trying to comprehend the words coming from his mouth.

"You really don't act like a freshman," Darren said, kissing her neck. He reached for her and pulled her closer to him.

Feeling like a rag doll, Azerica flowed with his movements. She had no control over her body. She couldn't utter any words and she couldn't feel her lips brush against his when he kissed her. All she could remember was hearing him say, "You really don't act like a freshman."

Chapter 14

"Craig, I'm serious. I need to do whatever your dancers are doing tonight. I need some money now," Candace pleaded.

Craig smiled. This was better than he'd imagined. She didn't put up half the fight he imagined she would. *I still have it*, he thought. The gift of game was his most valued gift. He knew how to offer a woman the most degrading job and make it seem like the most honorable.

And to top it all off, they beg him to take it. Craig smirked.

"Stop looking at me like that! I need to at least do something." Candace continued. "If I don't I can't work Monday morning."

"What do you need the money for?" Craig asked her, pretending to be sympathetic.

"Daycare for Chauncey. I have to give them $160 when I drop him off Monday," Candace said. "And I have to have it. I don't have any other sitters for him."

Craig went into his pocket and handed her eight 20-dollar bills. "Here, take this."

"Are you sure?" Candace asked him, a little surprised at the gesture. "This is a lot of money to just give away."

"I'm sure. I know you need it and I don't want you to start working here until at least next week. I can't let you get too caught up in the money. I know it's good and easy, but I can't have you living for it," Craig sounded sincere.

He had to play the caring friend role with Candace. It kept her hanging on and even more desperate to work at Eternity.

"Thank you," Candace looked at him and smiled. She was happy they were friends.

"Excuse me," interrupted one of the security guards. "Dr. Pearson, you have a call from the hospital."

Seeing the aggravation explode from his face, Candace knew the call meant that Craig had to go into work. That would happen when they were in the midst of planning her role in his club. But, she knew their little meeting was worth it.

When he saw how serious she was about doing more than just serve drinks, he was excited and took her into the VIP room to discuss the details. They agreed she would start as soon as she was settled with her job at the hospital and she had proper childcare for her children in the evenings.

Now, they were being snapped back into the reality of his career.

"Hell, that's why I turned the damn beeper off," Craig muttered under his breath, when the security guard left. "They act like they can't call any other doctor to work emergencies."

Candace watched him get up and walk out to take the phone call in his office. When he returned, he gathered his things and prepared to leave.

"Wait a second," she said. "How am I going to get back to my car?"

"I'm sorry Love. Come with me. I'll take you after I see about this patient. There's no telling what happened. Things get crazy on the weekends," Craig complained.

Candace followed him out the door and they climbed back into his Ford Explorer.

Craig drove frantically trying to get to the hospital to tend to the emergency. The city and streets seemed to whiz by her. She tried to follow the signs and admire the view, but then she lost herself in her thoughts. If only she could make half the money the women made at Craig's club, she would be financially stable again. She hasn't been able to take care of anything since Jeffrey was locked up.

God, thank you for sending Craig back to me, she found herself praying.

But she couldn't help it. Craig was providing her the opportunity to become financially stable and well off without being dependent on anyone.

When they arrived at the hospital, Candace quickly followed Craig as he rushed off to his office on the fourth floor. She couldn't remember all the turns they took and the hallways they turned down, but she was happy when they finally made it. She walked over to the burgundy sofa and sat down.

For a hospital office it was beautiful. The view wasn't that exciting since all you could see was the parking garage, but everything inside made up for it. Every piece of furniture was made from cherry oak. He had silver lamps and light fixtures and a huge Thomas Kincaid painting above the couch where she sat.

"Does everyone's office look like this?" She asked him.

"What?" Craig automatically responded. "Oh, no. I think I just make more money than the other doctors because of the club."

Seeing that he was preoccupied with getting himself ready, Candace decided to reserve all other questions for a normal night. She took off her shoes and made herself comfortable.

"Hopefully, I'll be back soon. I'll have someone let you know what's going on," Craig said and rushed out.

"Ok. I'll see you when you get back," said Candace.

She felt so comfortable bidding him goodbye and waiting for his return. It just felt natural to her. She could actually see herself being Mrs. Craig Pearson one day. Daydreaming about him and the life they would have together, she started to doze off. But then mother's intuition woke her up and she got up to use Craig's office phone.

She knew it was well after midnight, but she just had to check to see if her babies were okay.

"Hello," answered a sleepy voice.

"Hey, Azerica? Is everything okay?" Candace asked, not paying attention to the voice.

"I'm sorry Ms. Christian. This is Devin."

"Oh." Candace said, a little surprised. "I didn't know you would be there tonight with Azerica. Did Chauncey and Melina give you any problems?"

"No, they were great," replied Devin. "I loved being here with them. They are so funny."

"I know." Candace agreed. Her Melina was a hand full. "Well, how did the game go?"

"USG won. I forget by how many, but we won. My brother and all the rest of the team were so happy," Devin said, her voice becoming stronger as she kept talking.

"Ok. Well I just wanted to check on you guys. Azerica must be sleeping real hard. She usually gets right up when she hears the phone ring," Candace said, a little surprised. "The phone queen must be tired."

"Ms. Christian," Devin said hesitantly. She didn't want to get her in trouble, but she was worried about Azerica.

"Yes." Candace paused.

"Azerica isn't here."

"What do you mean she isn't there?" Candace asked. Her heart jumped to her throat.

"She's not here. I knew the only reason she asked me to help her baby-sit was so that she could go to Darren's party, but I thought she would have been home by now. She thinks about herself, but she's not that inconsiderate to not come back at a decent time. I didn't want to tell on her, but I'm worried. It's almost 2 a.m.," Devin rambled close to tears.

"You did right Devin. I'm sure she's okay, but that child might want to wish she were dead, because when I get through with her, she'll be pretty close. Do me a favor and call home and see if your brother came back. Let me know when he last saw Azerica and where. I'll call you back in ten minutes," Candace put her fears in check and took control of the situation.

"Okay." Devin said and hung up.

Candace was very concerned about her daughter. She clearly told Azerica to go home after the game. Azerica knew better, but for some reason she felt she didn't have to follow rules anymore. Candace decided Azerica's new friends must be influencing her, and that scared her.

She didn't know her daughter's new friends that well. She just knew they all cheered together. She had no idea how old they were and what grades they were in. She just knew Azerica and Devin were best friends, but now that she thought about it, Devin hadn't been over as much or called the house as often as she used to.

Sitting in Craig's office chair, Candace glanced at the desk clock in front of her and saw that only three minutes had passed. Time could not move fast enough. With each tick, she grew more worried until she couldn't wait any longer. She grabbed the phone and called her house once again. This time Devin answered on the first ring.

"Well, what did he say?" Candace asked as soon as she heard Devin's voice.

"He said Azerica left with his friend Darren an hour after she got there and they hadn't seen her since," Devin repeated the information given to her minutes prior.

"He didn't know where they were going?" Candace grew anxious. She needed more information.

"No, he said he had to get a ride back to the school with another one of the football players to get his car," Devin reluctantly relayed what she knew.

"Where was the party at?" Candace kept asking questions.

"In Riverside at Darren Lewis' house." Devin replied.

"Do you have the number? I'm going to call there." Candace said.

"No, Ms. Christian. You don't have to. Jason is calling them. I told him I would call him back after you called."

"Thank you so much Devin. Go ahead and call him and I'll call you back."

"Alright, Ms. Christian. But don't be worried. I'm positive she's okay. I've been praying for her ever since I noticed she hadn't come home. God will protect her." Devin encouraged. "We've got to let faith take over now. I know it's hard, but remember faith is the substance of things hoped for and the evidence of things not seen."

"Thank you so much Devin. Call your brother back now."

This time when she hung up with Devin, she was at peace. There was something in Devin's voice that let her know Azerica was truly okay.

"Thank you God for speaking through Devin. Please just produce my daughter and I'll be okay. I'll do anything. I just need to know she's alright," Candace said softly beginning to feel a reconnection with God.

As soon as she spoke those words, she could feel God tugging at her heart and telling her to take better care of her family and spend more time with Azerica.

"I will. I promise," Candace answered. "Please make sure she's okay."

She reached for the phone again and called Devin back. Her heart beat quickly with anticipation of good news, but Devin didn't have any more information to give. She said no one answered at the Lewis home when Jason called. Candace thanked her and told her to try and get some sleep.

Now Candace was really afraid. She didn't know what else to do, but cry out to God for help. She walked back over to the couch and knelt down with her face in the seat. She prayed and prayed, asking God to protect Azerica and keep her safe. She admitted her faults and her carelessness as a mother. All she wanted was to provide for her children, yet along the way she'd forgotten to give them the attention they needed...especially Azerica. With her heart open to receive all that God was telling her, she knew He'd forgiven her. How He could do it and still love her, she couldn't fully explain. It was the power of Jesus Christ her Savior and she was grateful for salvation.

"Lord thank you for hearing me and accepting my prayers. God keep me close to you. Keep me close to my family so I can be a better mother and provider. Please don't let my neglect be the cause of this ordeal," the words flowed through Candace with an intensity she hadn't felt in a long time. "Jesus, Jesus, Jesus, Jesus, Jesus, Jesus."

The name repeated over and over in her head.

She don't know how long she sat in that position, but when Craig came in some time later, her eyes were swollen and red with tears.

"How did they find you in here?" Craig asked her. "I didn't tell them where you were. It doesn't matter. Come with me."

Craig rushed over to where she was and pulled her up and out of the office. They walked quickly to the elevator and rode down to the bottom floor where the emergency room was. He seemed to be speaking gibberish the entire way there and Candace didn't get a chance to tell him Azerica was missing. It wasn't until he stopped to speak to another doctor outside of room 108 that she wondered why he'd dragged her down here.

"Craig," Candace said softly, not wanting to interrupt his conversation.

"Thanks Doctor," Craig said nodding his head and turning towards Candace. "We can see her now."

Still puzzled, Candace followed him inside the room and saw her 14-year-old daughter lying on the hospital bed. Candace quickly ran to her side and kissed her forehead. *Thank you Jesus*, she said silently.

Her heart rejoiced. Azerica was here. She wasn't missing.

"What happened to her? Is she going to be okay?" Candace began asking, with a million more questions running through her head.

"One question at a time," said Craig. "The ambulance brought her about an hour ago. She has a large quantity of GHB in her system. GHB is an illegal substance that is used as a date-rape drug that can be bought as a liquid or powder. We're not sure which she had, but the effects are still the same. When she came in, her heart was beating faster than normal, and her blood pressure was slightly higher as well. She's been stabilized and her body is working normally. We're just waiting for the rest of the drug to wear off. That can take up to six hours."

"Who would put that in her drink?" Candace said, devastated that someone would be that cruel to take advantage of her daughter.

"Do you know where she was?" Craig asked her.

"A high school party." Candace said, not believing teenagers her age could be a victim to date rape.

"Unfortunately there are some sick kids out there. That can happen. I'm sorry it happened to Azerica, but she'll be fine." Craig reassured her.

"Thank you so much Craig. I don't know what I'd do with out you," Candace was relieved that she could depend on him during all circumstances.

"No problem. The hospital needs your insurance information as soon as you finish. I'll give you a few moments alone with Azerica and then I'll bring the paperwork to you." Craig said and walked out the room.

Oh God, she thought. *I don't have insurance. Please bring me another miracle.*

Not knowing what her payment options would be, Candace became worried and her thoughts clouded over with other unresolved money issues not yet handled. She knew she started working at the hospital Monday, but that wouldn't solve her existing backdated bills. It would give her stability and the chance to keep everything current, but this hospital bill is a nightmare to her already bad credit. She didn't know how much it was, but she knew it would be expensive.

Craig walked back inside with a clipboard and some papers.

"Candace, you don't have insurance, right?" He asked her knowingly.

"That's right," she replied apologetically. "I'm sorry. I don't even have Medicare for my children."

"You don't have to worry about them pulling the plug. She'll stay here supervised until she wakes up. Sometimes the hospital encourages us to send home patients who aren't insured, but they aren't going to mess with Azerica since you are a good friend of mine. They aren't as lenient with the bill so what they will do is send it to you in the mail. Now don't worry. You'll be able to make all the money in a few months once you've started working at the club." Craig reminded her.

After everything he'd done tonight to treat Azerica and keep the hospital from releasing her, she owed him that much. But the look in her eyes, told him she was ready to back out.

"I don't think you fully understand what happened here tonight," Craig said menacingly. "If the hospital had not called me to this emergency, Azerica would not have received the help she needed. The other doctors don't care about uninsured patients and the hospital won't force doctors to treat them because they know the patients could never pay them back."

Was he threatening her? Was he really telling her she had to work at the club because Azerica didn't have insurance? Candace couldn't believe he would do that to her under these circumstances. The evening had made her an emotional wreck. In the past three hours she'd been nervous, excited, desperate, disappointed, worried, relieved and now she was in shock.

She felt as if she were backed into a corner. How could she work at Eternity now? She just promised God she would spend more time with her family. Her heart wanted to recommit to Him and her children. Part of her ached from God's absence in her life. For so long she denied that she ever knew Him. She didn't think He was as powerful and knowing like everyone claimed…until now. She just experienced a miracle and she owed her life to Him for eternity.

Unfortunately, she'd already told Craig she wanted to perform, and now that she didn't want to, he was going to make her. She had to. If she didn't, she would never be able to pay the hospital bill or anything else.

If she didn't play by his rules, Candace had the sinking feeling that Craig would give away her job at the hospital.

God, what do I do?

"Craig, thank you for your help," was all Candace could manage to say after his comment. She swallowed hard and said, "I really needed it and I think you know that."

"I do. That's what I'm here for," he replied pretentiously. His tone remained unchanged. "I'll leave you to the paperwork. Just bring it to me when you finish."

"Okay." Candace said.

For the next 20 minutes Candace filled out medical documents. As soon as she finished, she kissed Azerica's forehead again and stepped outside the door. Across from her sat Craig and a few other doctors. She walked over to them and handed the paperwork to Craig. He began explaining everything to her that she'd just signed to make sure she understood it. When he started explaining the last page to her, two men in suits walked over to where they were sitting and stood over them.

"Excuse me. Are you Candace Christian?" One of the men asked.

Nervously, she responded, "Yes, I am."

What more can I go through tonight? Candace asked herself in anticipation of something bad. Could the evening get any worse?

"I'm Lieutenant James. I need you to come with me." He said sternly.

"What's the problem officer?" Candace asked him, this time frightened.

"Grab your things and follow me." The officer replied, not giving her any more information.

"Candace just go with them. I'm sure everything is fine. I'll keep an eye on Azerica for you and take her home as soon as the hospital releases her." Craig sounded like her friend again. "It's okay."

Dumbfounded Candace got her purse from Azerica's room and followed the men outside to the patrol car. They opened the back door for her to get in. Then they drove downtown to the police station.

The Walker Diaries: secrets

By Alicia Caldwell Henderson

Preview

Jacksonville seemed a different place at three in the morning. The streets from University Boulevard to the police station downtown were scarce. Candace didn't know what she imagined it would be like; she hadn't been out on the weekend in years. But that was the last of her worries. She still wasn't sure why she was being driven to the police station. The officers never made it clear to her and every time she asked them, they brushed her off. So she rode in silence and listened as they made conversation from the commands that droned through their radios.

God did I wait too long to come back to you? Candace looked up into the sky. She felt built-up emotions fall freely from her eyes. *I'm sorry. I'm very sorry I haven't been what you wanted me to be. I'm sorry I didn't listen to my mom. I'm sorry I blamed her for everything. God, this is my life. I know. She's not the reason I became what I am. God protect me. I'm scared.*

As they approached the city jail, Candace dried her eyes. She didn't want them to see her broken. She needed to appear strong. There was no telling what lay ahead of her.

When they finally pulled into the parking lot of the police station, she couldn't wait to get out. She followed them inside as they guided her to a waiting area. A few moments later, Lt. James walked back into the room with a teenage boy following behind him.

"Ms. Christian, thank you for your cooperation," he said to her, then turned to the boy and commanded him to sit down.

Candace just watched, waiting to hear their reason for dragging her from the hospital to the police station without any explanation.

"I understand you are unaware of the events surrounding your daughter's hospitalization," he paused to clear his throat. "Now, you already know Azerica was hospitalized because of an overdose of GHB, the date rape drug. However, you also need to know that we found her with this young man in his car on private property. The intent was too scare them and send them home, but we saw Azerica and she seemed barely conscious. We instructed her to get out of the vehicle so we could test her blood/alcohol level and she passed out shortly after standing up."

"Ohmigod." Candace covered her mouth with her hands. She felt her heart stop.

"Immediately, we rushed her to the hospital," Lt. James continued. "And we questioned and searched Darren Lewis."

Candace looked at him blankly; still shocked from the information the officer pumped into her. She felt like a teakettle: warming quickly and starting to boil.

"Candace, meet Darren Lewis." Lt. James said sternly and nodded his head in the direction of the teenage boy.

She stared hard at him. The young man just looked up at her and quickly looked away. He looked exhausted and afraid. She knew whatever Lt. James was going to tell her next meant serious trouble for Darren Lewis. To what extent, she didn't know. But whatever it was, she was sure Azerica had some part in it whether directly or indirectly.

After all, the child did lie and go to the party anyway, Candace remembered. Azerica did skip school to hang out with Trish and two guys. And Candace had a strong feeling this guy was one of the football players she was with when she should have been in school.

"In his possession was three kilograms of GHB, the same date rape drug Azerica had in her system. The state plans to prosecute him. Whatever you plan to do as a citizen is different, however, you do have the right to take him to court." Lt. James said matter-of-factly.

Candace heard everything the lieutenant said. Yet from looking into Darren's eyes, she knew there was more to the story. There was something someone wasn't telling her and they hadn't been telling her from the beginning. So she decided it was time to ask questions before she became enraged.

"How did she get the drug in her system." Candace demanded to know.

"Normally the drug is slipped into a drink and dissolves," said the lieutenant.

"I know," Candace responded, feeling as though he were trying to belittle her. "What was she drinking and how did it get in her drink?"

"Mr. Lewis. I think you owe it to Ms. Christian to tell her what you put in Azerica's drink." Lt. James said firmly.

Darren looked at the lieutenant and then turned his gaze toward Candace, but he said nothing. His eyes seemed to plead with her, but they weren't telling her what she wanted to know.

"Ms. Christian, he has been advised that he doesn't have to talk until his lawyer is present. You may press charges at any time, but you don't have to decide this minute. We're still waiting for his brother to arrive," Lt. James said. "Here's my card and you can give me a call in the morning when you have decided. I suggest you talk with Azerica and help her go over the events of the evening."

"Can't you tell me what she was drinking? I know someone placed the drug in whatever it was. I just need to know what she was drinking!" Candace exclaimed, extremely aggravated.

Lt. James cleared his throat. "Ma'am, please calm down."

"You dragged me here to tell me nothing! You can at least tell me what she was drinking," Candace said outraged.

"Ma'am. The report states that her blood/alcohol level was 0.06. She was not over the legal limit, but she is a minor," Lt. James responded condescendingly.

"Thank you, Sir. I was aware of that."

"If you'll excuse me," Lt. James grabbed Darren from his seat and turned to leave the room.

"Lt. James." Candace said frustrated with the entire situation.

"Yes Ma'am."

"First of all, I don't have all the answers I want. And second of all, I think you're forgetting that you brought me here from the hospital. I have no way of getting home.

Are you going to provide the transportation for me?" She asked.

"I'll take care of that for you. Have a seat and someone will be back for you." He replied and quickly left.

Seething, Candace didn't know what to think. She was mad. Not only was her daughter in the hospital, but she was there because she was drinking. Drinking! Candace knew it wasn't Azerica's fault that Darren or whoever else drugged her drink; but Azerica knew not to drink. Azerica was more responsible than that. She'd always been more responsible than that. Candace could not understand what went wrong or why Azerica would risk so much to do what she did.

Her daughter came close to losing her life because she chose to drink alcohol. She risked her brother and sister not having a baby-sitter to go to a party, drink and do God knows what else. Candace knew it wasn't Azerica's fault her drink was drugged, but she was furious with her. And she was furious with Darren for being there. She didn't know for sure if he was responsible for it all, but she did know he planned to take advantage of her daughter when the drug took affect.

Yet no matter how many ways she twisted the story, Candace realized her anger boiled down to disappointment. This experience made her realize she didn't know her daughter as well as she thought she did.

Depression started settling in her heart and before she knew it, Candace began feeling an entirely new set of emotions. Her mind took her heart through so many whirlwinds that she didn't notice when a woman police officer entered the room.

"It's late," the woman said. "Let me take you home."

Candace looked up at her appreciatively and grabbed her purse. She was ready to get home. She needed to make sure Mel and Chauncey were okay. She knew Azerica would be fine once she got home. She hoped she'd been released and Craig was able to get her home. Candace didn't worry about them getting in because she knew poor Devin would probably be awake watching TV.

And I didn't call her, Candace thought. She felt horrible and inconsiderate. *She should've been the first person I called.*

"Do you mind if I make a few phone calls before we leave?" Candace asked the officer and stopped walking. *She had to make the phone call before she could go home, but first she needed to call Craig.*

"Go right ahead. It's over there on your right," the officer pointed to a phone sitting at the end of the hallway.

Candace searched for Craig's phone number in her purse. She didn't quite have it memorized yet, so she kept it in her wallet.

"Hello?" Craig answered.

"Craig, it's me. How is she?" Candace asked.

"She's fine. The hospital just released her. We are on our way to the car," he responded.

"I'm so happy. Thank you so much Craig. I don't know what I'd ever do without you." Candace said earnestly. "Will you put her on the phone?"

She needed to hear her daughter's voice. Her last memory of Azerica was seeing her laying in the hospital bed sleeping. And before that, she was arguing with Azerica in the car after school.

"Hi Mom," Azerica said groggily. She still felt weird.

"Hey Baby." Azerica's voice never sounded so sweet to Candace's hears. "I love you so much. How do you feel?"

"Weird," Azerica replied. "What happened?"

"We'll talk about it in the morning." Candace said. "I'm so glad to hear your voice."

"Where are you?" Azerica asked. She wanted to be with her mom and not some strange doctor. *Where do I know him from?* Azerica asked herself. But it hurt to think.

"Dr. Pearson is taking you home, Dear. I'll be there as soon as I can." Candace consoled her. "Can you put him back on the phone."

"Ok." Azerica handed the phone back to the strange man.

"What happened at the police station?" Craig asked immediately.

"Nothing." Candace said feeling slightly irritated again. "They brought me here to tell me she was drinking and she was in the car with some guy who had the date-rape drug in his possession. They wouldn't tell me what she was drinking. And the boy wasn't at liberty to talk because his lawyer wasn't present. And they didn't force the issue because he is a minor."

"That's fine. We'll find everything out tomorrow. Do you need me to come get you?" Craig asked her.

"No. One of the officers is taking me home. I just needed to call you first. I'll meet you there," Candace said. "Thanks again."

Before she dialed her home number, she breathed a sigh of relief. She knew everything would be fine with Craig on her side again.

"Hello." Candace heard Devin's voice after only one ring.

"Devin. I'm so sorry it took me so long to call you," Candace said apologetically. "Azerica is fine. She was in the hospital because someone put the date-rape drug in whatever it was she was drinking."

"Oh, God." Devin gasped.

"Don't worry sweetie. She's fine. She's on her way home. Dr. Pearson is bringing her. I'm on my way now too. I'll let you know everything else when I get there.

-ydn-

"Hello." Trish answered her phone quickly. She was still mad that Darren and Azerica disappeared. They ruined her after party.

"Trish it's me, Jay." Jason said nervously.

"Hey, what's up? Why are you calling me now?" Trish asked annoyed. "I wanted you to come over earlier. It's too late now. This hoochie is in bed. You haven't earned enough points to get a booty call whenever you want it."

"Trish they know," Jason responded, ignoring attitude and comments. There was more to life than sex. And they could be in big trouble.

"Know what? What are you talking about?" Trish asked him.

"Don't you even know what happened to your girl?" Jason asked in disbelief.

"Azerica?"

"Yeah, Azerica." Jason said.

"I know she left with Darren. She was supposed to spend the night with me so we could have an after party with you and Darren, but I guess they're having a real good time. I guess she didn't need me as much as she thought she did," Trish sighed. "I'm proud of her. She caught on quickly."

Jason rolled his eyes. "Trish, they put her in the hospital."

"What!" she jumped up from her bed. "What happened?"

"Darren's brother gave her a Smirnoff loaded with rope and somehow she ended up in the hospital." Jason explained to her.

"Well, where's Darren?" Trish asked, seemingly unconcerned about Azerica's health.

"Yeah, Trish. Azerica's fine. They're bringing her home from the hospital now." Jason responded sarcastically.

"I knew she was fine. She's my girl. She can make it through anything. Where's Darren?" If things didn't work out with Jay, Darren was next on her list. Azerica wouldn't mind. She didn't know what to do with him anyway.

"I don't know where he is. I haven't heard anything," Jason said scared.

"Do you know why they left the party?" Trish asked.

"Yeah, Darren's brother wanted him to get more rope. He was running out." Jason knew he should've gone back to Beaver Street with Darren. But Darren grabbed Azerica before Jason could even say anything.

"Oh," said Trish, a little surprised. "I didn't think you guys were going to give her some rope for real."

"You told us it would loosen her up so she could have fun. What else you thought we would do? Darren is feeling her, but he know she too shy and won't do nothing without it," Jason defended himself and Darren.

"*Well, I don't know about it and neither do you. I know Darren's your boy and all, but that's on his brother. You didn't touch the stuff, did you?*" *She asked him. If Trish didn't tell him what to do, he would probably start feeling guilty. Sometimes Jason could be just as bad as his sister.*

"Naw, but I saw him put it in her drink. He gave her extra cause he said he wanted his brother to get some," Jason played the conversation over and over in his head.

"*L'il nigga, 'dis stuff can get you all the pussy you want.*" *Darren's brother pulled a zip lock bag from his pants pocket to show Jason. There were only three pills left in the bag.*

"How many does it take?" *Jason asked. Personally, he didn't believe in the stuff, but he was curious to know since they were giving some to Azerica.*

"*One pill for women who like sex and two pills for the hard to get pussy like Azerica.*" *He winked.* "*I'm a hook Darren up.*"

Jason wished he would stop referring to Azerica as pussy. He hated that word.

"*Don't call her that Jevon.*" *Jason said taking up for her.*

"*Grow some balls. You're a man.*" *Jevon laughed and opened up a new Smirnoff for Azerica.* "*Stop being so soft.*"

Jason watched Jevon drop two pills in the bottle and laugh.

"*If this don't work, I'll have to start using the stronger stuff,*" *Jevon said and rushed out the kitchen to take Azerica her drink.*

Jason sucked his teeth. He could've stopped Jevon, but he didn't. Why didn't he do more to stop Jevon? Azerica was supposed to be like his little sister. When was he going to start treating her like one and not some trick? He needed to start now. It was too late to go back and change history.

"We gotta do something." Jason stated. *know*

"No we don't. We gotta act like we don't about it and pretend to be surprised when we hear." Trish stated, trying to confirm their positions in the matter. "Unless you want to be an accessory to the crime."

"Alright, fine." Jason gave in. Even though his heart was convicted because they'd done wrong. "What about Darren? You told him to give her some. He ain't gonna just forget. You can't put that all on his brother, it ain't right."

"You gotta talk to him. We can't afford this. I'll never cheer at USG again and you won't get the scholarships you want. We gotta think smart. One person has to take the fall. Let it be Darren's brother. He don't do nothing but play video games and chill with his boys. We've got our whole lives ahead of us. He must know that," Trish pleaded her side.

"Well, I don't know. I guess I need to find Darren and talk to him. I'll talk to you tomorrow." Jason said and hung up the phone.

On the phone, Trish tried to play it cool, but she was really concerned. She was scared. She didn't want to get in trouble. Not for this. It wasn't worth it and it wasn't her fault. She couldn't help that Darren's stupid older brother actually did what she told him to. She hoped Jason would be able to talk to Darren to see what was going on and soon. But just in case, she had to get her plan together. They weren't going to take her with them.

Made in the USA
Columbia, SC
08 June 2019